flighty

jamie nicole

flighty

Quirky House Press – Florida

This is a work of fiction. All characters, events and organizations are either products of the author's imagination or are used fictitiously.

ISBN: 061593188X (Quirky House)
ISBN-13: 978-0615931883 (Quirky House)

DEDICATION

To my boo…you are my lobster…

ACKNOWLEDGMENTS

This book is a collaboration of love from all of the people in my life whom I've laughed and cried with through the years. I thank my Nana who always loved listening to me tell my crazy stories, and the many women in my life who always inspired me to be my best self: Aunt Pat, Loni Brown, Cindy Guin, Barbara Taylor, and Irenie to name just a few. To my children's Godmothers (my sistas from other mistas), Yo-Yo and Jamie 2, you make my life full and I thank you. To the girls with whom I've had so many fun journeys through my life that have in turn lead to so many funny experiences, that will undoubtedly lead to my inspiration for some great stories in the future: Shanny, Kelly, Kristin (with an I), Niki & Mel. Thank you to my parents who love me for exactly who I am at every turn in my life and always keep me focused on being the best version of myself because "I am my families tent pole". And last I'd like to give a big hug and kiss through my sloppy words to my husband, Tim. He is forever behind me in whatever crazy endeavor I've chosen to undertake at the moment. He loves my crazy and I love his back. He gifted me with the three loves of my life: Regan, Luke and Walker, whom without my life would not be nearly as interesting. How else would I have learned about glutton, lactose intolerance, sleepless nights and so much vomit…so, so much. You are all the reason I have a life full of humor and I love you.

one

My life as of today…

I'm only twenty-two, starting over should be easy. Mysterious. Exciting even! My physical resume reads pretty good. NO, pretty great! I have no cellulite…yet. Pretty hair… still. And, I'm a brown-eyed girl… always. There's a song heralding just my type and people all over the world love this mysterious girl. They skip about with Sha-la-la's and la-te-da's running through their minds all day because of this girl and her happy brown eyes! I am well aware that things could be worse. My eyes could be blue. KIDDING! What I was going to say was that I could be dying. Like dying, dying, not just hypothetically dying, which is all this broken heart really is. I know tomorrow will come. The sun will come up…blah, blah, blah. I'm aware of what the masses will say. I've seen enough chick flicks and read enough love stories to know my family will worry and my friends will come to my rescue. Unfortunately that is not, at all, what I want! I want him and his yummy, salty, skin and perfectly solid muscles and big hands and oh gosh, I could go on for days. He's pretty perfect and did I mention yummy? I did. And he is.

It really bears repeating. He's yummy. Wait! Was, was yummy! *Him* doing *THIS* will change everything. It will change me and it will forever change us.

The Moment…

Think Ellie, think! How can I make this moment memorable for him? Kicking him in the nuts is too easy, completely predictable for a heartbroken girl but alas, not my style. Ripping up the things he's given me and putting-a-whoopin' to his truck is too cliché. How can I show him just what he's done so he believes he's actually made a mistake? I got it! I'll just pretend I don't care and he'll NEVER see that coming. Ever! He's been my boyfriend since tenth grade and he knows better than anyone that sometimes, ok, most of the time, I'm a bit nuts. Not nuts in the conventional bad way, just in the unpredictable kind of way, you know, flighty. Focus Elliot. All I have to do is fake it til' I make it. Let the pretending games begin… At least until he leaves my room then I can show how I really feel and cry my Mary Kay straight off and get to destroying all the stuff he's given to me since we were in high school. Pretending sucks because I do totally care, I now hate that stuff like I hate the gas I get from the yummy pepper steak at the mall.

It's go time. I do not care, I do not care, I do not care, watch out Oscar here I come….."So, like, this is it?" Pause and collect, "Wow, um, I need a sec," I say breathing in deeply and scratching my chin while staring down at my newly painted cherry red toenails, freshly coated for our date tonight. "Ok." I look up at him with my eyes all wide and resigned, shaking my head yes like a bobble head caught in the high beams of this break-ups oncoming headlight of destruction.

"What do you mean, ok?" He says. His stupid, beautiful face showing shock and confusion.

"What? Did you think I'd go all nutso on you like some whipped, codependent ninny?" Ha! Take that!

"No Ellie J, but I did come prepared with an explanation. I mean, I thought you'd want to at least know why we're breaking up." *We're* not doing anything. YOU ARE! "We've been together for six years Ellie J, I know you. Or at least, I thought I did." Man does he look confused! Point me! He's totally winning though, because I'm dying inside! D to the Y to the freaking ING!

"Having never had my heart broken before Danny, I have no clue how to react. So I'm just going with it. You know me, go with the flow. If you'd feel better telling me why you've come to this decision, fine by me. Whatever. (Not at all whatever, more like WHAT THE &@!*). Is it going to change your mind?" I say this all cool like Vanilla Ice… or better yet, Marvin Gaye, he's so chill. I'm not chill at all though. I'm more like death con five hot! ON FIRE! Burning alive! Scorched in pain! You get the point. I'm not good. Burn unit here I come. Get a bed ready and may I request a hot doctor….PLEASE! (insert whiney voice)

"No, I'm not changing my mind." His eyes are now staring down at his black biker boots that he knows I love. They make him look so rad, but I'm not telling *him* that again. I should tell him they make his legs look fat or something. That would totally make my "not-caring-plan" sound fake though, so I won't. He knows they turn me on. Now that I think about it, not cool for wearing them to break up with me you big JERK! You know your shoes will turn ME ON!!!

There are officially like 30 seconds left until I die at his feet. I must now compose myself and get him out. We're on a cry countdown and it is starting, now! "Okee-dokey, if that's it, then I guess you should go because I need to make some new plans for the night." I'm literally pushing him out of my pretty bedroom that now reeks of death like composted manure. Ugh! Now I need a new room too! This sucks! Bad! I continue my rattling with, "at least Becky will be happy you're out of my "me circle" so she can finally take me out to all those - and I quote - "jamming new clubs" she's so crazy about. But I digress." T-minus 20 seconds. On to nervous chattering, I push harder. He's solid muscle, ugh! "Hope your life works out." I totally don't. "Tell your mom she's the best." That's true, she's really sweet. "And oh, you can keep my Foo Fighters shirt (even though they are my FAVORITE band ever) I'll just get a new one (I will, for sure)."

"So that's it? We're just not gonna see each other anymore after all these years?" Why does he look like this is a shock? HE JUST BROKE UP WITH ME! He may truly be a moron, huh? I may actually be better off. Note to self; must think on this whilst crying to death.

"Yep, with that whole break up thing comes us, you know, breaking up. No longer being together, see ya later alligator, so on and so forth." HA, surprised much.

"And you're sure you're alright?" Ten seconds left. Lip may or may not be trembling I am numb now and am officially in the red zone. Three feet until the door. *Hang in there* is what I am shouting loudly to my tear ducts and now probable wobbly lip.

"Yep, it's all good." Open the solid door, smile the smile he loves the most to drive the "not-caring" point home and shut it gracefully in the face of the only boy I know I will ever love. Scene close. Fall to foyer floor, thank the heavens all family members are out, wait for loud truck to start and ....lose my mind. Ouch! Everyone is right. This really hurts. Breaking up is, in fact, hard to do. Damn those true lyrics Neil Sedaka. Cue sad song. End scene and previous, perfect life.

Parental fall out…

"Honey, I'm worried," my mom Jan says while rubbing her temples and taking a slow breath in. "She's been up there for 3 days and has only come out to eat and get more tissues and that's after I told her no more food in her room! What should we do? Elle's never been one to mope," she finishes plopping down on the chaise in our spacious sun room, thoroughly exasperated with my heartbroken behavior.

My father is quick to get my back, "I suppose we should be grateful this is the first time this has ever happened. Tom from work said his daughter has been going through this almost monthly for the last 2 years, and she's only 15. Let's count our blessings and give her space, okay? These things have a way of working themselves out. Let's just give her some time, okay?"

My phone sits powerless next to my bed for several days while I mourn the life I'd never get to have. Danny and I had big plans to one day run his family's bed and breakfast. It's nothing swanky but it draws a certain kind of crowd, the rich kind, and Danny is a good business man. I knew without a doubt a life with him would have been secure. Recently he and his father decided they wanted to add a pub and brew their own beer for the locals. Because of the valuable location of the Inn, the "locals" are well off and what's in their wallets is what they're after. Danny's double degrees' in business and hotel management are really paying off for his family and the Inn has been increasing in popularity over the past year at a very steady rate. I just finished school as well, receiving a bachelor's degree in hospitality services for this very reason and poof! The reason is gone! Like sands through an hour glass, so are the days of my life. Gone…gone..gone.

Staring up at the stars that Danny stuck on my ceiling, I'm brought back to reality when my dad, James, the one man I know for certain will never betray me, pops his head in to check on me. He eyes my wild mane of long dark hair, always loving my corkscrew curls that remind him so much of his mother, but is stunned when he takes in the scene that has unfurled around his one and only child. "Your mom was not joking. This is something else. Go big or go home, isn't that what you always say? Cause this is big and," as he pinches the bridge of his nose, "stinky. Don't ya think?"

I puff out the long stream of air I've been holding for the last minute hoping fruitlessly that I could die painlessly that way, and give my dad a good look at the saddest, most pathetic eyes he's ever seen me wear. "Dad, did you ever do this to someone?" He was struck dumb by the intimate question about his past love life.

"I sure hope not, but the chances are pretty good that I did. Your mom was not my first lady friend," he says waggling his eyebrows while I, in turn, make gagging faces. "And honestly, as hard as this is to hear, the reality is you will be a better person after this hurt has healed up a bit. Danny's always going to matter to you, but you will actually live and thrive without him you know? You're a Hallowell for goodness sakes; we don't go down without a fight, right?"

"I love you dad, but you're full of it."

"I know, but you're starting to stink up the whole house and that's a good amount of square footage. So how about a shower and mom and I will help you pick up this….hole. First, though, here's your favorite chocolate chip muffins and the newspaper in case you want to catch up on life, seeing that your phone is dead," he hands me a plate with two muffins and this outdated thing called the paper while bending to kiss my stinky head. "You know I love you, kid, and I got your back," then he turns and closes the door on my den of stink.

Perfect is relative…

"I've got it!" I scream while I run and jump down our long curved staircase. "You'll never believe what I just read in the paper. First though, you really still read the paper that is made of paper? Cause that's banana's, you know they have them online right? And you are a lawyer, dad. Just saying. Anyway, I was flipping through your paper periodical from the past and sure enough there was a wanted section and I believe my papery prayers have been answered." My parents are watching the homeless-looking girl before them with a shared clueless expression.

"Okay, don't get weird on me here, but I think I've found my perfect job."

"Well," my dad starts, "that's fantastic news since

you've just gotten home from college. What a great way to get started on that new life you wanted. Let's hear about it."

"It's perfect! Wait, I've already said that. But who cares? It is! Blue Skies is hiring for …..da..da..dahhhhhhhh…..flight attendant. Isn't it brilliant? I mean, I've just gotten a degree in hospitality services, and I'm naturally hospitable anyway, so it just, like, fits. And…I'd be able to leave this Danny-coated town to some new girl who wants a broken heart and start an Elle- covered sky somewhere else! I mean its freakin' brilliant!" A whole lot of excited jumping and screaming ensues. Obviously, I'm the only person in the room who finds my plan brilliant because my parents are staring at me like I've grown a second head.

"Wow, I just don't know what to say sweetie," mom is trying to remain calm but the idea of her only child flying all over the place to God knows where with God knows who is not sitting well with her, at all. "You do remember what happened the one and only time you flew right?"

"Mom, I was 15 for goodness sake. I was afraid of my own shadow back then. Besides, everyone's afraid to fly, and my personality will get me through.

I'm cheery, or at least this will force me to be; which is EXACTLY what I need. This moping and pain is for the birds, and I'm sure Danny's not sitting at home missing me so, I've got to go. It's the only answer and it got served to me in my pit of stinky-despair alongside daddy's amazeballs chocolate-chocolate chip muffins. I'd say that's a sign."

"Jim, are you going to say anything here?" My mom says, horrified, waiting for the backup she needs from her partner in plan destroying.

"Well, honestly, I think it is a brilliant idea. I mean, when will she ever have such freedom again in her life?" He turns and kisses my cheek and says the most brilliant words I've ever heard, "I've got your back. Now for the love of all things holy would you please go shower and then..." with a huge, supportive smile adds, "go get that job."

two

Interview don'ts 101...

by Elliott Hallowell

The corporate office for Blue Skies Airlines is in Palm Beach and as luck would have it, it's only twenty minutes from my parent's house near the ocean. As I'm exiting I-95, my fully charged cell phone rings with one of my favorite Foo Fighters songs, *Walk*. It's my best friend, Becky, frantic for news on my mental health and relationship status. The gossip gears of the eternally stupid in Palm Beach Gardens are working at full tilt and I know Beck is furious that, after having been ruthlessly gutted by the love of my life, I have not called her even once to share in a good cry. I'm screwed.

I answer and start speaking before she can, "Okay, I'd like to claim temporary insanity." Then I hear Becky bellowing into the speaker phone like my parents yappy shi-chi puppy Zha-Zha does every morning since they'd gotten her three weeks ago.

"I will KILL him, and then I may kill *you*! Do you know how stupid I looked when Alex's friend Kelly came up to me at Duffy's the other night and said how sad Alex was that her tool belt brother broke up with the best thing that had ever happened to him? I was all, yah, he can suck it and she was all, I know right? But you know what? I was really like....WHAT THE HELL is she saying? Then I called like a zillion times and you never called me back!" She finish's on a high pitched squeaky note.

"I kinda lost it, Beck's. Please don't hate me." That was the perfect blend of sorry and pathetic wrapped into one little plea package.

"Obviously I could never hate you stupid, but I can be seriously pissed for like another minute." Long pause while Becks cools off. Continue driving.....there's the building. Twenty minutes until the appointment leaves just enough time to clear up things with Becky, then I'm off to meet a Mrs. Wilson. Her phone voice sounded like a billion years old, but

I'm gonna kill it. Old people like me and let's not forget I'm trained in hospitality, so it's all good.

"Alright, I hate you no more. Now when are we meeting up to cry and eat pie? Yay, that totally rhymed and I'm winning because that's like my fourth spontaneous rhyme today! Boo-ya! Seusical Whosical?"

"How about I call you in a couple of hours? I'm running a bunch of errands and I'll catch up with you tonight, kay? Oh and if you see Danny or Alex, I'm fine. No hard feelings. Got it?"

"Hell's yah. I like what you're doing there. The "I don't care" card. Perfect. He's gonna rue the day he left you. Mark. My. Words. So I'm off to the current boy toy's house, wish me fun times. Oh, and I'm winking. Get it? "Wink, Wink!" I wish you could facetime and drive, then that would have been way more awesome. Oh well. Catchya lates baby." And she's gone. Becky the love machine, a new boy every week because if anyone has commitment issues, it's good ol' Becky. She is, however, the bestest friend a girl could ask for!

"I'm here for an eleven o'clock appointment with a

Ms. Wilson." I say this wearing my most sincere cheerleader smile. Wait - oxymoron. Whoever heard of a sincere cheerleader? Whatever, ADD alert.

"Ms. Wilson will be ready in just a couple minutes. She's finishing up yet another interview today. Things are not looking too hot, so I wish you luck," the mean receptionist says to me in the most insincere way she can. Mean much, gosh! Within five minutes the steel door into Ms. Wilsons (who I'm officially terrified of now) swings open abruptly and a beautiful blond walks out looking very pleased with herself. *See? Things were looking up,* I say to myself, regaining my recently shattered courage. But as my eyes look up through the door of doom I am met with the steely, not at all encouraging eyes of one Ms. B. Wilson, as the fancy faceplate on her desk shines back at me announcing. I stand, try to control my trembling limbs and put on my pretty yet increasingly insincere smile.

"You must be my eleven. Elliott James Hallowell. What kind of name is that anyway? Very masculine." Phone perception correct, a billion years old and meaner than a… um..I don't know, just a really mean thing.

Talking too fast and not at all businessy, I ramble,

"I'm named after my dad's mom Elliott, she was the best really, you would've loved her (not really, this lady probably doesn't even think puppies are cute!) and my dad's name is James so see? Elliott James. Family name with a masculine twist I guess you could say. I've always liked it and...," but she stops me mid sentence with a hand quickly shot out in annoyance to shut me up, pronto!

"Yes I see. Well, what brings you to my office today Ms. Hallowell?" She's glaring. Yikes!

Wow, I thought this was the obvious part, considering I told her on the phone just yesterday that I'd like to have an interview for the flight attendant position, but whatevs, I'll remind the old coot, "I saw in the paper your company was looking for flight attendants and I thought I'd be perfect for the job."

"What makes you perfect for the job? And please keep in mind every girl I see tells me she's nice, loves to travel and can't wait for all the new opportunities. Go." Wow. To the point much. Gee whiz, way to kill a girl's spirit.

"I was going to say all those things so I'll go with the truth instead, then I'll be out of your hair (wasps nest, really. Did she look in the mirror?) Not that those all aren't true but. Well actually funny story. I've only flown on an airplane two times, back when I was fifteen. I passed out before I got on the plane on the way to our destination and had a panic attack on the way back, true story. But I think we should focus on the positive in that situation, which is I did get back on the plane to come home even though I had a panic attack. That showed real courage, I think. And, well, the other terrible truth is that my boyfriend of the past six years," why is my lip trembling? WTH is going on? Stop. Stop now, I demand it. My brain is screaming at my unrepentant mouth. And then here it comes, "dumped me. Like out of nowhere. Like how we dumped Pluto as a planet. No one saw it coming; I guess maybe the astronomers did but not the rest of us."

Now I'm crying ridiculous tears and hiccupping out my words while the Mary Kay is getting a chance to run again in less than a week, awesome. "I mean he's been the only boy I've ever loved. I went to college with him. We had plans and well, we almost bought a puppy recently," mental breakdown and understanding strike full force. "That explains why he didn't want a puppy with me. AHG, I should have realized. See he knew then! And I'm all "we're gonna be together forever", blah blah blahk!! Oh My

God!" Major gagging faces are going on. No way did Ms. "scary face" Wilson see this coming today.

This is usually the moment when one is kindly lifted off the floor they have collapsed upon and escorted out of said interviewer's office. But, oddly, this is not at all what happens next. "I have to agree with you," Ms. Wilson says leaning over her dark, deep, desk of misfortune while staring down at me with what looks like an upside down frowny face, also known as a smile.

"Wait, what?" I squeak out while sniffling....on the floor...at an interview. (Bears repeating).

"Getting on that plane was extremely courageous. I think your odd behavior leaves something to be desired but you have certainly entertained me. And, well, your boyfriend sounds a bit like my ex-husband. Actually that's when I became a flight attendant. That's been well over twenty five years ago, but as you can see, I'm doing wonderfully. So, there is hope for you dear." She ended with a term of endearment. Wow, guess I shouldn't have judged a book by its terrifying, scary-faced cover like everyone always says. Man, sometimes cliché's are right on!

"Oh...." I say at a loss. I can actually see Ms.

Wilson's demeanor returning to flat and scary as I sit back down into my apparently very slippery chair and reach for a Kleenex from the box on her desk. She's actually annoyed I'm touching her tissues. Unbelievable! Surely she doesn't want me sitting here with snot dripping from my nose into my mouth and the mascara…well, I suppose even a tissue can't handle that mess.

"We'll be in touch," is what she says in the middle of my tissue napping. Just like that the compassion she held in her eyes just seconds ago has been discarded and replaced with disgust. She is coolly asking me to leave before I steal more items from her desktop, who knows what I may do with that staple remover. Maybe she's imagining me pinching my eyes out in agony or something equally alarming and psychotic, because Wilson here definitely has me pegged for the big, all capitals, PYSCHO type. I can tell. P.S. Who could blame her after the emotional fit I just threw her way.

As I head for the door, I turn back to look at Scary Face. I turn the brass knob with my trembling hand and end my interview with, "It's a good thing this didn't work out really. Because all I kept thinking about while I was waiting to see you was how getting on an airplane truly does scare the bejeezus out of me.

Anywho, thanks for the interview, and please just forget that you EVER saw me."

"Impossible," is all she says in return. I swear as I turned to shut the door I saw a genuine smile on Scary's face as she sat back down at her desk of torture. What in the world could that mean?

three

A plan takes shape…

Several days of despair have gone by and I swear even Becky's uninterrupted peppiness has not been able to bring me back from devastation station. She's yet to convince me to go out since the big dump -Ew, sorry that sounds so gross- or the job interview from you know where. I lay in my shabby chic styled bed day and night, wearing my new Foo Fighters shirt my mom lovingly purchased for me since I obviously will never get my favorite one back. By the way, that's one of my worst decisions EVER, in the complete history of my life. *"Oh, and you can keep my Foo Fighters shirt."* Who does that? Who gives up their most prized, perfectly worn in, FULL OF MEMORIES

FOO TSHIRT!!!? I do, that's who. The dummy who also thought she could outsmart her boyfriend into not breaking up with her during said breakup by acting cool. Where was this precedent set in my mind? Since I've never been left for dead by the love of my life, I have no freaking clue. Maybe this is one of those things you look back on one day and say, *"wow, I really grew from that incident. I don't regret it at all!"* Cue dumbface-hippee-high as a kite smile. NO, I will ALWAYS regret him having my shirt. FOO FIGHTERS, I'm SORRY you're in the hands of the enemy..........cries more.

"Beck's, I'm serious. I'm going to let my pit hair grow out. It's so much easier to shower when I don't shave." I love that I have a BFF I can tell anything, well, almost anything based on the negative facial reaction I'm receiving.

"OMG, you are not shaving *anywhere*?" Becky actually gagged and almost barfed on my dirty floor, not cool Becky. Okay, so she can't handle everything. My lady hair issues are obviously too far.

"I don't think I will tell you anything else about my hygiene. I want to wallow a perfectly normal amount of time. I want Danny back AND I want to work with him and have his babies and live in the Inn together and all the other awesome stuff I had planned that he didn't even know was awesome yet!" My hands are perfectly perched on my hips now like a two-year-old and my big, pouty lower-lip is out. I'm growing in leaps in bounds from my pain here, BOOYAH! Take that, hippies and psychologists of the world!

"What if I told you I heard from someone that Danny isn't doing so hot either? Would that get you motivated to, I don't know, stand?" Snarky face from Becky. I'm so putting her on my you're not my BFF anymore list.

"Who said that?" I say, so hard up to hear of his merciless melancholy that I literally almost jump for joy!

"Doesn't matter. It's credible and I believe it, because if I lost you, I'd feel wrecked. UGH, this is way too sappy for a Friday. Now could you please for the love of Mary, go shave all your girly bits and go out with me? I beg." She is actually on her knees, prayer pose style.

Who would've thought that was my get out of heartbreak jail free card? His pain is my neutralizer. I'm up and in the shower, suddenly ready for the night of my life. Unfortunately I don't hear the voice in the back of my head shouting *"BAD IDEA"* because I'm so deliriously happy due to the fact that Danny is suffering. This may seem harsh or like maybe that I am a bit meaner than people think, but you know what they say about a women scorned. Clichés score again. I don't want him to die or anything just, you know, feel like not eating, sleeping or shaving would be good for now. Maybe he's smelling my t-shirt right this very minute and is all like *"what have I done, I'll never smell her yummy smelly smells again"*....do boys do that? Here nor there, I feel better.

Leaving the house good?...or bad?...

"This club is amazing Beck's, you were not lying!" I scream/slur at my booty shaking BFF. The atmosphere is typical but the thing that makes it cooler than most clubs is that it's two stories. "I love that I can dance up here while I people watch below, genius club builder!" I say this all sing songy and slurry and then realize the railing is my friend. I am a bit tipsy and wow, these rails were really smart. Hmm, actually I'm drunk, yep, that's what I'm feeling. Oh well, at least I'm happy and dancing, which I LOVE to do and haven't since the incident in my stinky room.

"I'm so glad you're here. I've been a bunch of times with that girl I work with at the salon, Kennedy, and she's cool but I really wanted to people watch with you. I can't be as mean with someone else. You let me be a bitch. Hey, you're my bitch wingman." Beck's is slurring too I realize. Not good.

At this precise moment, I look down and see him. *The HIM* who has my shirt. I can't even say his name. He's my own personnel Voldemort! Hey, WAIT? If he was sad he'd be home. That's how sadness and heartbreak works. You stay home and cry on my t-shirt -I mean pillow- and don't get out of bed. How is *he* here when the only reason I'm here is because I heard his ticker was as fractured as mine? I look at Becky and she has followed my line of vision to see the apparently not so bereaved Danny himself talking to an overdone bimbo who happens to be making seductive eyes while squeezing his beautiful (I mean ostentatious) bicep. What happens next is a quandary to be sure. And not the kind you should be in when drunk, freshly shaved and in your most prized cowboy boots. EVER! The drinks have very unfortunately made me forget THE PLAN! The I'm NOT supposed to care, carefully thought out and implemented plan. Oops…..Does kicking a girl in the shins in a jealous rage always mean you care? I mean who made that rule up? It could just be that her hair is stupid and I don't like stupid hair. Who uses that much hairspray?

The next thing I know, I've done it. I've gone and kicked a bimbo in the shin with said shit-kicker boots and have subsequently had a very alcoholic drink thrown at me. Now, we all know that when you shave, if alcohol gets poured on you, it will hurt. Well maybe you didn't know, but you do now. IT FREAKING WILL BURN YOUR SKIN RIGHT OFF! At least that's exactly what it feels like is happening. I need a fire truck, I mean fireman, stat people! Instead of waiting for some genius to call 911 I flee quickly whilst jumping up and down, grabbing my legs and making ridiculous drunk pain noises, the score is now Bimbo-1, Ellie-0. This all happened so quickly that Danny didn't see it was me kicking until I was already running away and by then Becky was giving him the eat poop and die eyes from behind my running body. Danny didn't catch up to us until we were outside and by that point my razor burn was causing me more distress than the idea of seeing him again but lucky for me I'd get to confront both at the same time. That whole perfect timing thing I got going on.

"Ellie J, stop! Would you please stop? Please?" he sounds so ridiculous. And hot. Me = Sad face. Him=So pretty! STOP! STOP! He's Voldemort!

I stop and look at his empty eyes and think I see something there but I can't place it, I've always known his eyes and now, I don't. That realization is a bitter pill, my friend…that pill can suck it! "Ok, I stopped. What?" I reply, slur firmly intact.

"Why'd you do that?" All I can think is he looks so handsome. All beefy and yummy with his perfectly caramel hair color and blue eyes that make my heart shimmy. I'm serious; it shimmies when I look in his eyes…..so pretty…..Right now though, they have turned to angry eyes. I know those.

So I say the thing I was thinking a minute ago. "Her hair was stupid." This falls way flat. Flattest, flat, ever…

"You're drunk." Statement of fact.

"HA." Not really a good comeback. Oh yah, I'm drunk, so also, not super witty.

"Have you lost your mind?" duh, *oh, and my heart, you butthole,* is what I'm thinking in response to that stupidface question.

He's seriously going to start a fight with ME when the floozy ruined my FAVORITE BOOTS, and he knows this. He now has my Foo Fighters shirt and is the person responsible for this bogus boot catastrophe. Ok, I know you're thinking I'm responsible for the boot thing but he absolutely should not have been out. "Excuse me, we were just leaving. If you hadn't noticed my boots are wet with BIMBO JUICE!" I may be shouting. YEP! Definitely shouting!

I can tell he's starting to feel sympathetic by the way he drops his head and sticks those delicious manly hands in his pockets. He suddenly notices my boot situation and he knows what these shoes mean to me. "Ellie J, how are you getting home? You shouldn't be driving."

And that's it. As I turn and walk away I see the thing in his eyes that I hadn't recognized a moment ago because I'd never seen it before, from him....pity.

The next day is uber painful as I lie in very real physical and emotional pain and watch my boots slowly dry out, just like my love life has. Who knew boots could be a metaphor for my love life? I'll always remember the day I got them. It was one of the weirdest and most exciting days of my teenage life. It's cryptic how the beginning and the end of these past six years of friendship and love can now be remembered through one pair of shoes. I'd heard a saying before that went something like *"you should never give someone you love a pair of shoes because then some day they will walk out of your life."* I really never thought that cliché's were created from reality in my past, but now I'm a believer. Memories.

The day we met…

"EJ, you have to buy those boots, they are fierce on you. I mean, they make your legs look rad! High-Five."

"Becks, that's why we'll always be best friends."

"What? Why?"

"You totally love my legs. That's precious. I mean it. What kind of person gives you awesome-leg high fives?"

"You are so weird." She says this straight faced but I can tell that what I said makes her feel loved. Being with the same foster parent for several years in a row now has

been a good thing for Becky's belief in people but she still doesn't feel like she's part of a family. It's only her and her foster dad and he's okay but really.... I'm the closest thing to real family she's got.

After shopping all day we're exhausted and starving. We're upstairs enjoying some of my mom's delicious homemade brownies and looking through all of our purchases when a knock comes from down stairs. As I'm coming down to see who's here I see a truck pulling away from the front of my house through the glass door. When I look through the beautifully etched glass as I get closer I see a box sitting on the top step of the porch with a note taped to the top. It's handwritten in super sloppy script on a scratch piece of paper and all it reads is your legs did look "rad" in these. I couldn't imagine them on anyone else. Call me 555-4477. I pick up the box and run upstairs to show Becky the mysterious note and to try on the only thing I can imagine to be in this boot box. And there they are. Beautiful. The boots smell so amazing when I lift the lid. Good Lord, what smells better than brand new leather cowboy boots...mmm. I'm a sucker for cool boots. Always have been, but it'd been years since I had a new pair and these are the best money can buy. I wanted them so badly and with the little money I'd saved for guitar lessons there was no new boots for me anytime in the near future. Especially ones like these.

"Where did those come from?" Becky says jumping happily up and down in the doorway of my extremely girly bedroom. All covered with white fluffy things from rugs to duvets with small splashes of a shabby chic pink rose pattern throughout the décor. I Loved it.

"The box and this note," I say impatiently flinging the note into Becky's excited face, "were on the porch when I went to check to see if someone knocked! Read it!"

"Gee whiz, take a chill pill." She glances over the short note and looks up with a mischievous grin. "Call him. Now!" She says handing me my highly crystallized covered cell phone that has been hastily cast aside on the nearby desk.

"Holy Snap, I've never called a boy, that's so desperate!"

"We won't tell your mom, just do it while you have me here to be your backbone. Come on you weenie."

"What a wonderful way with words you have, butt face."

"You're totally stalling, do it." Love pushy Becky.

"So testy, read me the number." Ring… ring… ring… "well, no one answered.."

"Hello," says the most agonizingly charming male voice I've EVER heard! After several seconds of silence he tries again. "Hello?"

"What, oh. Hi." Totally startled, suddenly shy and feverishly blushing everywhere, I rattle out, "I don't know who this is but my name's Elliott and well you left me a note today I think? I mean did you?" rambling is so unattractive!

He laughs a rich laugh…mmmmmm, yum. "So you got the boots. Are you happy? Because when you walked out of the store without them I was shocked. They looked amazing on you and then you put them back and just walked out and I was like whoa," he stopped then. Ha now he's rambling a bit. I like it. A lot.

"My girlfriend and I, I mean my friend who is a girl. Gah, I mean Becky." Ugh, make my mouth stop being such a b-hole. Try again, sound prettier, "we were just window shopping really. I'm saving my money for guitar lessons when school starts back up."

"Guitar huh? I can teach you that and save you loads of cash if you'd like."

"Are you for real? I would more than like, I would love that! Only, I don't know who you are still and well, you could be really weird and stalkery and, well, just generally

icky for all I know." God, I'll be so sad if any of that is true. Pout.

"Well, lucky for you I happen to be none of those things, but so you can see for yourself, how about I pick you up tomorrow night and take you out? After that if you think I'm at all icky or weird I will bid you farewell without any sort of stalkery. Deal?"

Oh heavens to Betsy Johnson, I'm in boy heaven. If he's cute, I will be, for the first time, screwed. Literally.

"Deal."

The times, they are a changing…

After our unfortunate club night, the rest of the weekend is a blur. I've never in my life been the kind of girl who sits around and feels sorry for herself! But, I am also aware that I never understood how painful life could be before Danny tore the one organ that fuels the rest of my body out through my nose holes. Positivity and chillin' are both my thing. I'm a beach bum, jeep drivin (top down, doors off) kinda girl and Danny has really put a hot spot on my chill vibe. Bastard, turd-face, hot-bodded, loser! I feel so much better when I verbally abuse him in my mind! Is that wrong? I'll have a think on that.....nope, its fine. He is all those things and I never lie, if I can help it.

Monday morning starts off with a bang. Actually it's a ring but it will soon feel like a bang! The phone rings at nine sharp and since the looser –me- is the only one home without a job or boyfriend, I answer it. This is a big deal, because I've decided today that answering the phone is back on. I'm adding it back to the list of things I must do in my own personal game of life that I quit on just one week ago.

"Good morning. Is a Ms. Elliott Hallowell in?" Great, a solicitor.

"This is." Please don't be mean, whoever you are. I'm just starting to answer the phone again.

"Hi," she's curt but not mean. Curt, I can do. "This is Sandy calling from Blue Skies personnel department and I'm calling to offer you the Flight Attendant position that you recently interviewed for," dead silence. I'm stunned, cannot open mouth. So she continues, "If you're still interested?"

"You said Elliott Hallowell?"

"Yes." Annoyed is the emotion I read from her now. She definitely thinks they've made a mistake.

"Okay then. Can you give me just a minute? Thanks." I slide down the wall trembling without waiting for her acquiescence. This is my moment. I can go, I'm free. I should leave Danny in my past. I want to barf even thinking that aloud in my head. If I go, I'm saying goodbye for real and the I-don't-care-plan takes on a very different meaning. Like, it becomes the sayonara to the love of my life plan. I'm essentially quitting on us. Him. I'd never do that. I can hear Becky, the street smart one, shouting in my head to GO. RUN. FLY. WHATEVER. JUST DO IT! THIS IS WAY COOL! You will be cool too. And - this is where she gets me (mind you, she isn't really here, just in the old noggin) - you can fly wherever you want to see the Foo Fighters! Brain Becky is a freakin' manipulative genius!

"Yes, thank you," I almost shout. The now nice lady, Sandy gives me all the info I need and it's done. I'm off to flight school in only three days. Holy Moly. What have I done?

four

Time to go...

Three days later is here and the place I fear the most in the world is coming into view through my parent's pristinely clean Lexus SUV windshield; the airport. It's a clear day, thank the flying gods, and I have anxiety meds on standby in my carry-on just in case a cloud pops up. Unfortunately, when I become an actual stewardess, I won't be able to take these meds due to all the passing out I do within minutes of swallowing one. But, whatev's, that's later. Today's only plan is to focus on today. I've found lately I function best in small increments of time.

There it is, Palm Beach International Airport. And

on the tarmac, I see several Blue Sky planes taxiing into position both on the runway and into their terminal parking places. I want to cry. Becky totally senses the fear creapin' into my fragile mind and leans in to help, "EJ, you know this is going to be hard and stuff, but I totally believe in you. Okay? Anytime you think you can't do it, know I am somewhere thinking you are so awesome for being so brave. Also, when I see Danny I will totally kick him in the nards if you want me to, just let me know and it's a done kick. Capeche?"

"Capeche. Don't kick his nards though, because he's going to want me back one day and we'll want kids and that could totally put a wrench in my baby makin' plans. Oh I know, maybe you could launch a drink or two his way? YES, do that! Throw one right on his cool black boots that I love? Oh, and if he's clean shaven……his pretty face." This one small plan of vengeance fuels me through parking, check in, the inevitable frisking and the agonizing, panic inducing, waiting to board.

Mom and dad are doing their parental duty trying to talk me out of this craziness, well really just mom, and I get why she's doing it. She loves me and is worried about my death, but I'm not having any of it. The night I got the pity eyes from the pretty-boy, butt-face, boot wearer, this ticket was signed. I'm outta here, and my sweet parents can thank Danny and his cold, dead heart. I've decided to be brave and I'm not backing out now. I've never been a pushover and that's not changing. The last thing Danny said to me is seared into my newly sensitive psyche, "how are you getting home Ellie J? You shouldn't be driving." Well I'm not Danny boy; I'm flying to a home that you are no longer tied to and you don't even care. *Maybe you never did* is my last thought before the intercom is pinged on through the unnecessarily loud PA. *Hello, we're right here.* The only three people in front of you!

I wait until the last boarding call before I get up to board the Boeing 737 jet. The agent looks right at me and my family and says last call for flight 214 to Atlanta. Our love fest is seriously putting a hamper on this lady's day. "Last call," she screeches with one last glare, I swear, get a new face Meany. Your job sucks! Daily...- no, hourly- she separates people from those they love through a scratchy intercom with the words *last call* reverbing off the windows and bouncing back at you like word swords piercing the lovely goodbye you were having and inserting her ugly voice in its place. She's boarding my flight and if I don't get on now I'm not going anywhere. I've got an ex to run from here, so I take her reverbed words seriously and, with one more round of kisses and through lots of tears, I say my final goodbyes to my loved ones.

I'm not proud to admit it, but like every other dumpee in the known universe I have the fantasy playing in my head of Danny being here to say goodbye. Or, better yet, he runs through the terminal shouting my name as I'm about to board and I turn and he falls to his knees begging me to stay, admitting how wrong he was. But reality kicks in when I turn for my final look around the terminal, and my heart shaped dream bubble is popped. I'm going to have to board this dog gone airplane. Even though, I swear I can feel him here. Gah! Enough! I grab my guitar case, which I stubbornly refused to check when I found out the flight was nearly empty, and start up the ramp toward the aerial locomotive of death that is to be my new mode of transport as of today.

Little do I know that at this very moment Danny is one terminal over pressed to the glass, getting ready to watch my plane do what I want it so desperately to do....separate us and fix me; bring me back to life.

Danny, hours earlier…

At a party the night before I'd been trying to have a good time, get my mind off of my parentally coerced breakup with the love of my life when the girl I'm talking to says, "So, since Ellie's leaving maybe we can, you know, go out sometime or go back to my place tonight if you're interested?" My mind is putting her words in order when the warning bell in my man brain rang. Something about the way she said that sounded strange.

After an awkward silence I asked, "Did you say Ellie's leaving? Leaving where? Is she here?" I went a little stupid faced, frantically looking around because I didn't want the sneaky shin-kicker to pop up out of nowhere and cause another scene. This girl and her five inch heals and mini skirt stand no chance against a P.O'ed Ellie J and her shit-kickers.

"No, gosh, haven't you guys, like, been together for-ev-er?" she drew out the word like a moron. Though I was the one who looked pretty dumb right now because I was clueless as to what this girl could possibly know about Ellie J that I didn't. I knew everything about her or at least I used to and I was just now forced to see how naïve I was to think that wouldn't change the day I broke her heart and her trust in who we were.

"What *do* you mean then?" I say putting an emphasis on the word *do* all while trying to stay calm, cool and collected. Unfortunately, as usual when I'm nervous, I start to sweat.

"I mean, she's heading off tomorrow to become a Blue Skies flight attendant. Seriously, it's like you don't even know her. Whatever, I've gotta go. You're looking weird. You okay?" She says without a single ounce of real concern coming from her over-made-up mouth. The fact is I think I may vomit. I've got to get out of here and away from these people. I've got to think.

"Um, yah. Feeling a little queasy, too much tequila. If you see my sister, would you tell her to call me? I've gotta get outta here. See ya," God Ellie J….What the hell? You're leaving? What am I going to do?

The answer to that question is…nothing. Remembering my parent's ultimatum brought my truck to a screeching halt only a couple houses down from Ellie's. They had a point and I knew it. Ellie J and I were young and we've been together since we were kids. If what we have is real, and I know it is, a break won't destroy it. I can only hope Ellie doesn't give up on me, on us. What else could I have done after my parents "talk"?

"The talk"...

"Here's the deal," dad starts. "Your mother and I really like Ellie, she's a sweet young lady, but," always with the buts. Little "but" bombs were Dad's number one ammunition.

"But what? She's not good enough for me? You know she's not using me for my money. I told you she has no clue. She only knows we live at the Inn and that we run a tight ship. So, what the hell's the problem?" My mother flinches at my aggressive tone and ugly choice of words and my dad continues, unimpeded by the outburst. It was expected from me.

"The problem is not Ellie son, it's you." Blunt much? Now, I'm pissed.

"ME? WHAT DID I DO TO DESERVE THIS?" My

shouting is only proving his point and I'm seeing red. Shit…damnit to all…..motherf….. I've got to pull it together quick here. My mom loathes cursing; it's only safe to do through inner monologing.

"We are soon going to be turning this operation over to you and heading home, and when you're with Ellie you're just not responsible. Now your mother and I hate to have to butt into your love life like this ***but****: drastic times call for drastic measures, and to us this is a drastic situation. We built a multimillion dollar empire to have something substantial and forever to pass on to our children and their children. It's given you kids nothing but the best in your lives. It's time you act like a man and make tough decisions for the sake of your career, but……more importantly your family."*

And there it was, the simple truth was this, choose her or us.

The rest is history……as they say.

I remember his words as well as the brutal choice I made as I stand to touch the thick sound proof glass separating EJ from me and a single tear drops from the corner of my eye as her plane takes off speeding down the runway away from me and into a future of which I may never be a part. I hope she can feel me here. I'm broken.

five

Apparently flying is not optional…

"Ladies and gentlemen we are only a couple of minutes from landing in the greater Atlanta area, if you would at this time please lift all tray tables and fasten your seatbelts to prepare for landing. We hope you enjoyed your flight today on Blue Skies and Ellie, welcome home." With that I receive a wink from the peppy flight attendant in the front of the cabin accompanied by a very warm smile.

I survived and I didn't have a panic attack or pass out. Score Ellie-1, scary plane-0! The song *Learn to Fly* by my beloved Foo Fighters is blasting through my headphones at this very moment and I know this is where I am supposed to be. My Foo Fighters never lie.

Flight school is nothing like I imagined. We sit in a classroom day in and day out listening and learning directly from a flight attendant manual that is to be carried "on your person" at all times. That is the stupidest phrase ever by the way. Who says "on your person?" Really? Anyway, they really mean in your carryon luggage bag with all your other flight stuff, but I digress "per usual" (*who says per usual? The same people who say "on your person"*). The only part of this school that's tolerable is all the new friends I'm making. Charlie, aka Charl`ay was my first friend, current roommate and a very gay boy that I not so secretly love and gush all over. I've left my Zha-Zha at home and Charl`ay has taken her little furry place. Except unlike my furry little puppy he is shaved clean of any and all hair. And I mean ALL hair.

My parents think Charlie's a girl. Not that they will care in the slightest, they're cool like that but he's going to be quite a surprise. Our room is all done up like a queen's circus. Pink tiara's and boa's cover every available surface and there is no shortage of animal print. Now you would be correct in thinking this is not my style, it's not. However, I am trying to look at life through rose colored glasses lately, or, in this case pink colored boas and tiaras, and it seems to be helping my dreary mood swings quite a bit. After only three weeks I now only cry at night into my always-there-for-me pillow. It's going great!

I think Charlie and I get on so well for several reasons. One, he reminds me of Becky, he's a complete commitment phoeb. And two, he's completely out of his mind and over the top, which I admire. Then there's number three: he knows how to get me out of my head when I turn psycho. Right now this is his most endearing and useful quality.

Thank the good Lord he didn't judge this book by its mascara smeared cover when he first met me, because my book jacket would've hung me. He flung the door open with a "TA-DA" only to see me in my undies and bra on the floor crying, the ability to stand up and finish the tricky task of dressing for bed completely gone. I say tricky because all my limbs were like lead anchoring me to the floor. I was essentially a concrete block in panties, unmovable, a wasteland where tears went to die and evaporate from.

After I'd gotten to the room that first afternoon, the weight of what I'd done had begun to settle into the sensitive landscape of my newly heartbroken mind and what I had become. What's the characterization he used? Oh yes, the very famous "bat shit crazy". It was love at first insult for me. I needed someone to call me on my very real B.S. and slap me around a bit, even if it was with a Swarovski covered paddle. Poor guy had just flown all the way from L.A., which now I know as LAX, and he was lucky to land crazy #1 as his new roommate for the next six weeks. Lucky for me the fates knew I needed him and his sparkly outlook on life.

"I can see that under those puffy lids lies a very pretty girl, but girlfriend when was the last time you washed your face? I see mascara and zits on your cheeks and, well, I could gag. You're disgusting," this is what he said right before the "bat shit crazy remark." Why do I like him?

"Danny," I squeaked out between hiccupping sobs and he had it figured out. He knew it was cupid's nemesis, stupid, that did it. He said all boys were struck by it from time to time and clearly this Danny had been because he could see through my currently engorged face that I was a looker with a "killer bod" and gave me a high five. That's when I knew we'd be okay, just like Becky, he high fived me for my body, I loved my new gay Becky.

Fortunately, we've come through those dark days and things are starting to look up thanks to all the new distractions in my life. That is until we arrive at class the next morning. It was inevitable; alas, flying is part of the job description. But, it had been so easy to ignore that bit when we were in class every day studying boring manuals. Today however, on the brightly lit smart board in the front of the classroom is a schedule with all of our names scattered around on it. Two things jump out at me immediately. One, my name is nowhere near Charlie's and two; there are flight numbers next to each of our names! This is going to rock my shaky world clear into oblivion. I do NOT want to go on another airplane. Fiddlestix!

Clearly the teacher thinks we should be thrilled about this. She's got her annoying I love flying smile spread across her ridiculously made up face and is looking rather pleased with herself for the big surprise she's suddenly thrust upon us. I personally think her surprise sucks but I'm pretty sure I may be alone in my feelings because these people seem genuinely excited.

"We don't even get twenty-four hour notice? Seriously what kind of ship are they running here?" I say out loud to no one in particular.

"I know. Isn't this exciting!" Says perky teacher's pet down in the front. I want to punch her in the ponytail, also, her throat!

The powers that be haven't even come to ask if we're ready. I mean, if it were my company, I'd want to double check that people were ready for this kind of responsibility first hand, face to face; eye-ball to eye-ball. Not at Blue Skies. They're all, here's a manual. Go fly now! WWJD! My first training flight is this evening from Atlanta to LaGuardia and back. Charlie, aka the big betrayer, jumps up and down clapping his hands making everyone laugh. They all love him. *"HE'S MINE,"* I shout in my head while glaring at the room full of bellowing beauties. I'm pathetic and maybe just a wee bit possessive.

I have a sudden and very real understanding that I may actually need to know all the things they've been teaching us from *THE* manual, you know, in case of an actual emergency. What if I do have to deliver a baby? OH MY GOD, or put out a FIRE, in a STEEL TUBE IN THE SKY?

Raising my hand excitedly (not in a happy way) I blurt out, "what happens if suddenly we come down with something?" I shout this from the corner I've been shivering in, as the class is about to be let out. I believe I could have found my no-flying-today loop hole.

"If you miss the flight tonight you'll just be rescheduled for the morning, but I'm sure that won't happen. I know your excited so don't worry about what-if's just go back to the dorms and get ready ladies. Today you show us what you're made of!" I have hated her optimism for three weeks. Today we're way past hate and moved into the land of shut the blank up and back up b-ATCH. I'm still in my hate-filled diatribe when she continues with, "can't wait to get the reports from the trainers tomorrow. Have fun, and remember, FLY FRIENDLY!" she's almost singing with excitement….EW!

You can't make this stuff up…

"Well aren't you a cutie pie," says the perky Barbie doll in front of me who is my judge and jury for the day. Awesome…..I'm dripping with sarcasm.

"I'm Elliott," I retort curtly without slapping on a perky smile in order to please her, I'm incapable of being fake at the moment. I *so* don't belong here.

"Goodness, let's have a Blue Skies smile, shall we? This will just not do," I swear she's smiling and giving me the finger here at the same time. Damn southerners have a way of saying you're an arse and being nice at the same time. If I'm being honest, I wish I could learn this. It's just not in my DNA. I'm perpetually walked on.

"Sorry, just a bit nervous is all." I flash a smile that is as contrived as a Scientology Recruiting Event and she humors me for trying.

"Well, I'll give you a tour of the plane and then we'll get to it. We're boarding in five." Tour? I think to myself. I mean, it's literally a metal tube with seats. What is there to tour? We continue on in spite of this fact and I act all, 'great and yep and OH, that's where you stow the pillows and blankets?' DUR!

After the walk through is finished, we board and do our presentation of air masks and how to hold it to your face, you know, for the eternally stupid. This goes without notice by the handful of passengers aboard, which is probably why this flight was picked for a trainee such as myself.

Then the inevitable happens. We are cleared for takeoff. Triple-Fried FISHSTIX!!!! Barf bag at the ready between skirted, sweaty thighs, we hurl down the runway in the aforementioned steel tube and lift into the air at an alarming pace. Everyone else on board looks bored. What the GOBSTOPPERS!!! Does no one understand what's happening? When I die, Danny better feel bad for having pushed me into this, and if I hear he's dating when I'm an angel, he's screwed! I will so angel stalk him and his lady friends, he's screwed angel style!

"Are you okay?"

"Huh? What? Why? What's happened?" I say frantic while trying to unbuckle the crazy harness I've got pulled between my thighs like a four year olds booster seat. Seriously?

"Nothing's happened, sweetie. The Captains turned off the seatbelt sign and we need to set up the service cart, come on. Up an' at em'." I hate her drawl. Truly I do. My cynicism is out of control around her.

"Great. Can't wait." She glares at me and my newly acquired companion, aka Chip, who lives on my shoulder.

"As soon as we finish with the service we'll have time to sit and relax before landing so come on, let's hurry it up."

We scurry up and back in less than five minutes. Barbie wasn't lying, we get to just sit and chill, *unless* someone pushes the call button. I may actually like this job. (Leave me alone, I can dream). Then a call light goes off and I'm told to get it by snotty-face. My position on the totem pole is firmly planted in the dirt here so I'm up and heading to the one dim light on in the dark cabin. It's so dark outside I can't even see the stars I'm feet away from. I realize moments later that it's not so much night as clouds. Then *IT* happens. TURBULENCE.

"HOLY MOTHER!!!!!" I cry and fall into the first person's lap I see for comfort. I should be embarrassed, but I'm not. I'm just so grateful there is someone nearby to comfort me. I should have boundaries or maybe shame would be better, but nope, just happy for a strangers lap. Don't judge my fear, look at your own.

"WHOA!" stranger boy looks stunned and then a look resembling humor passes across his face. He thinks this is funny! The nerve. Need I remind you we are currently, falling out of the sky.....in aforementioned TUBE! I'm mind screaming!

"This is NOT funny! We could DIE!" I am hysterical and may be shouting, but my pulse in my ears makes it hard for me to judge how loud I'm actually saying things.

"Okay, okay. It's fine, just some turbulence. Are you serious? You're not just trying to pick me up here?" He's smirking. I currently hate smirkers, though sometimes they're really hot.

"Do I look like I'm kidding? My blood pressure is off the charts and I'm pretty sure, I may be having a heart attack! OH MY GOD, do you know CPR? Because Barbie will not do it on me, she hates me!" He's laughing and then the plane jumps again! I am clawing his back pulling him to me bear hug style. His face is firmly planted in my cleavage and honest to God I could care less. Live it up buddy, cause this is it, we're TOAST!

"Um, I can't breathe," he says pulling his face from my breasts. He's red faced from his near death by cleavage. Of which, I'm sure there are worse ways for a guy to go, just sayin!

"Sorry. Is it over?" I now have my arms secured around his neck and my face cuddled near and almost into his armpit.

"Yeah, it appears to have calmed down. You okay? I could go get your partner over there if you need me to." He says pointing to one very irate Barbie wanna be.

"NO, PLEASE DON'T. Is she looking?" I say frantic.

"Do you really want to know?" Stranger says lifting my chin to look in my eyes. I shake my head in the affirmative and he asks to make sure, "yes?" I firmly shake an affirmative again.

"Yes." He's frowning while shaking his head in the affirmative as well. I think he's figured out it's not good for my career that I'm currently camped out, scared for my life while in a passengers lap. He'd be right.

"Crapstix, double poopscoopers! I'm dead meat here." I hiss out between my very clinched teeth.

Through his quiet laughter at my word choice's I can literally feel the pressure of her glare on me. I look up from the safety of said armpit to see Barbie looking at me, no lie, hands on hips, all school marmyish, face contorted in complete disgust with a finger out. "This will be going into your assessment," and she turns and walks off. I've failed at being a stewardess. Unbelievable.

The only positive in this scenario was the making of my new friend, Tanner Stanton, aka, boy who comforts strange flight attendants who are clearly not cut out for said job. Unfortunately, I'm too broken currently to take any usable notice of his hotness, but I can tell that he's the trendy, cool type and I adore his personality. But, he is going to have to fit into my current life plan under the heading of good contact and a lot of fun, also, really helpful to complete strangers. We get to talking and I learn quickly that he's from South Florida as well and is currently on his way to New York City to work for his uncle's realty company. We exchange info. You never know why people land in your lap (or why you land in theirs), and before you know it we're preparing for landing, THANK MY LUCKY STARS! And Tanner Stanton.

The next morning, Charlie and I are walking to class and he's telling me all about the hottie from his flight yesterday that he hooked up with in the lavatory-GROSS! Only after he was sure there was no one looking, of course! Doesn't matter, still GROSS! I don't hear any of the tawdry details because as soon as I enter the room I hear the voice of one very annoyed trainer.

"Ms. Hallowell. Monday morning, in my office. Before class. Eight sharp." She looks pissed. And now I have the entire weekend to get myself worked up over what kind of punishment she's going to dole out, for what? Stupidness. Gah. Would they really fire me without a second chance? I really am very pleasant when I'm not horrified. I just hope I get the opportunity to convince the people who hold my job in the palm of their perky hands. I guess we'll see this Monday, eight sharp. I fear groveling is something I am going to have to become accustomed to. OH DUCKS!

six

Danny's world…

"Tonight? You in?" Ryan asks breaking through the looping daydream of Ellie J I've had going on since the night I saw her last outside that stupid night club. The look on her face, God…she hates me. I hate me.

"Sorry dude, just thinkin'. Yah, I'm in. Where are we going again?" It's embarrassing how often this has happened since I've stopped seeing her. I've been assured by my younger sister, Lex, that this is the first stage of the heartbreak grieving process. She says this stage will end soon, being that I'm a male and we suffer much shorter periods of time since our hearts are so small and empty. Also, and I'll quote her here, "because you're a bloodletting heartless leech." Ouch, obviously mom and dad didn't let her in on the "ultimatum" making me look like exactly that. Good description, little sis.

"That new club Downtown. My sister and a bunch of her friends are heading there and I thought we'd meet up with em'." The sympathetic look he was giving me let me know he knew I wasn't doing a good job of acting like everything was cool.

"Stop with the look dude, I'm fine. Just working things out in my head having to do with an ex. It's all good." Not. Even. Close.

"Been there man, you need a night out. You'll have forgotten her name by tomorrow morning if I do my job right tonight. My sister has been dying to meet you. And to be fair here I should warn you, she's a piranha, very crafty when it comes to the opposite sex. I hope you're prepared for what you may be up against," he says with real concern behind his laughing eyes. Great, just what I need. I have no idea how to deal with women, NONE! Everyone assumes I do because of my long relationship with Ellie but she's all I know, all I want to know. I can't play the games. Anyway, what the hell is wrong with

Ryan, trying to get his sister laid? Weird. But hey, maybe I'll take one for the team. I'm in need of a serious Ellie J distraction.

Ryan wasn't lying. His sister is very crafty and handsy. Man, her hands have touched exactly every part of my body, and I mean EVERY part. I'm no angel, I mean Ellie and I were each other's firsts but we weren't exactly innocent in that department, we were fun; she was up for *it* anytime, anyplace! WE *were*....A LOT OF FUN! But this girls' roaming hands weren't flirty or fun, they were like having a pair of five legged tarantulas crawling all over you and they were givin' me the 'hebee geebee's', as Ellie would say. Who told this girl men like to be touched like this? Lord she wasn't a piranha; she was a poisonous hairy spider! SHIT! I Hate spiders!

"So, Ryan says your single. How is that possible for a hunky guy like you? I bet women throw themselves at you all the time." Like you are right now I think? She's purring in my face and spittle (hate that word but its appropriate here) is flying into my mouth. God, I had no idea this is what I'd been missing while I'd been in a monogamous fun relationship all these years. I get why guys are being told they're heartless. Dealing with girls like this all the time could do that to a guy.

"Actually, I've just come out of a long term relationship. Not looking for anything from *ANYone* (Take the hint)." Maybe that will do the trick. Nope.

"Oh. I was hoping you'd take me home and teach me some manners later." HOLY HELL, did she just ask me to do her? "Am I making you uncomfortable?" she breathes into my ear while her dancing tarantulas roam around my pecs' slowly heading south....again.

Unfortunately this is the exact position I'm caught in by the flash of an iPhone less than five feet away. "What the hell," I shout covering my eyes, momentarily blinded in the dark night club.

"What the hell is right YOU....YOU...... ASSFACE!" Becky's on a roll now. "To think Ellie has cried over you! CRIED! I thought you were different, I've actually told Elle to be patient that surely you were just panicking and that this whole thing would blow over in no time, but if this is what you'll be doing," she says pointing hostilely at the spidey-fingers next to me, "then I WAS WRONG!!!!" She ends her tirade with a bitchslap that I did NOT see coming, storming off before I have a chance to explain how she has severely misjudged the situation. Who am I kidding? It wasn't like I lifted her hand off my crotch; I am a man…….aka "heartless leech".

EJ, moments later…

A text beeps through at two am. I am a working woman now people and the schedule they're keeping us all on here is driving me nuts. I'm venting to no one in particular, in my head of course, so as to not wake up Charlie, he's a real bi-atch when he's sleepy. We've been getting wake up calls for class at all hours of the day. It's rather genius really. They're trying to prepare our internal clocks for this type of unexpected punishment. Being on call in the world of flight attending, which we all will be for several years, at least until our seniority in the food chain of stewardessing increases, is like having a newborn baby, except you get no cuddles or baby kisses, just phone calls giving check in times and number of days gone. It sucks.

I digress. Text….that's why I'm up and dialoguing. Maybe it's from Danny…begging me back! YAY! Okay, I see Becky's kissy face on the glass front of my iPhone and I smile, I miss her craziness so much. I'm only a little disappointed. Maybe she's texting me a shot of a new boy toy she's found for herself. After all it is a Friday night. I smile to myself as I slide on my phone and watch as the grainy image in front of me comes to life and loads to perfect clarity.

Thought you'd want to see this so you can get on with getting over him. I'm sorry. I'd want to know if it were me. Call me when you can. Hell, call me now if you want. I have no idea when you're awake anymore. Whatev's, ANYTIIME. Call me. Xx's……b

I don't call Becky. I cry. It seems that's all I'm capable of anymore. I can't keep this up. Can you die from crying? If you can, I'm a dead woman walking, actually laying, but that's only semantics, really. *My* Danny and *the guy* in *this* picture are two different people and I don't want this one. He's disgusting. I let Charlie sleep, which shows I'm making progress in my mental health because a couple of weeks ago I would have been way more thoughtless, (ok selfish) and woke him intentionally with my loud wailing just for some comfort. I decide tonight though that I will be different and I will cry quietly into my pillow, which is starting to stink of stale broken-hearted tears.

I think of it as a fluffy hanky now. And with that thought I realize I must get a new pillow soon….ewww, in a good cry I'm letting loose way more than tears…double eww!

I must have fallen asleep because I'm woken by – OF ALL FREAKING THINGS - a fire drill, and the sun is up, laughing at me in all its sunshiney ways. Someone up above is getting a real giggle out of my life, I'm sure. Unfortunately I am incapable of finding much humor in either 1) my systematic ongoing heart break, 2) my swollen cry face, also ongoing or 3) the inexcusable amount of sleep I've been getting. I'm in my new Foo Fighters shirt and polka dot boy short panties, stumbling down the stairs with my newly detested iPhone in my hands holding onto Charlie who's dolled up in his pink feather boa and tiara at noon on a Saturday. Lord, do we make a pair. And seriously, that's what he grabbed? A boa and a tiara? Good God!

"Girls and… boy. This is not a drill. There is an actual fire in the cafeteria and due to the fact we are all housed in the same building as the cafeteria we will be waiting for clearance from the fire department on when we can go back to our rooms. Sorry for this horrible inconvenience. Clearly," glaring right at Charlie and me, the only two in our sleeping gear *and* boas, she continues, "some of you had a long night and were not planning on being productive today anyhow." Everyone laughs. There is no sufficient way to describe the humiliation happening to me right now. I cannot imagine a scenario where I would feel less stupid.

My phone startles me when *Everlong* by, of course, the Foo Fighters starts playing, alerting me to Becky's call. I walk away from Charlie and his adoring harem of friends into the shadows of the nearby magnolia tree. "Hey," I say solemnly as I slide on the phone.

"I'm sorry EJ. I hated doing that, but I was a bit punchy with too much drink and I was so pissed. I just wanted you there to handle it and I hope you don't hate me, forgive me," she rambles quickly, thinking I'm mad at her? She has no idea how badly I needed to see that. I had a come- to-Jesus moment in the night and woke with some real clarity this morning. I was not this girl, the one who was no fun to be around and so whiney. Gahck. That girl can suck it! If this is the life Danny wants then I'll have to deal with this once and for all. I must be boarding the acceptance phase of grief. ALL ABOARD! LAST CALL FOR THE ACCEPTORS!

"You have nothing to apologize for. Looking out

for your best friend is always the right thing to do. I love you Becks, kay? We're good."

"What do you want me to do now?" She asks me in her quiet, worried voice.

"About?"

"Danny. He has left like, I don't know, a zillion messages on my phone this morning. All like…"you don't know what you saw. It wasn't what it looked like. You're not going to tell EJ right? That'd only hurt her…" you know typical boy BS. Blahblahblah."

"Oh." I have no energy to care at the moment. I'm emotionally wrecked.

"Elle, you okay for real? Hello? Ellie, you still there baby girl?" I can tell she's just as sad for me as I have been, yet another reason why I trust her so much.

"I will be. I'm just probably about to be put on probation here…. and now this. I feel like a total loser. You should have seen me on my flight yesterday."I'm currently tapping my head on the side of a beautiful magnolia tree that are so prevalent here in Atlanta. "I am getting well acquainted with making a fool of myself in public. For example, right this minute I'm outside with a slew of model types in my polka dot pink undies and non matching t-shirt, Foo Fighters of course, it's really the only thing that gives me any street cred, and I've got one of Charlie's beloved boa's wrapped in triplicate around my neck. I'm hopeless." I'm very swiftly moving backwards in my grief stages.

"Tell ya what. I'm erasing his messages. He can figure this out on his own. Let him live in the mess he's made. And you, my very bestest and coolest friend, go and party ASAP, it's an order." She is very forceful now. "Where is this Charlie character you live with right now?" I pan around and find him talking to one of the instructors who doesn't hate either of us and he waves when we make eye contact.

"He's talking to an instructor. Why?"

"Could I please speak with him?" Long pause. ".... Lord you are helpless."

"Mean," I say walking over to my new BFF and passing him my phone wearing an apologetic look on my face. He excuses himself from the instructor and walks off......with my phone *and* MY FRIEND! The NERVE! At least let me hear one side of the conversation. So Rude!

"You people are acting like I'm some helpless ninny, I swear," I say to no one in particular, I thought under my breath, but apparently not, because said comment earns me an exasperated stare down from Charlie over his shoulder as he rounds the corner. It didn't take long though because only a moment later he returns from around said corner in a much better mood.

"Becky says '*Bye*', and I see why you love her so much by the way. She's fierce girl." One finger snap in a Z shape coming up.

"Well, what did she want with you?" JERK! I am really mean with little sleep. True story.

"Don't worry about it. Just know that we've got your back and what comes around always goes around. You trust me?" Not with that wink!

Girl's night out…

"This is going to be so FUN," I'm singing from the bathroom while finishing my "go-out" makeup. Right now I'm fun Ellie. She's my favorite. She can Par-Tay!!

"Damn girl you look Bangin'…HOT" Charlie draws out the words all cool-like while spinning me for a loop, appraising to see if said club attire is to his liking. It is. You cannot go wrong with cowboy boots. It's true. Boys love them paired with a mini. This should not be considered an opinion. I have never seen a girl not pull a guy while wearing this attire…..EVER.

When we get to the club it's almost eleven. Perfect. No class tomorrow so this is going to be raging like the freakin machine! A quick looksie proves this to be your typical nightclub. The difference tonight is that there must be a rodeo in town, because cowboys abound and I am swooning all over the place. This is your proverbial fish in the sea scenario. I have found the island from *Lost,* the promised land of milk and honey, Noah's ark, whatever. You get the point...its MAN manna from heaven. *Danny who?* is my last thought before I start accepting drinks from one cowboy after another. Yee Freakin' Haw!

"You wanna dance sweetheart?" God yes, Studs voice just undid my bra, I swear.

Charlie has been watching me all night; actually protecting me is more like it. I see Becky written all over this party. I knew the two of them were up to something. She probably found out about this place and everything. I LOVE HER! She really is my sista from another mista!

Me and cowboy-who-undoes-bras with voice are all over each other on the dance floor. We are making quite a scene and I am numbly in a conscience free zone, thanks to all the nice cowboys and their free drinks. Mr. Hot and Sizzlin voice slides his free hand down my thigh, lifts my knee up and pulls me all the way into him. I'm currently wrapped around this stud all python style and I throw my head back giving him full access to my neck. He gets the signal and takes full advantage of the meal in front of him. I think I'm humming sounds of pleasure but the steady beats of Will. I. Am are drowning out my love noises. Ahhhhhh……

"Come on lover girl, time to go. Sorry handsome. She's with me," says Charlie as he disengages my locked arms from around this head-to-toe lollipop. Lover boy is not too pleased about Charlie stealing his sure thing. I was totally a sure thing and he knew it. Thank God for Charles and his slut-protection enforcement program.

"But I love him," I slur reaching back for my yummy cowboy snack as Charlie drags me away.

"No, honey you don't. You love Mr. Does NOT deserve you. But I let you have a treat tonight. You're too sweet. Tomorrow you'd regret that" he says pointing over his shoulder, "and I'd pay for it. Come on, I've called us a cab."

"k….." How could I regret that?

Danny's wake-up call…

I'm going over the latest plans for the new brewery and I can't help but be excited about what we're doing here. Not that I feel great about having given up Ellie J, because I don't. But I have every intention of getting her back once I've proven myself sufficiently to my father. Whenever that is. We'll be fine. She's a good girl, she'll hang in there and then one day I'll ask for forgiveness and explain to her the whole situation and I'm sure it'll be fine. She knows how important this job is to me, to us.

Beep.

It's 2:30am. I don't recognize the number that pops up on my cell screen but I see a grainy picture attachment and have a sudden urge to rip some cowboy's balls off. Namely this piece of shit with his hands and mouth pressed all over Ellie. And she's wearing THE cowboy boots. OUR boots. This is not Okay. NOT! OKAY!

seven

Ellie J and Pain are so, not friends…

"It hurts."

"What does honey?"

"Everything," I moan while rolling over, finding Charlie looking at me with Cheshire cat eyes. Oh no, what have I done.

"So good to see your face still intact after the vacuuming it took last night. That guy was freakin' suckin' your mouth off...Mmm...in the most delicious way. You were the envy of every girl and fancy boy in that place, myself included. But, I got just what I needed. You were way better than either Becky or I gave you credit. Really....I didn't think you had *THAT* in you." He finished feeling very smug.

"Thanks. I think. What exactly did you get that you needed? Oh, did you find a boy toy too?" I sit up ready for all the juicy details, and my head is not in agreement with this plan at all and I immediately take notice and lay down before I hurl on Charlie and his boa-wrapped body. He's so weird.

"No. No boy toys. Just a few pictures." All innocent like.

"Of?" I'm shivering from either vomit chills or what I fear I may hear. It really is a toss-up. Ugh, don't say toss. Vomit gods, have mercy on the broken hearted....

"You. Wrapped all koala style around the hunk who puts to shame all other hunks." He's delighted with himself and me. He's literally taking turns clapping and patting himself on the back. I'm currently... concerned, scared, horrified, you get the picture.

"What was done with these pictures? Wait. Before you answer. Do I want to know?" My instincts answer first with a resounding NO!

"That depends on whether you believe in clichés. Do you?" DUH? They're real.

"Lately……more so than usual. Oh God, why? You're making me NUTS, GO!" Don't, shut up!

"Well I did say what comes around goes around and all that yesterday. Remember?" Head shakes in affirmative. Ouch. "Becky and I made a command decision that we thought maybe you'd disagree with. Only because you've never been at the dump-end of a relationship crapper and, well…..Danny needs to see what he's up against is all." And there it was. OH. MY. G!

"Let me see the phone. NOW," I shout scaring the three of us; Charlie, myself and my very dehydrated brain. I quickly open the phone and find in the message box a sent photo at 2:30am from this phone to Danny's. I click the image to enlarge what I cannot decipher in this small - ridiculously small - photo box, and up pops the most alarming picture of myself that's EVER been taken in the history of my life on earth. I look like this guy is playing me like a fiddle and is bringing things home, like in that song *Devil Went Down to Georgia*. Oh my G, I'm in GEORGIA! Damn. That's kinda hot, actually. Gah, that's not what I mean. Danny is in possession of this picture.

Right now.

"Say something, I'm dying here. Becky is waiting for a call from us. Are we friends, enemies, frenemies? SAY SOMETHING."

"I....I....just. I don't...what is he going to think?" I'm going to barf..For sure, that's happening.

"What anyone who see's this picture would think. DAMN! THAT'S HOT! Then it'll click in his arrogant brain that it's not him making YOU feel like that and my guess, and Becky's is that he's NOT going to like it one little bit."

It was like my hangover and bad morals summoned him in revenge for my very bad behavior. My phone rang his newly programmed Foo Fighter theme song, *The Pretender.* And I almost threw up. For real this time...I dry heaved! Charlie ran for cover after throwing me the garbage can. I had no clue how to handle this situation. I am in over my head. I wonder if Charlie answered if he could get away with pretending he was me. No good. Way to girly to play me. SHOUTY CAPITALS coming.........FLIPPIN A!!! MOTHER DUCKER!

Charlie passes me the phone calmly and says, "Be cool. Tell him the truth, that you had no clue I was going to send a picture like this to him, Becky must have put me up to it and that you're sorry that I was so callous. But never. Never apologize for the face sucking and general fondling fun that was going on. Got it. GO. He slides the phone on, quieting my lovely Foo Fighters and puts the phone into my trembling, sweaty hand.

"Hello." Thank God my voice isn't shaking. Be cool, don't barf/gag.

"That hurt." Flat. His voice is a stranger's. I just don't understand why he's hurt! HE BROKE UP WITH ME! I'm starting to think what we're doing is causing too much damage to fix *US* later……… if there ever was an *US*…. Or worse thought yet, a later. That was always my hope, but he NEVER said it was his. This thought comes in and crushes me. The crying countdown has returned. End the call or he's going to realize I'm a phony and I miss him more than my pride! 10…..9……

"Listen, I had no idea Charlie was going to send you a picture like that. He and Becky thought it would be a good idea. I never would've agreed to that. You know me better than that." Good job. No tears, lip trembling or projectile vomiting imminent.

"Oh." LONGEST SILENCE ever……..8…7…6…

"Okay. Listen. I gotta go. You saw the picture. I need a shower." He's not laughing at my completely inappropriate joke……this is *so* bad…. "It was good to hear your voice." Still silent. "Bye." Hit red end button. Cry…..again. I need a Bed Bath & Beyond for a new pillow. STAT!

A guru comes a callin'…

Monday morning, eight am, finds me in a world of trouble. I've gone and gotten myself put on probation for the "lap incident" on my training flight to LaGuardia. Of course they don't take into account that I've made a new friend in said lap partner and he seemed to enjoy the "incident" quite a lot, but whatever. Rules…Regulations…Appropriateness….

"Well, how'd it go?" Charlie is frantic to hear if I'm canned. He really does love him some Ellie.

"I'm not fired….today." I wink. Winking is stupid. My eye must be twitching.

"I swear you have nine flight attendant lives. One more training flight and we're placed. Can you please keep it together long enough to get permanent placement? Some of us kinda like having you and your crazy around. It makes us feel less weird, more normal. Ya know?" I know.

As luck would have it, today we get our flight assignments for our final training flight, and I'm off to Los Angeles. The longest flight out of everyone it turns out. Someone's out to get me, I can feel it. To add insult to injury, I'm without a training partner, again. Geesh. Charlie has a Miami turn with one of the other students who we both really like, SO NOT FAIR (it is, I deserve this, I'm a terrible flight attendant). All I can think about is how much fun they're going to have and how much NO FUN I'm going to have with my stupid new Barbie trainer. Someone ask for a whine sandwich? Cause I got one for ya. Order up!

I arrive to my flight an hour before takeoff to get acquainted with the crew and my aircraft. I like the 757. It's sleek, with clean lines and more importantly, this particular plane looks new. YIPPEE! This is refreshing. Then I hear the captain and co captain complaining how they hate flying new aircraft because all the kinks aren't worked out yet and I plummet right into pre-panic panicking. Who the HECKFIRE flies a plane they feel like has "KINKS"?

Maybe I should call Danny right now and pledge my undying love because fact: I'm dying, soon. On a kinked aircraft. Holy Mary Mother of God, PRAY FOR US SINNERS!!!!!! There are not enough Hail Mary's to calm my nerves.

"Hi. Elliott Hallowell, nice to meet you. Did you know this is a new airplane? Kinks and all." I'm rambling on as I extend my shaking hand to introduce myself to the senior flight attendant who's just boarded, scaring me half to death with her polite shoulder tap, as she catches me eavesdropping on the pilots of death.

"Well Elliott Hallowell, it's a pleasure. Mary Phelps." She is smiling at me and dare I say she looks…kind. Her hand is also not sweaty when she takes my shaking one into her own, another plus for the possibly kind, non-sweaty Mary. It's obvious she isn't afraid. Good on ya, mate! Why am I rambling in Australian now? I need help.

"Thanks, pleasures mine. So…You're not worried about this being a new aircraft are you? I mean, who worries about such things, right?" Trying to be cool is NOT working for me. I'm in a panic induced inferno.

"Elliott, I see you're on probation and I've read the

report from your last flight. I get the distinct feeling you're a bit afraid of flying and I'd like to help you with that tonight okay?" I must have rubbed this genie before me out of a bottle because she will need some serious magic to cure my fear.

"That'd be great, except I think you'll be wasting your time. Just keepin' it real here, Mary Phelps." I've found if I say someone's name three times after meeting them I remember it. Anywho, "Generally, I'm very optimistic," not lately, lately I suck at positive thinking. "But, when it comes to this whole flying thing I lose all ability to see reason and logic Mary Phelps. It would be better for us both if you just knocked me out cold and lied on my report Mary Phelps." She's laughing, but jokes on her because I totally stored Mary Phelps name now.

"Elliott, you are funny! I needed this tonight." She's still giggling. Did I really say something that funny? She continues with, "I'm on my last day of a three day trip and this is my long day, then I'm home for a week thank goodness. Having you as a partner is going to make this so much more tolerable for me." She used the word partner. She's the funny one. I'll be partnering the toilet as soon as the seat belt sign goes off. She's screwed.

Our preflight checks are done. We've done all safety demonstrations, meaning I've been lucky enough to perform charades while Mary reads from the card that each passenger has handy, directly in front of them. Then we buckle into our baby seats - it's what they feel like. Just sayin. Only one thing left to do. Takeoff, also known, in my mind, as the "kinky" aircraft voyage of death. No, not that kind of kinky. Geeze! Mind-gutter.

"Lesson number one," whispers Mary next to me. "Relax the white knuckles. You're scaring the passengers," she's smiling at me, she thinks I'm hysterical funny, not the mental kind of hysterical. She's wrong. "Also, breathe. You'll find that helps." She has the best smile and because of it, I almost believe her. Almost.

I do what she says and shock of all shockers, breathing actually helps; must always remember this breathing idea, hmmm. I look over and see Mary smiling at the baby in front of us, no cares in the world, and make it a goal to gain this kind of relaxed confidence whilst flying on a death tube. This is a light bulb kind of moment for me. I think I just assumed everyone on the plane felt like I did. To see that some people actually are not afraid gives me hope that I too can be like them; fearless. Just the thought helps me, and as I feel us speeding down the runway and lifting into the evening sky, I do the unimaginable. I smile.

Since this flight is so long we have a lot of down time. Mary uses this time to help me with my fears. She gives me a simple list of ideas to keep in mind when I'm up in the friendly - or not so friendly - skies, depending on your perspective. Currently I'm more of the NOT type but, sweet Mary has faith. Silly girl. The first two tips she's told me already, relax and breathe, both worked wonders on takeoff and they are filed away as To Do's from now on. We sit to relax when the cabin lights go down for the movie portion of our flight, and Mary asks if I'd like to continue with my fear training. Yes please. If she can help I'll owe her big time. Maybe I can find sexy voice guy and give him to her! Who wouldn't love that package? Eyebrow waggle. Oh my goodness I said package. HEE HEE. Charlie is turning me into a perv.

"First you need to better understand turbulence, because it is the number one issue for most nervous flyers. Think of turbulence as speed bumps in the wind because that's really all it is." This is a revelation to me.

She laughs, again, when I blurt out, "Believe it or not, speed bumps don't scare me!" I say this with an unnecessary amount of enthusiasm since no one is afraid of speed bumps. "This metaphor will change my life. YEAH MARY!"

We are interrupted from our chat by passengers needing drinks, blankets (must be noted, they can reach these themselves), and begging for something to eat even if there are only stale, small bags of pretzels to ration out to theses poor trapped souls. I mean, at least I'm getting paid to be here with nothing to eat. They've actually paid a fair amount of money to get handed stale salted carbs. But, to each his own. This is another point for driving: Fast food is so much better than airplane fare. It's not even a contest.

The flight flies by. We're prepared for landing and strapped in when Mary leans in to give me my last two pointers.

"Remember to drink plenty of water before, during and after all your flights. One, your skin will thank you and two, your brain can not think clearly in a shriveled state. Flying is super dehydrating. Oh, and just a side note to this one, don't eat food that makes you gassy while flying. Your stomach will blow up like a balloon and it really makes for a "stinky" flight," Mary says giggling. Who knew she'd have such a silly sense of humor in that reserved brain of hers. I like her so much.

"Water, no gassy foods. Got it." I say seriously, ticking the points off on two fingers while giggling along with her now.

Then she gives me one last nugget of Mary Wisdom. "This one seems like common sense, but it helps to hear it. Look at everyone else." Like I have a choice when I'm stuck facing forward in this dumb harness from Hades.

"What if everyone else looks like they're about to die?" Serious question.

"They won't be. Half the people will be excited to be going somewhere and the other half will more than likely be asleep. A few will be showing real signs of fear and now that you have my handy list, comforting them can be your job. Actually this will help you, too!" Mary is a Saint. That's another total truth. It may be a different Mary but clearly she's influenced this one because she is just what the doctor ordered.

"I will never forget you Mary Phelps, and I promise to pray for you every day for the rest of my life. I don't know how to thank you for caring enough to help me and not just hang me out to dry like the last trainer did."

"You don't have to thank me. Just remember to pass it forward when you see someone else struggling onboard. Also, don't give up on yourself. You are going to go a long way my friend, you've got something special that not many people have anymore."

"Oh really, what's that?" I say waiting with bated breath.

"You seem to have no ability whatsoever to bullshit. It's beautiful." Holy Toledo, Mary curses! Then we both start laughing, and before you know it the plane is making a landing as smooth as Danny's backside..... I miss it. Not the landing. His backside.

Charlie is so happy for me. I've been in such a grand mood all week. These are my first consecutive days of joy since arriving at training, and I'm starting to be a better version of the old me and it's just brilliant! After the whole Danny texting incident he thought I'd never bounce back, but my newly acquired resilience is even surprising to me. I'm starting to gain some of my old confidence back, thanks to one seriously productive training flight with one long lost Jedi-master, Mary Phelps.

Everyone in class is giddy when we arrive, right on time. They're about to lock us out just like they would for a real flight. You learn real quickly not to be late; there are serious consequences when you are! Anyway, there in the front of the classroom is none other than....wait for it.....one Ms. B. Scary Face Wilson. BUM, Bum, BUM!!! Cue scary music because she is looking right at me with her glaring interview eyes! Surely she is wondering what I am doing here. She has just put together that this is an accident and I was not supposed to be here and someone has made a terrible mistake. OH SWEET TWIX, the gig is up!

eight

Danny and the eternally stupid day…

After smelling Ellie J's Foo Fighter shirt for the thousandth time I stick it back under my pillow, where it's been since the night I sold my soul for shares in my family's empire. I don't know anyone who wouldn't have done the same thing, but that's neither here nor there. I sound like I'm turning into a chick. I haven't gone out since the night Ellie J's "friend" Charlie sent me a photo of my girl getting dry humped by a dude that wasn't me. UNCOOL, CHARLIE. UNCOOL! I haven't even met this dude and I've already decided he's dead when I lay eyes on him. I've been playing my guitar all day trying to shut out the mental pictures that are running through my head of what must have gone on the rest of that night when someone knocks at my door, room 3555. I open it and hit my head against the wall when I see who it is. Note to self, use the peephole, that's why God made them!

"What's up?" I say shortly.

"Good to see you, too, handsome." Flattery will not work here. Not with senora spidey-fingers.

"Ryan and I were just going to spend the day by the pool." Then she adds happily, "Your parents were kind enough to give each of us a keycard for whenever we want to come hang by the pool. Cool huh?" Nope. "Anyway, Ryan thought I should run up here and see if I could convince you to come down and hang out with us." I can't help but look her over. I am a guy. With eyes. She's wearing nothing but a barely there white string bikini and anyone would notice that she's insanely hot. Forgive me, again, I'm only human. The problem is that I'm also aware of the fact that she's completely without scruples, and let's not forget the spidey-fingers, AKA Carrie, the girl who helped ruin things even more for me with Ellie.

I surprise myself, and her, when I say, "Let me get on my suit and I'll be right down." A normal person would leave. She didn't. She let herself right in, and I can tell by the look in her eyes that she's hoping for a strip show, but no such luck for her. She makes herself comfortable on my bed rubbing my white, fluffy duvet while giving me some serious do-me eyes, so I speed things up by grabbing the first pair of board shorts I see and enter into the safety of my deluxe, oversized bathroom. I must've agreed to this because my subconscious is hoping to get laid. There is NO doubt that my rational brain would not have made the same decision to hang with lady nimble fingers all day. No doubt I'm gonna have to keep my wit's about me. Because "Dan the Man" has other plans today and is leading this ship. He's starving without EJ's attention.

"Hey man, what's up?" Ryan says as I throw down my white and blue striped hotel pool towel five minutes later.

"Not much man. Glad you came by. I've been so busy lately I haven't had a chance to check on the progress of the newest brew you've been foolin' with. How's it going?" Ryan's offered to do some sample brew recipes for us. We need something new and light seeing that we're on the beach. He's had some really close calls, but nothing that says this is our signature beach brew yet.

"I think I've got it man. This last one is the one. It's got an orange note to it and it's a pale, which is what you seem to like the most. You can serve it with all sorts of seafood appetizers. It's good man. Carrie and I both agree. This is it."

"Did you bring any to sample?" He looks at me like I'm an idiot. I deserve that.

"As luck would have it, I did. Your parents have already tried it and gave it the thumbs up, so it's your call."

"I'll go get us some frosty mugs from the bar. I see you brought a big cooler. Nice. Be right back," I finish, noting the largest Igloo cooler on wheels they make. I can use some/a lot of those today. I need to be careful here because "Dan below" is paying close attention for my weak moment so he can make his move on Carrie and her string bikini that is not double knotted. He noticed, not me.

The beer is exactly what I've been waiting for. It meets all the requirements I asked for and now that I've given it the seal of approval Ryan's been waiting for we can chill the rest of the day. This is one of those South Florida days when you can't imagine why anyone lives anywhere else. The sky is the same color as the ocean and it's impossible to tell where one begins and the other ends. There's just enough of a breeze to keep you comfortable without blowing sand all over the place. The only thing missing to make it a perfect day is Ellie J. She was the perfect beach bumming partner.

Most people wore flip flops to the beach, but not EJ. She'd always wear her boots to the beach as well as everywhere else. She gave no care to the sand that undoubtedly filled the bottoms up. She'd just dump em' at the end of the day and hop into her jeep, screw the sand. To add to the effect, she'd wear the same short cut offs every time along with one of her many tank tops, she drove me crazy and she knew it . "Dan the Man" misses her but, P.S. so does big Dan. She made my life fun and I'm slowly beginning to realize that I am not one of those lucky bastards that get to have it all. My parents have made sure of that, and let's not forget that I was the one to nail the coffin into our relationship the day I signed their agreement.

Sensing my mood starting to shift, Ryan hands me yet another beer. Who knows what number I'm on, I've lost count. All I know is that I'm starting to think Carrie and her roaming hands both look all right about now. Her near nakedness isn't helping my testosterone filled brain, either. She's been keeping her distance today and I can only assume that Ryan warned her to back off considering the last time we hung out ended so awkwardly. Unfortunately for me the 'get-me-laid' subconscious part of my brain is starting to take charge of the situation. He had a plan. I knew it.

My "other brain" makes the next move when he directs me to say, "I know it's been a long day but you guys wanna go upstairs and hang out? I gotta get outta the sun. I'm burned." I can't feel my legs anymore either, but I don't say this. Also, I'm drunk.

"Can't man, got a date later. That is if I can sober up first. Dude, I'm wasted," Ryan says, rubbing his legs like maybe they're numb as well.

"I'll get Danny to his room. Who's picking you up RY?" Carrie's already packed their stuff up and oddly is the most sober by a mile.

"I called John, he's probably here already." He stumbles to an upright position flicking two fingers from his forehead as he salute's us goodbye and stumbles out the side gate to meet up with his ride.

"Come on, I'm starving. Let's order pizza." And

just like that, I'm following Carrie up to my room, pizza sounds amazing - and *her butt looks good* too. My subconscious licks its lips. Or maybe I do. I'm in serious trouble. Suddenly I want to lick her butt. No, I don't…I do…I DON'T. Me and my 'main-man' are squaring off. God I hope I win but he is in it to win it. SHIT!

I hear *Learn to Fly* as we enter my suite. *Where the hell is that coming from?* my foggy brain is thinking as I look around for Dave Grohl and his band currently playing in my room. Carrie figures it out before I've had a chance to work out the puzzle and is snapping open my phone and answering it without any thought. Whoa, I'm just drunk enough to suddenly appreciate that there is no way that this is going to end well for me. Not on any planet in any world does this situation end well for any man, not even George "can do no wrong", so I've been told, Clooney!!

"He's right here. Next to me actually, here ya go," Carrie says while passing me the phone and wearing a huge "I WIN" grin, looking me up and down like I'm the pizza we were supposed to order.

"Hello." I slur. Covers blown.

"I'm sorry I've interrupted. It's just…well I was

just calling to tell you I'd be home for a couple days, but never mind. I gotta go." Click. This is NOT HAPPENING AGAIN! After two months without a single productive conversation between us she's hung up. Then again, what do I really think I can say to explain any of this? It's not like I can tell her the truth; that I know my subconscious and the traitorous 'other Dan' had big plans and I almost went along with them. I wouldn't want to talk to me either if I were her. I suck and so do ultimatums and backstabbing penises.

Ellie After…

I don't know what I was thinking! Why in the world did I think he'd want to see me? With everything working out so well around here lately, I was taking a gamble that Danny had come to his senses. DUH! What I keep forgetting is that he broke up with me. HE doesn't want to be with me! I cannot get myself through that pesky denial stage of grief. I've done pretty good lately with the other ones. Like 1) I've totally been getting on with my life. Hello! I'm a flight waitress, I mean attendant. 2) The anger part has gotten way more manageable especially since that revenge photo. Becky and Charlie are good at this because they were right on, that did help quite a bit. 3) The crying has slowed way down, as evidenced by my new pillow which does not smell one bit of stale tears or snot. This leads me to 4) I thought I'd accepted it. Nope, my acceptance/hope phase was really me accepting that he didn't mean it. Sorry… WRONG ANSWER! You cannot pass Go or Collect $200 or your EX-boyfriend. Matter of fact, you just picked the go to jail card…..you LOSE!! I am not winning, Charlie Sheen. Not winning…….

"Packed up and ready to blow this Popsicle stand." Charlie says all singy like he does when he's really happy. Screw you Charlie's happiness. I am not a good person today.

"Let's hope these three days go by warp speed like. I wish I could just beam myself into my room all Star Trek style, grab my things and beam right back out to our new place. But, alas…the smart people have still not figured this out. Bummer for me."

"Elle, you listen to me." Charlie has on his super serious face, meaning..Well, this is super serious. He takes my face into his cherry blossom, lotion-lathered hands and says, "DO NOT LEAVE THE HOUSE WHILE YOU ARE HOME! Do you know why I say this? Because you will do something appalling. How do I know? I know what you're thinking even though you don't and quite frankly girlfriend, I've seen what you're capable of and it's better left inside…THE HOUSE," he shouts for effect. GEEZE Lou-ISE!

"What do you mean you know what I'm thinking? I'm not thinking anything." Yes I am. He's good. Really, really good!

"You weren't thinking of doing the same thing every other heartbroken psycho ex-girlfriend does, like a drive by or a hundred? Elle, I'm telling you right now NOT to do that." He's sounding a little demanding. I pout, lip fully extended. "I've talked to Becky and she's in charge when you're home. Understand?" I obediently shake my head up and down like the two year old I'm sure to look like.

"Fine." I'm mad at his superiority and rightness. Changing subject now. "By the way, I finally got through to Tanner, aka lap boy, and he said he's got a couple places to show us as soon as we get to the city! You should have heard him, he was laughing at me. He said and I quote, "I can't believe they let you graduate after the disaster you were." The nerve.

He's right though, I totally wouldn't have graduated me either.

"Can you blame him? Really?" He should be on my side here!

"GAH…you sound just like him! Both of you are Big. Fat. Butt faces! No one was more shocked than me when Ms. Scary Face herself came to tell us we'd all passed. She was giving me the stink eye the whole time, I swear. All that matters now is me getting to New York City without any further incident with Danny. I'll stay home, okay. I want to get better." Take that, Charlie bossy pants, who only cares about my well being and loves me…..Thought bubble: I really need to be nicer to Charlie and I should really take his advice on the drive-bys because I don't think I can, but I guess we'll see.

nine

The Stalkers among us…

This not doing drive-bys is proving to be way harder than I'd anticipated. Who knew I'd be compelled to get into Daisy and drive by Danny's at all hours of the night and day! Becky and Charlie knew, that's who. But, I've actually gotten really good at sneaking around behind Becky's back and am starting to feel just a little bit guilty about all the lying that's been going down. After twenty four hours things take a nasty turn and it becomes clear why I was told to stay inside. I never listen….dumb…dumb….dumb.

It's almost ten at night and nobody's cars were in

their designated parking spots at the Inn, which, by the way appears to be growing by leaps and bounds since the new pub addition. It's beginning to look more like a swanky Hotel than the Inn it used to be. I guess our breakup has been working in Danny's favor. I thought it would be safe to sit and stare at the ocean while parked right in front. Top and doors are off my jeep, typical, and I'm listening to my Foo Fighters, duh, staring at the wave breaks in the distance. Then I see them, headlights that turn in my direction momentarily blinding me. Jesus, Mary and Joseph! It's him and I'm in plain sight. I'm not at all a seasoned stalker. I'm totally busted.

I duck down in my seat, like that will help with there being no door and all, but whatever. I'm clearly not making any good decisions at the moment. I should have zoomed the hell out of there but nope, I stay. Seconds later, Danny's door opens and out comes his beautiful strong legs with his black boots and worn jeans on, followed by his hulky broad shoulders that appear to be struggling to escape his favorite billabong T-shirt. I swear this is happening in slow motion and I may or may not be panting. I'm having an out of body experience here. Two long months without seeing his gloriousness have tipped the scales of my love to CRAZY TOWN. Finally his shaggy head of hair that always looks perfectly messed comes out and he's standing his full six feet two inches all loud and proud like, BAM! Mmmmmmmmmm…..

BUZZ KILL ALERT. BEAUTIFUL club bimbo steps from the other side of the truck in stiletto's a mile high that I could never pull off, because I'd face plant for sure, and a dress that is grazing the bottom of her evidently perfect butt cheeks. I want to die. Unfortunately for my currently dissolving mental health, his parents pull into their spot right next to his. His mom, whom I've always loved, gets out and does the unthinkable, she hugs the bimbo. THE FREAKING BIMBO! Just like she used to hug me. It was all lovey and sweet like his mom is and this is the moment the whole thing blows up in my face. His mom spots my terror stricken face over bimbo-girls shoulder and looks confused for a minute before she releases said HOE-BAG and I see her saying something to Danny and in S..L..O..W M..O..T..I..O..N…….he lifts his face and now they are ALL looking… directly…. at ME.

It's obvious by the shocked expression on his perfectly suntanned face that he was not expecting to see me, and why should he be? Especially since the last time I talked to him I told him to never mind the fact that I was coming home and hung up on him. Suddenly the shock is gone from his face and is replaced with what looks like frustration. I realize that there are always two options in this kind of scenario: fight or flight. I'm not stupid! SHUT UP! No opinions please! I do the obvious one and choose the flight. I mean who wouldn't? Plus, who wants to go to jail for stalking, because that's a real thing, I've heard of it happening. Not to mention I have a new city to be off to. I get the hint and do what any psycho ex-girlfriend does when caught red-handed stalking. I FLEE, loudly. My car roars to life and I would swear Daisy roars out of there in my defense. Sweet girl loves her mama. I pat her dash, she loves that.

As I look in my rearview mirror while speeding away I see his face lit up from my red taillights and I think of the lyrics from one of my favorite Foo Fighter songs, DOA.....

Take a good hard look for the very last time
The very last one in a very long line
Only took a second to say goodbye
Been a pleasure but the pleasure's been mine, all mine....

That's it. My last look of the only boy I've ever loved, and that's my tail light tinged final goodbye.

The morning after always sucks…

The next morning I come clean to Becky about my stalkery ways and she loses it. I get a serious talking to. Then she does the unthinkable, okay not really unthinkable, actually totally expected and necessary…She takes my cell phone and says I can only have it back when I'm at the airport leaving and, shocker, that I can no longer be trusted. Of course, I can't argue this point. I've been a lying lunatic since the moment I was back in Palm Beach and, truthfully, I don't even trust myself anymore. Traitor.

"Are you coming to my farewell dinner tonight?" I ask now that she's no longer screaming at me.

"Yah, your mom said they found this great new pub around the corner that they want to take us to." Pause. Emotional Becky arrives, "I just can't believe you're leaving, Elle. I mean, last time, I knew you'd be home, but this feels…like ….permanent." She wipes a tear and she thinks I don't see her do it as she turns around to put something in my suitcase. Always trying to protect me, she really is my best friend in the whole wide world. I can't imagine doing this without her. But, it's time I grew up and left my comfort zone. I need to learn to be self reliant and this is absolutely the way to do it! Go Big or Go Home is what we've always said right? Why should this be any different? She looks over her shoulder at me and smiles her most sincere smile and I know I have her support. I always do. I always have.

An hour later we're nestled (best word ever) into our booth and dinner is going great. The pub food is amazing and the home brews this place makes are RE-DOnk-U-LOus! The owner is some guy by the name of Ryan Stall and he's charming and not too hard on the eyes, either. He's come over to say hi and check on our food several times and he keeps looking at me like he isn't sure if he knows me. Maybe he thinks we hooked up and forgot my name, typical male thing. That would be extra awkward considering he clearly has the hots for Becky and she sure isn't holding back with the hair tossing and doe eyes. Lord, get a room at the hotel of obvious and screw me please.

"So you haven't seen or heard from Danny since you've been home?" My mom sure gets right to it after she gets a couple beers in her.

"Nope," I suck at lying but I have no intention of

surprising my parents with the new development that, SURPRISE, their one and only child is a psychotic stalker. Not happening. Not tonight.

"Huh, I see him all the time at the gym and he's always asking about you. That's weird that he didn't at least phone you to say goodbye." WHAT? He asks about me? She sees him ALL the time? I totally see why she never mentioned this before, says NO ONE EVER!

"Does he know I'm moving to New York?" I know I look all crazy faced. I can't help it. I may sound a wee bit loud and squeaky as well.

"Oh yes, I saw him after one of my zumba classes the other day, right after you'd phoned us about the big move. He seemed shocked. Now I know why, I didn't realize the two of you weren't speaking at all anymore. That's just so sad. You were always so happy together." She is really kicking me in the gut here. I have to be cool, this is my going away dinner and my parents have to believe they're sending me off in a good mental state or I swear my mom will move with me. She'll just curl right up into my suitcase and I'll have no idea until I unzip it and SURPRISE! I come by my stalkery ways honestly. DNA's a Bi-Atch!

"Well, HE kinda shocked me with that whole break up thing. So you know..." They so don't. "I just think its better this way for now. Maybe later in life we'll run into each other and be able to look back fondly on the whole him ripping my heart out thing. Ya never know." I know I sound bitter, but it's only because I am.

We are finishing up our meal, waiting for the waitress to return dad's credit slip when, as luck would have It, THE Hoe Bag walks into the pub, saunters over to Ryan Stall and kisses him square on the mouth with a loud MWAH, how romantic. Becky recognizes grabby-hands immediately and looks as taken aback as I do. She's heard the whole story about Danny and his date with the aforementioned home wrecker at the hotel and is as shocked by her betrayal of Danny as I am. First off, who would cheat on Danny, he's a Stud. Second, I liked Ryan and so did Becky. Not anymore that's for sure, not if he's interested in a tart like that. Looking at her long legs that end at the bottom of her perfectly shaped butt makes me feel completely inept. Note to self, work on recently shattered self esteem. Next thing ya know the two of them are looking all cuddly at a two top situated in the dark shadows at the rear of the pub gabbing a mile a minute. This girl is like a grenade in everyone's love lives. GO AWAY or EXPLODE ALREADY!

Before we are able to deduce what's going on with the cuddly couple the bill is delivered to dad and we leave bummed, having gained no new or useful Intel. Unfortunately Becky is a bit crest fallen about Ryan to boot, but I know my girl, she'll bounce back by morning. Who am I kidding, maybe even by later tonight. Lucky for me, Becky's man hunting plans for the night have changed and she's agreed to have a sleep over at my house tonight like when we were kids.

We drink wine and eat tons of chocolate at our adult sleepovers while chatting about our current plans for the future. Becky is still a stylist at a salon she hates and hopes to find a new place of employment sometime this year; I support this plan as she is to hair like The Bachelor is to T.V., unbelievable. I mean really those girls just don't appreciate the extent at which they are humiliating themselves. Not my business, I know, I did just get caught stalking like twenty four hours ago, BUT I did not do it on t.v. so it's way better! All I'm saying is that I have scruples about my duplicity and Becky rocks at hair doing.

It's well past two a.m. when Becky's annoying snoring starts and I'm quickly reminded why I haven't had a sleepover with her since high school! I may as well be sleeping beside a drowning gorilla and his wet, slurpy, snoring. Gross Becky, get one of those pap smear machines or whatever they're called that can help you with your monkey noises. I thought only fat old men needed those, gah. No wonder she never sleeps over with boys. After hearing this it wouldn't matter how smokin' Becky is; they'd run scared for their future sleep-deprived lives. I wouldn't even be able to judge them like a good best friend should, cause I'd know they were only self preserving.

Becky is good and sound asleep when I spot my newly Swarovski, thanks to Charlie, covered cell in her sleepover bag. Oops. She totally should have slept with that tethered to her person; she very clearly does not realize the depth of my fanatical lovelorn brain. I do what any irrational girl would do in this situation. I snatch back the phone, go into my walk-in closet and sit in the dark to ponder and maybe see what I've missed on my phone, but I absolutely will not make any calls. Nope. Not me.

When I see that there are ten missed calls and fifteen missed texts from Danny my heart starts in triple-time and my hands start sweating. Now I'm the nasty one. No one likes sweaty palms. They're just gross. Gag.

I try to think like Becky and Charlie would want me to think and it occurs to me at once what I need to do. The shocker of all shockers is that I do it, I DELETE THEM ALL, without ever looking or listening to a one. As soon as it's done I regret my decision immediately. Then I know I did the right thing because I did the opposite of what my instincts told me to do, which of course was to open them all in hopes of seeing and hearing of his undying love for me, laced with apologies and begging for forgiveness. The reality is he was probably explaining to me the details of the restraining order he's gotten against me, forbidding me to bother his new girlfriend, the woman who is now the love of his life (who I know to be a cheater!). He'll go on to inform me of how they are soon to be married and moving into the recently awesomized Hotel, so back the "F" off. You don't have to be so mean made-up Danny. Geesh. Curse much.

See Becky, I'm teachable… 8:30am Sunday…

"I still can't believe you deleted them without a single peek. I was debating whether to tell you or not and look at how you've gone and surprised us both with your brilliance! Charlie is going to be like a proud papa." I'm getting ready to board and leave this yucky mess behind me for good so I'm happy to hear Becky thinks I did the right thing. As soon as she got up I told her what I'd done and we called and had my number changed. Now I'm feeling much less anxious about Danny's curse-filled rages or his phantom restraining order. Phew, dodged those bullets!

Danny 8:35am same day…

"I can't believe she didn't even respond, Lex. It was a total shut out. I mean not even an icon of a smiley face to say she was okay or anything." My sister can see how torn I am here but doesn't understand why since she still believes I broke up with Ellie J for all sorts of other made up reasons.

"Well, all I can tell you is that I tried to help you

out big brother and when I called her this morning the message I got said the number has been changed. It appears she may actually be done with you, Danny. You are an idiot, if I haven't told you that already! I can't believe you thought you should date around before you settled down. I seriously expected better of you. Really?" DAMNIT! I wish I could tell Lex the truth but that wasn't part of the deal with our parent's so instead I just look like a total jockstrap here, worse, toe fungus… SMELLY TOE FUNGUS!

What I want to do is fix this whole thing with Ellie J. The situation is getting completely out of hand and it's becoming increasingly clear that we may be doing some irreparable, lasting damage to our once happy-go-lucky relationship and it's all my fault. The problem remains that I can't tell her about my parents' proposition. More importantly, it may be too late anyways and that fact's just not sitting very well with me. I have to do something. I just don't know what?

PART II

ten

I'm down with NYC, Ya You Know Me…

This cab driver is no joke. I don't kid in the face of death. Everyone must do this, this being a cab drive in NYC, before they die (you may actually die doing it, just FYI). This experience was never even on my bucket list or on my radar of top one hundred scariest things to try. It should've been, and it's definitely made my top *ten* scariest list, which also consists of eating bugs, bungee jumping, or generally anything where I may lose my stomach. I hate to barf. I thought for sure when I first saw the city I'd be all like, ewww… awww… but not even close. It was more like, *OH MY GOD I'M GOING TO DIE*! Someone clearly called a crazy cab driver and….I

MEAN WHO CARES about a bunch of buildings when you're facing death? I've since learned all cab drivers drive like this. They must have a pool going for worst cabby or something?!

Thank the good Lord the realty company I was meeting Tanner at was only a ten-minute ride from LaGuardia. I was seconds away from either begging the cabby to drop me at the nearest corner or barfing all over his already germy backseat. Who knows which would've happened first? I would've put money on the barf. Tanner was out the door the minute the cab stopped and I could not have felt more relieved or excited to see him. A couple things happened straight away. First, I forgot how much I really like Tanner. I mean we only met once but we've been texting, a lot, and we have this awesome texting connection plus, he's super sweet, also he has the best smile. Second, I also hadn't noticed how handsome he was the last time we saw each other. I was all terror filled and sorta couldn't see much through my fear-stained glasses or Danny tinted brain.

Also, on the airplane, he was in traveling clothes, which are not at all the same as his work clothes. He's wearing a light gray suit that's tailored to him with a crisp white shirt, top two buttons undone and the effect is that he is effortlessly casual and cool. Holy heart flutter, he cleans up well. He's a solid six foot and where Danny is kinda hulky and buff, Tanner is more like a runner, trim and lean but definitely strong looking. I'm a bit flushed looking at him and I can tell by his smirk he knows he's having an effect on me. How embarrassing, really! My humiliation lately in regards to him, or anyone for that matter, knows no bounds.

He greets me with said dreamy smile while opening the cab door. He reaches down to take my hand to help me out like a gentleman and…Zinggg, whoa, what was that? I just got a zap throughout the entirety of my body when he took my hand in his. I look up into his crystal blue eyes and notice for the first time how much they contrast with his dark, shaggy hair. I remember the last time we met he had on glasses and clearly I didn't get a close look at those babies because, mother of pearl, Wow, with the eyes! Before I know what's happening I'm being pulled from my daydream and into a familiar hug and my body responds happily.

I feel fevered all the way down to my toes and the small hairs on my spine have stood up on end like an army coming to report for duty, the duty of try not to be an idiot around recently realized hot friend. I feel his hand slide to my lower back right about where it dimples and he squeezes me a little closer. Holy Heck-fire! I pull back from him knowing I am all flushed but need to break the contact that is quickly beginning to unnerve me. He smiles down at me, puts his warm hand on my cheek and I think he's about to kiss me. I look like a lunatic because I've closed my eyes in anticipation when he says, "Is there something in your eyes?" Completely serious, GAH!

I quickly pop them open and fake like they were itchy, rubbing them all careful not to ruin my perfectly applied Mary Kay, *I love black* mascara. "Nope, all good, must be allergic to something around here. So itchy." More fake scratching. I'm met with another smirk. ARSE!

"Is your friend Charlie still meeting us here or can we start without him?" That quick he's in business mode. That fast he's recovered from our lover's embrace while I'm still tingling all over. Get a grip woman, he's clearly not interested and more importantly, for some reason, I still love Danny. Clearly, though, I have some lust issues with Tanner that need addressing ASAP.

I respond with a throaty, "He's not in till late tonight. I'm afraid it's just the two of us. Lead the way. I'm all yours." *I could be* is the dirty thought that pops into my mind. Good Gracious! Who's the hoe bag now?

After several hours and countless cabs of death, as I now refer to them, we've seen no fewer than ten places and I know the one I want. Since places go so quick in The City, Charlie told me that if I find one to put down the money and sign what needs to be signed. The shocker here is that he trusts me. Clearly I'm making progress in my life. Go Me!

"This is going to be so FANTASTIC! The Upper East Side is safe, the subway is two blocks away, and we're going to each have our own room, which neither of us thought was even remotely possible. YIPPEE!" I'm jumping for joy when the application is accepted and I know for sure the place is ours.

"Let me take you out to celebrate. We can go to dinner and out after if you're up for it. Cool?" I almost scream Heck yah, but I know I must not act like a fool anymore where Tanner is concerned. I must show that I can be calm, cool and collected like all the other New York girls he knows are sure to be. He's way too smooth to not have cool friends.

"Perfect. First I need to check in at the hotel the airline's set us up in for the next three days." I dig through my bag with a huge smile on my face and immediately start texting Charlie the good news.

"I'll take you. Come on, the company car can pick us up." Perfect.

An hour later, I've checked in to the hotel, added the four extra days we'll need to the reservation and changed out of my stale travel clothes and into my favorite halter style navy sundress that Danny always said made my chocolate eyes look so deep. Whatever that means? I'm not thinking about him. No more. Nope. Not when I have yummy Tanner waiting for me down in the lobby. I'm tingling in anticipation of another zap from him.

I get off the elevator in time to see he's already engaged in a conversation with a very pretty blonde from our training class at the bar and I may get a wee, tiny-bit jealous. I know this is a completely unacceptable reaction because other than said shared tingly hug from earlier, Tanner has been nothing but friendly and polite. Like a friend. She's rubbing his bicep and giving him eyes that say what she'd like from him, and it's not let's make friends, its let's make babies. So I march right over and put an end to *the* nonsense.

"Hey Miranda, I see you've met Tanner. We were just heading out." I take possession of his big hand with my own much smaller one and pull him away from her and right out the spinning entrance doors. He thinks this is funny. I can see him smiling, fighting to hold in a laugh at my expense. Men. So can't kill them.

"In a hurry are we?" His laughing eyes are taking in my pouty face and I can tell he's aware of my jealousy. You'd have to be a complete idiot not to be. Well, I don't find this in the least bit funny. Since I've met him I've done nothing but show him what a neurotic freak I am and right now I'd just like to eat dinner and try to gain back some of my dignity. I'm starting to question his sanity now since he still wants to hang out with me, the neurotic.

"I'm just starving. Do you know that all I've eaten today is airplane food? That is just perfectly unacceptable to my blood sugar. That must be why I'm suddenly so moody." One can only hope he'll be convinced that I'm just hungry and not at all jealous, even though I totally am. "Are there any good pubs around here? I could really go for a cold beer and some greasy food."

"As luck would have it we're only a couple of blocks from one of my favorites. Greasy food and beer are their specialty. You know, you just keep getting cooler." He winks at me. Wowzers, that was hot. Usually winking is gross but on him it's.....there's no words. "A girl who likes greasy food and beer makes me think twice about staying single." He smirks looking down at me sideways and I squirm remembering I've still got his hand entwined with my own small, feisty, possessive one. He's not pulling away though, so we'll just play a hand-holding game of chicken. I always win at chicken, and in this game it would be impossible to lose.

The food and the company are perfect. My first day in the Big Apple has been amazing. I'm in love with it already, minus cab drives of course. I only think of Danny in the quiet moments, which is a change of pace from the constant flow of memories that have been recently wreaking havoc on my new life. I know that this is exactly where I need to be and thanks to Tanner here, things are starting to look promising.

It's glorious walking through the city at night. It's all lit up and there's so much noise and the smells, my goodness there is an abundance of good food in this city, mmmm....it's fantastic. I can't believe this place has been here all along, while I've been sitting on the quiet beach at home. They feel like alternate universes, each with their own list of reasons for being the better choice to live permanently. Right now, though, I'm feeling quite blessed to get to have both places at my disposal.

Tanner and I are almost to the hotel and all I can think is how the walk has been as much fun as the dinner. This walking everywhere is growing on me and so is Tanner. I love sharing his company. His enthusiasm and love for the city are contagious. He's made a good decision coming back. Over dinner I learned he grew up here and is living in his family's walk up on the west side. When he headed south for college his parents bought a place in the south, ready for some warm weather, and fell in love with the beach. Now they live between the two places so they love having Tanner here to watch over the place in the city. It's worked out perfect for them, and quite frankly I can't imagine Tanner anywhere else.

When we get to the hotel I almost ask him up, and then think better of it. Charlie is probably here and we have an early day of training in the morning so it's better to leave my lust at the door. I can tell he's considering how to end the evening as well and I don't want this to get awkward because I really like him, he's been nothing but kind to me. So, I let him off the hook and push onto my tippy toes and give him a friendly kiss on the cheek. He smiles his dreamy smile at me and I'm almost certain I'll be leaving him wanting more....at least, I hope. Hope for something is a nice thing to have back.

When I get to the door of the hotel I turn over my shoulder to say goodnight one last time and he's just standing there watching me with the most unbearable smile on his lips, with the city lights shining around him making him a sight for sore eyes. For the first time in a long while, I will go to bed tonight thinking of someone other than Danny and deep down this makes me sad. But I know there's nothing to do about it; it's over and I'm finally starting to accept it.

Who knew self defense was so gross…

The next day in the self defense class that the airline set up for us, my good feelings about the Big City begin to change, rapidly. I cannot possibly make up what happens next, nor can I believe it's been taught to me, but it has, and I'll never be able to wipe it from my memory. NEVER…EVER. Apparently, if you're alone in the city and attacked, a good line of defense is to pull the bloodied maxi pad in your panties out and stick it to your forehead as a way to scare off your attacker. I KNOW.....GAH, GROSS!! But, as the instructor put it, being shot, bashed over the head or raped is worse...point safety instructor, gross point, but point nonetheless. The class continued on, scaring the wits from me and most of the other girls the rest of the day. They taught us ways to break noses, pop out eyeballs and bash in balls, which truthfully is very self explanatory. Charlie laughed and said what's he to do in the maxi department? Then he came up with some rather gross ideas that are too embarrassing to repeat. It's hard to forget, but he's such a boy sometimes. I love him in spite of said boyness because he so understands my "bat shit" crazy. His words, not mine.

When class is over I can't wait to take Charlie to the new pad and give him a preview of our good fortune. We decide to walk the ten or so blocks and are meeting Tanner there since he's the one with all the power, I mean, keys. On the way Charlie gets right to it. "So you got in late last night," wink, wink. What's with all the winking lately? NO!

"I told you this morning, we had a beer and some

food. Stop." He's so frustrating. All he thinks about is sex and is sure everyone else does, too. There are those of us who have *some* self-control, key word here being some. If he only knew what I'd been thinking last night, I'd be so busted! Don't even get me started on my Danny daydreams, I'd combust....So HOT!

"You didn't cry last night and I could feel you daydreaming about you know who from the next bed over. I can't wait to get a look at this guy. I bet he's yummy. I saw your type at the bar; you've got good taste my friend." More winking. That's it, he's got tourettes. That's the only possible explanation for that twitchy eye! He'd die if he saw Danny, he makes the bar guy look like a hobo. His twitching would go completely, shockingly, crazy!

"I didn't cry last night because after my trip home I've accepted Danny is over me and I'm working really hard to not be so pathetic. Could you please stop treating me like I'm such a baby? I know I deserve it after the way I've behaved since the moment you first laid eyes on me, but believe me, that is not who I am anymore. I was just grieving, okay? Geesh." I ended this with an eye roll. Yep, I'm not a baby at all.

"Got it, my Ellie's all grown up now and soon to

have yummy sex with that yummy new boy toy staring your clothes right off, and in the middle of the day in front of all us strangers. Now who's the perve?"

I slap him on the arm and take in Tanner in the daylight, and Charlie's right. He is yummy. Today he isn't in a suit but in a pair of worn in jeans. You can tell they are probably his favorite by the way they are worn in all the right and expected places. They sit low on his hips and he pared it with a soft t-shirt with a band name I've never heard of printed on it, nice. I love obscure music and sexy jeans. Two points Tanner.

"Hey beautiful," he leans down and kisses my cheek and my body does that zingy thing again, Bliss…

"Hey," is the smartest word I can muster in my flustered state. Charlie rolls his eyes at the pair of us and takes over. "Come on you two, I have an apartment to fall in love with, no time for sex." CHARLIE YOU ARE SO DEAD! Is what my eyes are screaming at him telepathically. He laughs and walks away before either Tanner or I can defend ourselves. I look over at Tanner and he is laughing too. Thank the heavens.

Charlie goes gaga over the place and now we have a million things to do before move in day. Tanner takes us to several home decorating stores, and then a few antique shops. The three of us are having an exceptional day with Tanner and I continuing on with our flirting and without noticing I'm more relaxed than I have been in months. My life seems to be sorting itself out beautifully. Then, my lovely little bubble gets majorly burst.

A replica of the hoe bag, perfect butt and all, is slowly sauntering towards us staring at Tanner with an intensity that makes me feel like I am infringing upon a very private moment. Apparently privacy isn't an issue because she reaches us a moment later and is instantly wrapped around him, talk about handsy, phew. Those spiders are everywhere. Tanner is not yelling "Stop! Rape!" or pushing her off, like we learned in self defense class earlier. Rather, he seems to be enjoying himself right along with her. It's disgusting. I can't believe I even considered liking him…PIG! OINK much? I bet he oinks her all the time!

Charlie makes an MMMHmm noise in his throat and the two of them pull themselves apart for some much needed air. "Hi, I'm Leslie. And you are?" She says sticking out a single claw to me, looking me over while simultaneously sizing me up. Clearly she doesn't see me as any sort of threat. I can tell by the way she's looking amused with my long, curly hair and my petite frame. Obviously I am no match for her long legs and glossy pin-straight, waist length hair. She is physically perfect, but a hoe bag none the less.

I know my dignity is in danger because I actually feel the pressure of tears forming behind my eyeballs. I can't believe I thought Tanner was interested in me. This is a devastating blow to my exceptionally fragile ego. Charlie is reading my body language and saves the day. "Oh good. I'm glad someone's here to take you off our hands, Tanner. Elle and I have a manicure appointment in thirty minutes and we were going to have to ditch you so this is perfect timing. Say bye Elle." He prods me because I can't move, speak, or blink for fear of spilling tears.

"Bye." And just like that I'm being whisked away by Charlie, my gay knight in shining Armani.

eleven

Distractions rule, boys drool…

"You have to go pick up the keys to the apartment. I can never face Tanner again. He must've thought I was some silly little fly-girl with a crush. How am I ever going to succeed at dating? I have terrible..NO..APPALLING, instincts. GAHHHHH!" I am currently sitting with my knees tucked under my chin, rocking back and forth like a total tool.

"This is what we're going to do. The car will be here in a minute to pick us up along with all these bags. You will stay in the car. I'll run in to get the keys, say you aren't even with me *if* he asks, and then we'll skedaddle, zoom away, gone with the wind.

You'll never even have to lay eyes on him, plan?" Did he just say skedaddle? Hmm, whatever. He's a saint and an amazing love doctor. He can say whatever he wants. He keeps my prescription filled.

"Yes, plan. Make an apology for me so he doesn't think I'm too embarrassed to come and see him. I've been avoiding his calls all week and I definitely don't want him to think I was jealous, okay?" He totally knows I'm jealous, he's not stupid. His brain is part of what makes him so totally hot. His brain is an aphrodisiac!

"Already thought of that, but I *am* proud you did too. You're learning, young one. Very good. Always remember where boys are concerned pride is number one. There may be hope for you yet. You're growing up. I like it." I love that he can see I'm learning through all this mess, I'm so proud of me. My pride and keeping it in tact are the goal here. Besides Charlie said he was thrown by the girlfriend, too. He could have sworn Tanner was feeling me. This has seriously messed with Charlie and his belief that he can read peoples sexual desires. Tanner is just one big fat giant question mark for us both, and we're over the mystery.

Charlie is inside spelling it out for Tanner while

I'm dying in wait. "She's in the car actually, but you're right, she doesn't want to see you."

"I knew it. Damnit! You have to believe me man, Leslie is an ex, I swear to it." Charlie likes watching him squirm. Why you ask? Because, he even squirms sexy. And now that he knows he was right about Tanner wanting Elle he's changing the plan…again.

"Well then it's your lucky day. For some reason my gut is telling me to trust you so I'll give you a hint. A grand gesture would help you out. A text isn't how to get a girl like Elle to talk to you. She's too good for that and her ex just doesn't get that either."

"What ex?" Tanner looks nervous which is great for team Elle.

"The guy she's running from. THE ex. And if I were you I'd work hard because she's still in love with him. You play your cards right you can swoop in and save the day. Flowers wouldn't hurt for starters and then maybe some light groveling. I know she likes you so don't be an ass here. Just fix it." With that Charlie takes the keys out of Tanner's startled hands and takes off waving Toodles over his shoulder. He knows what he has to do now though and that is to help Ellie get over this ex because obviously whoever he is, he's stupid enough to let a girl like her get away and he has no intention of making the same mistake.

The apartment…

"My room is unpacked, I'm wiped out and I go on call tomorrow. All I want to do for the rest of the day is relax. I'm not cooking, so what should we do for dinner?" BUZZ….BUZZ…pause…BUZZ…BUZZ….. So loud, what in the world? That is going to take some getting used to. I push the intercom button and almost shout a surprised, "Hello?"

"Flower delivery for Elle Hallowell." The delivery guy sounds so bored, poor guy.

"Come on up." I buzz him back and he's at the door a moment later after ascending the three short floors.

The expected knock comes and I run excitedly to see if Danny sent me flowers at last. I'm disappointed in myself for the thought a moment later because he'd never done that before, so why would he suddenly start now. I should be embarrassed answering in the small nightie I am wearing but hey, it is just going to be a delivery boy, why not make his day. I have no money for a tip anyway, skin will have to suffice. Desperate times and such.

"Hi, wow these are amazing!" Then I hear his voice. "I'm glad you like them." And there he is behind the delivery boy, who is currently drooling over my said lack of clothing. Great! Devious flower delivery boy deserves a big fat fluffy robe fist to the face.

"Oh my gosh," I toss the flowers back at the delivery boy and run off in search of the robe I know I just unpacked, but where? I hear the door shut and Charlie saying, "about time. I almost thought you'd chickened out." WHAT? I'm being set up? Not okay! Uncool BF move.

"What do you mean?" I say giving up on my robe in the heat of the moment and coming back into the room in a huff. Let em' look and see what he can't have.

"Listen, this is not what it looks like. I told Charlie all about the misunderstanding and I just wanted a chance to explain to you. There's no set up going on here, please believe me. I'll say my piece and get out of your hair if I can just have a minute first." He is a little grovely and I find I like that. Danny's certainly never groveled. Point to Tanner, he can explain, and I'm starving, too. hmmm?

"Fine, you can explain, but I'm starving. Feed me and it's a deal." Wow, go get em' tiger. Me-OW!

He agrees immediately and then his eyes are wondering over me and I realize I am still in my most delicate nightie, showing more skin than necessary to a guy I've yet to even kiss, "yet" being the operative word. Look at that mouth. ELLIE, Head…Gutter….OUT!

Holy Kiss!...

"I can't believe your parents live here. You don't act like a zillionaire or anything…." I look around at the opulence of the living room and can't get over how each room keeps getting better than the next. Being around Tanner, I never got the impression that he was a spoiled rich kid. I am seriously impressed that he is choosing to take me home and cook for me rather than showing off and taking me to some fancy place, because if I haven't made it clear, he can afford to. My opinion of him is growing bigger by the minute. He opens a beer for me and pours it into a frosty mug like he's already learned that I like. Clearly the few times we've been out he's been paying close attention to detail. Either he's a playboy who's very educated in how to treat women or he's genuinely interested. We'll see. The verdicts still out on this one. I sure hope the jury finds in his favor, though.

He smiles at me when he starts talking probably reading the thought bubble I've been rambling in over my head, "This is where I grew up, so to me it's just home. Don't get me wrong, I know it's nice but it's not like I earned the money. I can't take responsibility for any of this, but it doesn't hurt my cause if it impresses you." And then he flashes me a smile that gives me the shivers and I hope more than anything that I'll be able to forgive him for Leslie The Hoe and our future relationship's death.

We sit at the kitchen island and eat the most delicious homemade pizza I've ever had. The crust is just how I like it, thin and crispy almost to the point of being burnt and it's covered with fresh veggies, my mouth is in heaven. It's a flavor explosion of the best kind. We keep the conversation light while we eat but as soon as we finish and put everything in the sink he takes my hand in one of his and grabs the bottle of wine in the other leading me upstairs to an amazing outdoor patio. I really should congratulate him on his smooth moves. His confidence is a major turn on.

The patio is covered with potted plants, each one wrapped in delicate twinkle lights that sparkle a bright clean white. It's like being in a dream. The tiny lights are reflecting off all the modern metal and glass surfaces throwing light around like a disco ball, a sexy disco ball. The furnishings are modern but yet they're still homey with little splashes of color in the pillows and throw blankets; the word that best describes this patio is romantic.

He fills both of our glasses and sits down close to me on the plush, cushy, outdoor sofa. He's so close that our thighs are rubbing together in an extremely intimate way, causing me to grow increasingly nervous and very ready to hear his plea for another shot. "So Leslie?" I say, starting the much needed conversation we've managed to ignore until now.

"Leslie is my EX girlfriend, emphasis on the EX part. Our families have been close since we were kids and to them it was always a given we'd be together. We went out for a bit when I got here and I really tried to like her in a romantic way, for my parent's sake, but you met her. She's awful. I hated that you thought I'd like someone like her and then you wouldn't answer my calls, so I thought when you came for the key I could explain, but then you didn't. I hope you don't think I'm crazy for showing up at your place. I just really needed you to know I was sorry for the other day. I know I looked like a big jerk, I just didn't know how to get her off me politely without causing a scene so…." He drifts off watching me closely hoping for some kind of response. But I'm thinking…deciding. Making him sweat.

"Okay. So you don't like her even though she's beautiful and a bit hoey?" Lately, I'm noticing guys really seem to dig hoe's. It's a theme.

"You're beautiful, and oddly enough, I don't like the hoey ones. Kinda turns me off." He is teasing me now, but good answer!

"Alrighty then. Oddly enough I feel better with that admission and clearly you've now learned that I can be bought with a homemade pizza, some good wine and a romantic patio." While I've been rattling on nervously his free hand has made its way behind my back onto my opposite hip and is currently pulling me closer to him. Personal space is no longer an issue because there is none. Holy cow, here it comes. I am staring at his lips, I can't help it, I want to suck on them....BAD! No thoughts of Danny anywhere, except for that one and now it's gone. Go Tanner Go my brain shouts as it pushes all Danny memories away from its frontal lobe where it was way too close to kissing Tanner with me.

"I'm going to kiss the hell out of you right now, okay?" Then his other hand snakes through my hair at the back of my neck and it is on. Like On, On. My light is switched to full brights, amongst other things.

Holy cow can he kiss! Danny kissing me pops into my mind again for a moment, but I push, no drop kick that thought aside as fast as I can. I am going to give Tanner a fare shake here, so the *imaginary* Danny needs to back off, NOW! I become just as eager as Tanner, my aggressiveness surprising us both, but in a very good way. He growls and I love a man who growls in reaction to my moves. My hands are busying themselves exploring every line of his back, then move on through his hair, and currently they are progressing down to his oh so glorious abdominal muscles. Gosh, I love good abs.....ahhhhhhhh. This is the first moment I believe it's totally possible that I can get over Danny and that makes the kiss even sweeter. Good Lord did I mention his abs...those help too and I know it sounds like I'm using his body to forget someone else but seriously with the abs…

The Foo Fighters blare from my cell, startling us both back to reality. It's Becky's song, what the heckfire….gah! I grab the mood-killing device out of my back pocket, making an I'm so sorry face and holding my finger up to Tanner begging him to hold that thought.

"WHAT?" I say all breathy and frustrated.

"Good to hear your voice, too darling. What are you doing? Running on a treadmill? What's with the heavy breathing, you psycho?" I'm silent. I cannot answer this question with Tanner sitting right here so I just say "Becks, what?"

"YOU SLUT, you're hooking up right now. Who is it? Can I talk to him?" Her hook-up radar is crazy good! And heck no can she talk to him but she already knew that when she asked.

"NO. Are you crazy?" She's giggling. We both know the answer to that question anyway, duh. Then it's quiet and Becky quiet isn't a good sign. So I wait for the drama queen to get back to it.

"Well, we'll get to that later. I just wanted to tell

you I saw Lex today and she wanted to talk to you so I gave her your number, just a heads up to warn you. She is really p.o'd at her brother and I felt bad for her. She misses you Ellie. Don't be mad okay?" I miss Lex too. Breaking up with someone when you like the family adds a who other layer of suck to the breakup casserole.

"I'm not mad and thanks a bunch for the heads up. Listen, I really gotta go. It's so not a good time to talk about all this. Call you tomorrow sometime, kay?" Talking about Lex makes me feel sad suddenly. I lost her in a way as well and I don't know if I can trust myself to talk to her and not ask about Danny, so now I'm completely at a loss. THANKS A LOT BECKY!

"Kay. Love you EJ. Miss you bunches." I know she realizes she totally ruined my hook up and she owes me, BIG TIME!

"Miss and love ya back. Lates loser." Dig number one. Tanner knows something's up and I can see he's reluctant to ask so I put him out of his misery and tell him something that isn't a lie. "That was my best friend from home Becky. She just wanted me to know she gave out my new cell number to an old friend and wanted to give me a heads up. Unfortunately though, I kind of need to head home." I could tell that he did mind, but being the gentleman that he is he just smiles and offers me his hand as he stands to help me up as well. And that right there is exactly why I like him. Mr. Confident meet Mr. Manners. A killer combo on any man.

"Let me get you a cab. It's been a long day and I can imagine you're not in the mood for the public transit system tonight. Am I correct?" He gives me a one sided grin while lifting his eyebrows in question. He is so smart, he's clearly read his dating handbook and knows player one is in need of a time out. Just so he knows I plan on resuming the game after a cool down. I lean in and give him one last exploratory kiss before backing off and heading to the door, a lovely little reassurance peck.

"You are correct, but you don't have to get me a cab. I can take care of it. I'm a big girl." Actually, I'm kind of small in physical terms.

"Completely unacceptable, I've brought you over here and I'll get you home. What kind of schlep do you take me for? Come on; let's go find you a cab and that'll give me a couple minutes to pull myself together from that kiss." He looks down at me and I can see the impact I've had on him tonight and I definitely like it. His "impact" I mean. Mind wink.

"Thanks for the dinner and everything else." I say one last time as we're standing by the cab and I suddenly get shy, which is not typically my style. Quirky and awkward, yes. Shy, not so much.

"No, thank you for talking to me .....and the other stuff was pretty hot." He smiles and I can tell we both are thinking about the same thing, *THE* other stuff. "Can I see you tomorrow?" He moves fast, whoa.

"I'm on call so I can talk I just can't venture far in case I get called out. They don't give us much time to get packed and to the airport. Plus I'm totally nervous," as soon as I say this he laughs. Our first meeting pops to mind and I laugh with him remembering how ridiculous I behaved.

"I don't believe that for a minute. You're so cool on airplanes, you'll be great!" I can tell he's trying to make me feel better, but it's not working due to all his laughing, at me. Humor aside, I'm good and freaked out about receiving the dreaded call for my first trip. I've been meditating daily on the good advice from Mary Phelps, and dear Lord do I hope it works.

"Okay, well I gotta go. Talk soon." I get on my tiptoes, kiss him softly on his all too willing lips and touch his arm one last time before I get in the cab and speed away. I see him watching the cab until it's out of sight and I feel happy, and it's not the kind where you're fooling yourself. It's the real deal, I'm all lit up with like and lust and I feel like I could bust from heat retention. I'm like a jiffy pop bag on the stove of love waiting to pop wide open and spill all my buttery goodness.

twelve

Danny's World…

"Hey dipshit," my little sister Lex says, barging into my room using her skeleton keycard. "I thought maybe you'd be interested to know that I got her new number." She's looking at me all smug, hands on her hips.

"Who's? What are you talking about?" I think I know and I'm about to beg her to give it to me on my hands and knees?

"You know who. I can tell by your crazy eyes. Ellie J's obviously. I just can't decide if I should give it to you because Becky trusted me not to and I haven't decided if you deserve to know it." I deserve what she's dishing out.

"What do you want me to say, Lex?" I'll say or do about anything and she knows it.

"How about you tell me the real reason you broke the heart of the girl you've loved for most of your life." Except for that, I can't answer that. "It makes no sense how you went AWOL on her. I want the real reason, not the crap you've been feeding everyone else. I know you too well to buy any of that." I'm hung.

"I can't Lex. If I could you'd be the first person other than Ellie J that I'd tell but you have to trust me when I tell you… I can't." She huffs out an angry breath as she turns to leave, without giving me the number I'm dying for.

"Fine. Your loss. I hope you realize what you're losing because she's never gonna forgive you if you wait too much longer." When she leaves, I'm still phone numberless…

Twenty minutes later I'm heading down to the kitchen when I see Lexy talking all animated on the phone through the patio doors. It dawns on me that she may be talking to Ellie J and I'm suddenly not in a hurry to eat. I've got to hear for myself. I sneak out the side door where I can listen behind a nearby pillar. I can tell by hearing Lex's side of the conversation that it's Ellie. My heart is strumming like a bass guitar to a heavy beat and my skin is tingling with nerves and anticipation about what I am about to do. Knowing all I have to do to hear her voice is take the phone from Lex propels me to act, no matter the consequence.

I reach my sister and have the phone yanked from her hand before she knows what's happening. "Shit, give that back you giant ASSHOLE!" She yells, but I'm locked in the nearby men's room before she can get to me. "Ellie J? Are you still there?" Dead silence.

"Listen I know you don't trust anything I say anymore and I deserve that. I haven't been an awesome friend and if I were in your position I wouldn't want to be my friend either. I just…" just what? What can I possibly say to her to fix this? Then reality hits me. Nothing. Then I hear it and for the first time in months I can breathe deep. It's her voice. God I haven't heard her voice in too long and I'm flooded with memories. Memories of her singing silly songs to me during our guitar lessons, the sex kitten voice she uses when see's kissing me and whispering how much she wants me, the sound of the I love you's I know she's only ever said to me. And the weight of what I've done crashes down on me.

"Danny. What are you doing?" Keep her on the line jackass.

"I just wanted to hear your voice. I've been worried about you, if you can believe that? I was there when you passed out the last time you flew, in case you forgot. I can't believe you're doing this."

"Well don't worry about me, I'm fine. I've had lots of help from some great new friends." This is the killer; she has a whole new life that I know nothing about.

"Worrying about you is kind of an old habit I'm trying to break." No. No, not trying to break, why did I say that? Focus dude!

"Oh. Well. Good." I can feel her sadness and all I want is to fix it.

"Why didn't you stop by when you were home to say goodbye? The night I saw you I tried to talk, to catch up to you but you, just sped off. I thought maybe you were there to see me?" God say yes.

"Um, I didn't know why I was there. Then it felt weird and I just left," her answers are so short and they sound so....not Ellie.

"I tried to call you but then you changed your number. It's been weird not being able to talk to you. I mean we used to talk all the time and then you were just gone from my life. You literally vanished." Good so far. Maybe she'll settle for friendship until I can figure something out.

"Listen, I don't know what you want me to say, but you broke up with me and I just felt like after the amount of time we were together the only way was to make a clean break and, well, unless something's changed that's why I'm here and you're there." She wants to know if I changed my mind.

"I'm sorry. That's what I've been trying to say. I just needed you to know that. I'm sorry. I never wanted to hurt you, ever. It seems I can't stop though doesn't it?" I am such a jerk. I've literally just had to do an impromptu break up with her all over again. I have zero foresight. How did I not see this coming?

"Well, if that's it, then apology accepted and you can live your life with a clear conscience. My dates here, I gotta go. Bye Danny." And just like that she's gone…. Again. And to make matters worse, I now know she also has a date! FML!!!

Ellie's world…

"Are you sure you're okay? Because I gotta go sweetheart, check-in is in 30 minutes." Charlie is going on his first trip and he's trying to temper his excitement to fit my melancholy mood. I love the way he cares about my sanity.

"I'm fine, nothing a good six pack can't fix," he's looking at me like I need AA stat. "Just kidding, this is not the first time he's let me down. I'm getting better at this. Go, I'm fine. Really." The crazy thing is I am handling this much better than either Charlie or I could possibly have imagined. I think I'm just getting numb where Danny's concerned and it doesn't hurt that I have a Tanner sized Band-Aid in place.

"I can't believe I'm headed to Palm Beach on my first trip. Ironic? Becky's my bitch for the next three nights so it should be good." He kisses my cheek, smacks my hiney and sachet's out the door. What a girl. And, he is so Becky's bitch he just doesn't know that yet.

I run to the window and fling it open, "Charlie! You two better call me tonight!" I shout as he's hopping into a cab. He looks up at me and smiles, "Duh. Now go inside. It's raining and I'm off." With a final wink and a wave, the diva has left the city. Palm Beach will never see him coming.

Our tiny, no, let's call it cozy, shower is calling to me. I'm really working on positive self talk. No more wallowing. I really don't want to be the kind of friend that is all wrapped up in self pity all the time. I am going to embrace this new life and let the cards fall where they may. Cliché alert! Maybe tonight I'll be off to Europe where more excitement awaits. Come on phone...... ring.

Two days go by and I'm still home. *Home Alone in the City* should be the title of my new life. Tanner's called but I can't bring myself to see him after Danny's call. I haven't mentioned the whole I'm still crazy in love with my ex thing to him yet but I really ought to. The dilemma is this; I really want to keep sucking face with him. He's such a good kisser and I miss that so much. Danny is the best but Tanner gives him a run for his money, and he's available, which totally helps. It' just that I know his kissing won't stop me from loving Danny and that makes me feel a bit hoe-y, so I'm kind of sitting around ignoring Tanner, hoping he'll just give up. Then all my problems are solved. Head is currently parked deep in the sand. See that butt up in the air? Yep, that's me.

Finally on the third day of my four days on call I get my chance to fly, to....wait for it....Arkansas. ARE YOU KIDDING ME!!!? I've never even heard of El Dorado but this is my life story. El-freakin'-Dorado. Meanwhile, I get a call from Becky and Charlie giving me a play by play of their three day hedonism fest. Not cool B-to-the-itches! They both actually have the nerve to laugh when I tell them where I'm going. EXTRA. NOT. COOL!

On the way to the airport, I snag my hose on my new, apparently sharp, roller bag, step in a puddle while wearing my new leather heels and unfortunately I underestimated the heat and put on too little deodorant because now I have visible arm pit stains. The picture I had of myself entering into my first flight all glamorous and gorgeous is riddled with irony now. It's completely possible I may even get put back on probation for the smell of my pits alone.

By the end of my first day I'm exhausted and bloated. Tomorrow I must remember to follow rule five of Mary Phelps to do list and hydrate. Otherwise I've done excellent. No panic attacks, fainting or accosting passengers. Really I was brilliant. A fellow steward gave me a new pair of stockings and my pit stains have dried out with all the dehydration; unexpected dehydration bonus. The best part is that tomorrow we're leaving El Dorado and heading to Los Angeles. The irony is not lost on me that while I'm in Charlie's hometown he's in mine.

The pilots arrive the next morning and we all introduce ourselves before the day's flight. "I hear this is only your second day flying," says today's co-pilot, who introduces himself as Garrett, adding no last name. Obviously, he's way too cool for a last name introduction. He's a first name only kind of guy; I've met his type before, they're called collectively, Douche bag.

"You heard correct. Please fly straight and if you could help it, stay away from turbulence or anything else that's weird. I'm a nervous flyer." I say this in all seriousness but he thinks I'm joking, I can tell by his you're so funny laugh. So I laugh along to not give myself away and he's buying it. My Oscar please.

On the flight over things are going smooth. Literally; there's no turbulence. Smooth as a baby's behind until Arizona and then all hell breaks loose. Other pilots were reporting a bad area and unfortunately it's on our flight plan. In my mind I'm thinking change the damn flight plan but the pilots are like, "no problem we'll just pop on the handy seat-belt sign and problem solved." No, problem not solved!

I forget all the techniques I was previously given when we encounter the first "speed bump". Let's call it what it actually is: a free fall from the sky. THE SKY! I do the look around for support, and every freaking person on the plain looks terrified. So I move on to technique two, breath and relax. It just so happens I can only accomplish these brilliant moves when the plane isn't falling. Step three, hydrate. Not possible on current roller coaster ride I'm on. OH MY GOD, THESE STEPS SUCK! I normally don't take the Lords name in vain, but this is an actual cry out to Him, it's not in vain, so it's totally acceptable here seeing that the last step is to pray and that's all I'm capable of in my current state.

"Elliott, Elliott, wake up," why am I being shaken and what's that awful smell? "There you go, easy does it." Garrett is looking down at me with a concerned expression on his young face and an ammonia stick between his fingers. I hadn't realized how young he looked until this minute, and I agreed to get on an airplane he's flying, note to self only fly with old men. "I thought you were just kidding earlier when you said you were a nervous flyer but you weren't, were you?" Clearly, smarty-pants. My faint-fests are completely humiliating.

"Nope, I'd never kid about that. I've gone and passed out again haven't I?" I'm a tool. Screwdriver's have nothing on me.

"Can you get up? Sit maybe?" He's being sweet, maybe my douche-o-meter is off a bit. Jennie, one of the other stewardess's has brought him over a cool rag and he's holding it to the back of my neck while she fans me with a sky mall brochure.

"Yah, I think. I could use some help though, I'm feeling a bit loosey goosey." I reach up and put my shaking hands around his broad shoulders and am struck by a wave of déjà vu. Holding onto him brings me back to the last time this happened when Danny was the one to scoop me up into his strong arms. Not helping here, so I let go and pat his arm reassuring him I'm better now. "Just please tell me I've been unconscious long enough that we're through the worst of it."

"Yes, otherwise I'm guessing, we'd be in trouble here, wouldn't we? You know, considering I'm not in the cockpit." He's grinning but I can see his concern for my mental health. He really has no idea. But wait! He's not in the cockpit. HOLY HELLO!

I get my legs quickly back in working order and begin pushing him closer to the cockpit all the while rambling the way I like to do, "I'd feel much better if you were flying the plane. Stop worrying about me; I'm just going to have a soda. How much longer do we have anyway?" Please say less than an hour. I need the ground like Charlie needs his boas.

"We're not far, maybe thirty minutes." He's trying to pull away my crazy claws while laughing at me. "Okay, if you're all right I'll try to get us there in one piece." My face shows real horror so, he laughs harder. "What? Sorry, bad joke?" I'm slapping him repeatedly on his big arm and he just laughs more. Not funny, fly boy.

Luckily most of my hijinks have taken place behind the galley wall so the passengers are none the wiser to my turbulence induced fall off and I can get back to the business at hand. I'm quite capable of working again now that I've been informed by the youngest pilot in the history of flying that we'll be landing soon.

Later that night…

"Let's go out." It's a statement, not a question. Garrett is standing firm at the entrance of my open door dressed and ready for a night out on the town in dark denim jeans, a grey Henley t-shirt and a cool leather bomber jacket. He looks like a pilot in a top gun sort of way and I dig it. He's a cool cat.

"Yes, I'd love to!"

"I've called a cab already. Call it wishful thinking, but I had a hunch you'd like a night out."

"You are a mind reader. I just got off the phone with a friend who gave me instructions for a guaranteed fun night in LA and I was just heading out hoping to meet up with some of the girls at the bar downstairs but you'll do. Come on, let's do this." There's no way I'm sitting in this lonely room tonight contemplating the day I've just had. If so, I'd never agree to go to work tomorrow. So this is an easy choice. Go out or quit my job. For sure, going out wins.

The cab takes us to the first club on our list and Garrett and I have thankfully dressed the part to get through the door. Apparently, according to this bouncer, we are cool enough. I'm in black hot shorts and a white-collared button up bodysuit with black peep toe heals, which obviously works for said bouncer. I can tell by the way he is raping me with his eyes. PIG!

"Shots?" Asks Garrett as he already has an arm raised to get the busy bartender's attention.

"Why not? I feel like I can survive anything after today." When you stare death in the eyes, what's a shot or five?

Several shots later we are on the dance floor and I am officially drunk. Garrett saw fit to get me several shots followed by several beers. He is a very smart man; if his goal is to get me out of my head, then score Garrett because I'm out of my inebriated mind.

We dance for hours' or maybe it's minutes. I have no clue, as I can't keep time anymore in said inebriated state. I finally unstick my sweaty flesh from his, he's a very good dancer, and I let him know

I'm ready to go. I'm exhausted. Matter of fact, I've never felt this tired in my life. It's as if the last several months of stress have all hit me at once and all I want to do is go to bed. Hibernation sounds more like it, but I'll settle for at least ten hours of uninterrupted sleep.

He agrees and we're outside in a cab in what feels like mere seconds. I must have fallen asleep on the drive because he wakes me when we're in the roundabout of the hotel and helps me up to my room. He takes the keycard from my uncooperative hands and gets us into my room with a single swipe of his steady hand. I want to say thanks and goodnight but clearly we're on two different pages because before I know what's happening I've been flopped onto the bed all WWF style and am currently being dry humped and kissed by what appears to be a snake.

I can honestly say I did not think this was a real thing, the dry-humping. Danny always thought of my needs first, he said it made it more fun for him. What's happening here is beyond anything I've ever experienced. I've heard stories of 'it' happening like this before but they're more like the Lochness Monster or big foot stories; I thought they were legends, but apparently dry humping is a real thing and one can get to "completion" this way because that is what is currently happening to Garrett.

"YES!" He shouts and I'm thinking, yes, I'd like you to get off me now, you wanna-be Maverick. Mav would have never ended his flight test like this. He would have been all TURN AND BURN MAV, TURN AND BURN, until everyone was involved if you know what I mean.

"It's late, I think you should go," is all I'm capable of saying without laughing. I'm about to start in on a serious bout of giggles and I need him to get out of here ASAP or his manhood is going to be put in jeopardy.

"Yah," he says rolling over spent and in serious need of both a change of clothes and a shower.

"Okay, can you let yourself out? I'm exhausted." Don't laugh. Don't laugh. Don't laugh.

"You good?" Um, is this a trick question? How do I answer him without telling him he knows absolutely nothing about the female anatomy?

"Yep, all set. Maybe we'll work together again sometime. Thanks for everything today. You really helped me out of a sticky situation." Did I just say sticky? I can't keep it together ten seconds longer. I start having preemptive laugh spasms and swiftly shoe him out while shutting the door in his face in tandem. Dr. Phil would find my current state intriguing, considering I'm stumbling over to my now mussed bed, tears streaming, trying not to alert the entirety of the sixth floor of my hysteria. I can't breathe I'm laughing so hard. I can NOT believe that this is my life. So glamorous and sexy! HA! This thought creates more laughing. Then eventually I've laughed myself to sleep, on top of the icky covers, still in sweaty, freshly humped clothes. Today my life is called…….GROSS!

thirteen

Days later back in New York…

"Tell me again how long it lasted," bwahahahaha goes Charlie….. again.

"Not even long enough for a pre-flight check if you know what I mean," now I'm laughing again. The poor women doing our pedicures have no hope of getting us to sit still. I've already told Charlie about the legend better known as Garrett, but it put him in such a good mood the first time that we're now on our third replay. It just never gets old.

"Lord, after seeing your Danny I officially

understand what all the tears have been about. Mmmm, yummy! I would've cried for years, baby girl. And then to have to be exposed to a two minute, over the clothes attack like the one ol' Mav unleashed on you? I'm wiping your love slate clean sweetheart. You need a complete do over."

"I still can't believe you saw him. He never used to go out, and now it seems like that's all he does. You know that's probably why he broke up with me. We were like an old married couple and maybe all along he needed more excitement in his life. I feel like such a fool for thinking I was enough for someone like him."

"Clearly you've never looked in the mirror. You, my dear, are one fine girl and if I weren't so gay I'd be all over that," he says, waving his hand from the top of my head to my toes. "Don't you go thinking he's better than you, not even close." I love Charlie. He totally polishes my self esteem and pulls it from its case when I need him to.

"Let's stop all the Danny talk. It's depressing and I've been really happy lately. Kay punkin?" I say all sleepy while rubbing his newly manicured and massaged hand beneath my own. Cardinal red is so pretty is what I'm repeating in my mind while trying to wipe Danny out of it. *Cardinal red is so pretty, cardinal red is so pretty*........this is my final thought before I'm jerked back to reality upon hearing an obnoxious, familiar voice sit down beside us.

"Tanner's mom told me not to worry. He's going with me for sure. Apparently he's already got a new tux and everything, so it's done. He called last night and told me he'd pick me up so, YIPPEE," actual hand clapping is going on, yuck. Cheerlead much.

"I can't believe you. You always manage to get him back; it's like a magic trick. Your name is now officially Leslie the great Houdiness," says her equally annoying and squawky friend, sporting equally fake blond hair. Barf. My ears are pulling so hard to the left I am almost laying on Charlie's shoulder and he's almost lying over on Leslie's. We both recognized her at the same time, his recently manicured eyebrows told me so when they shot up at the sight of her and bimbo number two.

Bimbo number one and two continue on about all sorts of random idiotic subjects and Charlie and I make our escape without being recognized. If she had talked to us we would have instantly become stupider, no question. I am trying not to be mad because I've only kissed Tanner the one time and have been keeping distance between us since. Unfortunately the green-eyed monster is raising his ugly little face and I am undoubtedly jealous. Maybe this means I'm getting over Danny, because why else would I care? And I do. So I do what any normal girl would do. I finally call Tanner back. At the exact moment I know he's unavailable.

The call worked…

"By the way, I'm really glad you called, but I think I've said that enough. After you left last week I had a feeling I'd never see you again," I admire his honesty and the way he looks in that crisp white shirt with the sleeves bunched up at the elbows, so manly. I can't seem to bring myself to do the same honest thing in return and mention I'm completely emotionally unavailable for the rest of my life, but oh well. I'm on a jealous date.

"I'm sorry I left so quickly after my friend called and then I haven't called like I said I would. I've been a jerk. Still friends?" Say yes. I sound just the right amount of grovelly, I should know, I practiced.

"I wouldn't be here if we weren't. I like hanging

out with you, you're not like other girls. You surprise me. A lot. And it's refreshing to be with someone who is so themselves. You're a rare bird Ellie."

"Or an odd duck." I wink at him and when he smiles down at me I know we really are okay. I want to kiss him but after my recent hotel incident I'm officially concerned that not all men are like Danny. Clearly I was spoiled in that department so I'll be taking it much slower with Tanner; I like him too much to be disappointed like that by him.

All night I wait for him to say something about this Gala I overheard Leslie talking about but, nothing. He's not telling me or asking me to go so clearly Leslie's right, he's going with her. This sucks. The way she was talking it sounded like kind of a big deal with all the socialites in town invited. It would have been cool to get fancy and be all Cinderella-like for the night. I hadn't realized his family was that high up in the food chain of New York's social elite? It should've been obvious by the lavishness and address of their pad, duh. Clearly I'm not part of that circle and not the type that's acceptable to bring along as a date, either. Can you imagine him introducing me around and someone recognizing me as their recent flight waitress? They'd probably pinch their fake noses in disgust. Not Tanner though, he already told me he loves my smell. I use this great coconut body spray. I smell like the beach.

We eat out and walk through central park holding hands and people watching. This seems to be our thing, we're having a great time so I'm surprised when we get back to my place and he says he'll call me soon without so much as a single kiss on the cheek. As he turns to walk away I say, "wait" and turn his face to mine with one shaky hand and kiss him lightly just once, adding just the tip of my tongue to his, zinggggggg, wow, every time. Leave him wanting more is what I'm going for and he seems to like it too! He is smiling like the cat that got the canary, I just can't tell if he got the zing also. I suck at reading men, it's annoying.

"Bye Elle, see you soon." He smiles and suddenly releases the hand he's been holding the last hour and I miss him. I miss his strong hand. He's the dating Houdini, not Leslie. Geez, playing hard to get is a real thing that obviously works on me! You learn something new every day and I've just learned that I clearly like a chase and so has he. Tanner's not only pretty to look at, he's clever.

Tanner's friends…

"I can't believe you guys are finally coming back to town, it's been year's man." The phone in Tanner's hand beeps with a text while he's talking.

"Lex sure is looking forward to it, I can tell you that."

"And you're not? What's happened to the Thomas I knew and worshipped growing up? Don't tell me you're no longer a ladies' man! I won't believe it?" I look down to my now open text and see the word 'goodnight' glowing at me from Elliott. I've got it bad for this girl.

"First of all, we were kids, I left on my sixteenth birthday and I knew nothing about the ladies back then. Since then I've been schooled for sure." We can also add completely dumbstruck with heartbreak, but I can't tell my best childhood friend that or I'd never live it down. He thinks I was "the man" and the one thing I still have intact is my pride.

"Whatever, this news has just made my week. This party may be a good time after all. Thomas Lovelle…..about damn time, man, about damn time."

Nancy Drew has nothing on Elliott Hallowell…

"Okay Charlie, here's the plan. I've gone all Inspector Gadget. Wait, no he's a robot. Um, I've gone all Nancy Drew in *The Case of the Glamorous Gala* and found out all the details. It's this Friday night at the Plaza, of course, and it starts with light hors d'oeuvre's and cocktails at seven. I say to be safe we get down there at around six thirty. That way if they arrive early we can still catch them."

"You're scary. You know that, right?" Charlie looks a little concerned, but fear not, Charles. This isn't my first rodeo. Though we all know how my last "rodeo" went. I failed at stalking. Oh well, try and try again and all that nonsense.

"I'm not scary; I'm determined to get to the bottom of this drama with Tanner. If he likes me then I'll try a little harder, but if he's playing me, well then I think it's my right to know. A girl can only take so many punches to her ego before some serious trauma occurs. You don't want to live with that girl again do you?" I say teasing. I know he likes the new me way more, heck I like the new me better too and I'm in no hurry to go back to the stalkeratzee that I was. Just this once, then back in the drawer she goes.

"I'm only agreeing to this because my life has doubled in excitement since meeting you and well I do like a reason to get all dressed up. Plus, I totally agree that something's up with Tanner and I need to see how this soap operas going to end." He says all this while packing his overnight bag in a hurry to make his flight. "I'll see you Thursday, and for the love of Chanel, get a new dress! Something that shows off those beautiful legs and, just so you know, a little cleavage never hurt a girl, either." Wink, wink, air kiss and my Charlie's gone. YAY, a-hunting we shall go……

Unfortunately I get called on a two day flight before our mission, but no worries because as luck would have it I'll be laying over in Palm Beach and that means dress shopping with the queen of shopping herself, Beck's.

The next morning finds Becky and I at our first boutique at ten sharp. Opening hour. "Your job makes me so happy, Ellie. Not only do I get to still see you out of the blue I also get to see Charlie, who by the way is a gem. Love him."

"I know. If I didn't have to fly to do it, it would be the perfect job. That's the only annoying part of it." I say in all seriousness.

"You are aware that's the *only* part of your job right? The flying?" B to the itch. Rub it in, why don't you. Salt in wounds and so forth. Gosh.

"Whatever, I don't want to talk about that. I have until seven to get back to the airport, so let's get me a dress that will make Tanner wish he wasn't such a liar face."

"You're weird. But yes, lets." Wrapping me in her long, lean arms Becky leads me to the land of the shopping gods.

Carrying an extra bag through the airport is a wonderful feeling when inside of said bag is the most beautiful piece of clothing you've ever purchased. We went to a new boutique that, of course Becky knew everyone at, and we had the most fun trying on everything in the store. They served us wine while we shopped, and to top off the experience we got everything from the dress to the shoes and the accessories in one place. I hope now that I'm sober I'll like it as much as I did in the store. Oh well, too late now, isn't it?

Charlie is already back when I come rolling in at eleven Thursday night, and he looks exhausted so I quickly warn him, "you do NOT get to change your mind. Don't even think it, you hear me Mr."

"Darling, do you honestly think I'm not aware of this? I just need some beauty sleep and I'll be good as new. How was Becky?" He's stretching like a kitty over the back of the couch arm looking at me upside down. What a dork.

"Brilliant. Wait until you see what I got! SO PRETTY!" I'm holding the bag in his face and he grabs it, sits up and rips the zipper down in an instant. This has all happened in under three seconds.

"Oh girl, Tanner is going to wish Leslie was never born. This is going to be so much fun!" Then we're both jumping on the couch, me in my hosed feet and him in his fuzzy house slippers. I grab the remote and turn on the stereo and on pops *Walk* by my Foo Fighters, the lyrics singing out to me.....

I think I found my place

Can't you feel it growing stronger?

Little Conquerors,

Learning to walk again

I believe I've waited long enough.

Where do I begin?

I'm learning to walk again exactly as my Foo Fighters are telling me to do. Their wisdom knows no limits.

fourteen

Danny in NYC…nothing could possibly go wrong…

"Lex, hurry the hell up! The car is waiting downstairs." I hate that I'm the responsible one all the time.

"Carrie's still getting ready too, you know? It's not just me. Chill please!" Lex shouts down.

"Ryan, I'm having a drink. Want one?" He gives me the "duh" look I've grown accustomed to and we share a much-needed beer dressed in our newly acquired tuxes. All I'm thinking is Ellie J is somewhere in this town right now and I can't see her and I'm pretty sure she'd die if she knew I owned a tux. Especially after the fight she'd had to put up to get me in one for both our junior and senior proms.

"Hey, let's do a shot." Ryan says, grabbing my father's good whiskey out of the liquor cabinet while pouring us each a double.

"Sounds good to me man, I'm in need of something strong." Actually I'm in need of a mind sweep and if the whiskey can make that happen, I'm down.

"It'll have to be one for the road because I think I just heard the girls coming down. To good friends and the good times to come!" *How about to girlfriends we want back and the life we could've had but fucked up.* All I end up saying is, "sounds perfect, simple, I need simple." Then we both tap the granite island with our crystal shot glasses and throw em' back shooting to both toasts, he just doesn't know it. The one good thing about whiskey is it has a way of wiping things out, and tonight I need to wipe out Ellie J.

Let the stalking begin…

We get dressed with my Foo Fighters playlist

blaring obnoxiously from the living room surround sound. The windows are thrown wide open and the evening is glorious. It's the perfect night for a stake-out in fancy clothes. Thanks to the cool evening air, the humidity is super low and my curly hair is cooperating fantastically! The ringlets I'm achieving are a dream that I'd never imagine possible in the Florida humidity. This is a point for the northeast. Good hair.

I've shimmied into my dress and Charlie's zipped me in effortlessly, it's a perfect fit. The fabric hits mid thigh making my legs look long and lean like a gazelles. Then the waist pinches in tight and from there it's like a corset the rest of the way up my chest showing off the exact right amount of cleavage. I can see that Charlie is impressed! The entire dress is in a sparkly black fabric that is anything but typical. There's no discernible color in the sparkle because when the light reflects off of it, it reflects back like a rainbow. It's outstanding.

"If there was anything that could turn me straight, it would be you, in that dress. Damn!" I feel like that too. Charlie just verifies how I feel, and I haven't felt this good in months. Danny always made me feel like this, even when I was in cut off's and an old tank top. But, since he so brutally betrayed me, I've felt anything but beautiful.

"I can't believe that I've dressed like this to try and catch someone in a lie!" Thank goodness for friendly-style stalking. This is SO FUN!

"Not a lie, sweetie. He's never mentioned it so he's not technically lying. Remember you're dressed like this so he can see what he's missing out on. Big difference. We already know what he's doing. Focus." Charlie really is a genius, and I need him desperately to keep me centered. Where boys are concerned I seem to have gone a bit A.D.D.

"I must say you look rather amazing yourself. Where did you get that suit? It was made for you." He's gorgeous with a capital G and OUS!

"Gucci sweetheart. When I suit up, I only do the best." I've always thought he was attractive but dressed like a male model instead of a fashion diva gives me reason to swoon. He really is beautiful.

We split the cab fare getting out across the street from the plaza. It's six thirty on the dot and we're right on schedule. Good plans are essential when stalking properly. We're trying to decide where the best place for a stake out is when a black town car pulls up to the entrance of The Plaza and when the door swings open, I swear I almost pass out, I actually see stars and loose all sound. Everything's all whaa…wha..wha…Charlie Brown teacher-style. Time stops as I watch a long tuxedo clad leg step out onto the rough concrete walkway, followed by the body of the Adonis I've been in love with for the past six glorious years of my life.

Charlie grabs my arm as my feet have automatically started carrying themselves toward him. He's what they know and want. I'm stopped in my tracks when a moment later the long, lean leg of one hoe bag in a gala gown ascends from the same door as the Adonis I *used* to love (or maybe still do but he'll never know). My mind is trying to put together the facts it's been given and can't. This makes no sense. Think. Why would my Danny be here in New York City dressed like that with *her*? A parallel universe could not explain this. Nothing could. I can feel my mind shiver in shock – OUCH!

"Sweetie, hold on tight. I've got you. Sit." I hear Charlie through the loud ringing sound in my beautifully adorned ears. I feel like I've lost all sense of reality. I'm here to catch Tanner, so why am I currently looking at the love of my life with one dirty tramp on his arm? My skin feels tingly and I'm pretty sure the passing out is happening. I've grown accustomed to the feeling as of late, so I'm pretty certain I'm about to make a scene.

"Charlie.....I can't see you." I've got tunnel vision. This is no good!

"There you go. He's gone honey. Just breathe. He's gone." Thankfully he's found a bench to sit me on and pushes my head between my knees. So classy. That's me.

The next thing I'm aware of is another tuxedo clad stranger before me asking if I'm okay. "Should we call the paramedics?" He says to Charlie, very concerned, as I'm coming to.

"No, she's fine, just low blood sugar. This happens from time to time. We knew the food would be served at seven and she really shouldn't have waited but it seemed silly to eat twice." Charlie, you genius.

"Of course, Sir. The Grand Ballroom is open for guests; I'll help you get her inside then." The Plaza attendant saw what was happening and came to the rescue assuming this lovely dressed couple was here for the Gala as well. I could not have planned this better!

"Thank you so much. I know if she could, she'd

thank you herself. Her family will repay you in kind, I'm sure." At this point I'm being hoisted between Charlie and the other gentleman who is trying to save the day and the reputation of the hotel. Thank God Charlie is in a Gucci suit and I'm in this fancy dress, or we'd never have gotten carried into the party.

"Oh my goodness, what's happened? Where am I?" Acceptable amount of blushing occurs naturally and I need to thank the blushing angels above.

"Ma'am, you've passed out. How do you feel?" Duh.

"I just need some juice. Have I missed the party?" Feign exhaustion and my arm plays along going all *Gone with the Wind* style and throws itself across my forehead. Good move arm way to be a team player.

"No ma'am. We're just starting cocktail hour. Let's get you to a table and I'll bring you some food. There you go." He's left me propped up at a corner table with Charlie who's looking at me with sympathy and concern. He has every reason to....I've a terrible track record.

"I saw him, too. Obviously the plan has to change. Now we have to figure out how to stay hidden to do recon on both Tanner and Danny. Dear God, this is exciting! You are without a doubt the best thing that's happened to my life in ages!" Charlie is having a blast and I feel like I might throw up. How is this even remotely fair?

We're nestled in a corner, drinking New Castle Brown in perfectly frosted mugs when I spot Danny across the room. It's like a scene out of a spy movie. He looks like James Bond, which I guess makes me the bad guy who's secretly watching him. This is the most I've seen him in months and I'm taking advantage of the opportunity by drinking in his every move trying to recognize the Danny I knew, desperate to find him through this tuxedo-clad version I'm so unaccustomed to.

He's standing at the bar wearing an heir of authority and refinement I never knew he was capable of. My Danny was charming for sure, but in an easygoing relaxed way. This guy looks capable of taking on Mr. Trump himself and it's HOT and unnerving. Charlie and I are discussing this very thing, trying to come to a consensus on what it all means when Tanner walks right up to Danny and his date, his own hoe bag in toe and gives Danny a big ol' bear hug. NOTHING, and I mean NOTHING could have surprised me more than what I am witnessing at this very moment. THEY KNOW EACHOTHER!

Where's the feather to knock me over with?

I would give anything to hear what they are saying. They're both smiling their beautiful smiles while introducing each other to their respective hoe's and the whole scene is like an orgy of nonsense. The girls and their equally fake boobs and matching hairdo's are bouncing while they giggle and smile their fake smiles at one another. They shake hands, clearly excited at this friend-match-made-in-the-parallel-universe-of-hell that I am currently in.

"Well, heavens to Betsy Johnson, what in the world is going on here?" Charlie whispers, stunned, while his light green eyes are trying not to bug out of his beautiful face.

"I....I...have to pee." Is the only thing I can think to say? Genius. "How do I do that without being spotted? The bathroom is behind that bar over there." The motley crew I'm watching is keeping my bladder in distress.

"How about I walk you over? I'll block you from their view and then I'm heading to the bar to say hello to Tanner. I must make him squirm. This is my new mission in life. You call Becky from the bathroom. Sister's gonna flip the hell out." And before I know it, he's got me up on my wobbly gazelle legs marching us in the direction of my true love and current fling with a zing. HOLY CRAFTSTIX Martha Stewart!

"Tanner. Fancy meeting you here." Charlie is an evil genius, I'm so lucky he's on my side, I'd never want to be his enemy.

"Wow, um hey, Charlie, I didn't know you were coming tonight?"

"It was a last minute thing. A passenger on my flight last night gave me his ticket. He was supposed to be here, but as luck would have it, he got called away on business. So, here I am." I can tell Tanner's scanning the room to see if I'm here with Charlie and Charlie can totally see him doing it and lets him squirm. It's fantastic. Meanwhile, Danny's being mauled by his hoe and I feel torn between the two dramas unfolding before my hiding eyes. Thank God for fancy useless pillars that are large enough to conceal crazy women.

I still need to go to the bathroom. I just can't pull myself away from the drama currently unfolding. I really need to go… bad… and I should call Becky like

Charlie told me to. She's going to die. I may. It's completely realistic that my heart may still attack before this night's over.

In the bathroom, I quickly call Becky. I need to get back to spying on James Bond and the *Days of Our Lives* scene that is breaking out by the bar, but right now I need to give her a rundown of the last twenty minutes or so of my life. She is perfectly outraged by all of it and demands I call her the moment we get free of our current situation. What would I do without her and Charlie by my side? I'd probably be like one of those girls from The Bachelor, all crazy with not an ounce of self respect left and loads of mascara stains on my puffy cried all over cheeks. Okay, I did do both of those things, but true friends would never let you do it on TV, so I'll thank them for that later.

I'm about to open my stall door when I hear the lavish bathroom door swing inward, hitting its rubber stopper and coming to an abrupt stop, just like my heart, when I hear the voices of the two hoe's and their clickity heals file in.

"Your Danny is a fox. How's he in bed?" GAH! Don't answer, please GOD don't answer, let her be one of those hoes who doesn't kiss and tell! Ew, or better yet doesn't actually do it! A sexless hoe is what I'm hoping for.

"He's as good as he looks, and he looks pretty damn good!" They are hysterical; the two of them think this is the wittiest thing she could have ever said. Meanwhile, I am currently in one of Dante's nine circles of hell, the stall door I entered should have had a sign on it that reads *Abandon all hope, ye who enter here,* just like the famous line from his Divine Comedy, because I have just lost all hope and all faith in Danny. He is not the man I thought he was. He had sex with a hoe.

After a while Charlie comes and finds me in the women's room. He calls out for me, not caring in the least who's in there with us. I reach my arm up and unlock the fancy stall door from my spot on the floor. He hears the click and opens the door to find me on the pristine marble with my knees tucked to my chest, completely cried out.

"Well aren't you a sight for sore eyes." He says, lifting me on to my stilettoed feet.

"The hoe's came in. I couldn't leave and then I didn't want to....She slept with him."

"Who and with whom?" He's as aghast as I am

that either of those fabulous men would choose to sleep with either one of those desperate girls.

"The original hoe bag and Danny. She said and I'll quote here, "he was damn good", which I happen to know is true, so there you have it. He now carries a hoe card and I'm going to have to dump my daydream of our perfect reconciliation. He's just too gross now. I can't go where she's been. She ruined him. That was probably her plan all along." I say in a huff of complete defeat. "And Tanner, well he's just as bad. I should have stopped before I ever let those yummy lips touch mine. He carries the same card as Danny, and the two of them are officially on the list."

"What list is that? You have so many to choose from. Your first choice, I'm sure, would be shit list, but then you have the others: never dating again list, want to get back with list, hot stud muffin list, I like hoes list, I lie for a living list.... I could keep going here." He's trying to make me smile; it's sweet in a completely futile way. I'm never smiling again. I'm having a smile sit in.

"Your pick, they're all right. Truthfully though, I'd say it was more like the first one if you made me pick. It's like when you listen to the Foo Fighters, they put you in the best mood you know? Then when you really listen to the words you realize that all their best songs are about heart break and you've just never noticed before because all along you've been completely bamboozled by their awesome drum beats. That's what happened with Danny. I was just completely bamboozled by his totally fake awesome drum beats and I didn't know you could do that. You could never synthesize the beats that Taylor Hawkins plays, NEVER!" Okay, I may be becoming hysterical.

"We need to get you home and get some chocolate and wine in you. This is a level red situation." Then he pauses and looks me over. "Or would you rather go out and party. We wouldn't want to waste looking this pretty." Hmm? The old me would definitely go for the wine and chocolate at home scenario thing, but the new me is ready to party and that's exactly what we are going to do. I look at him with eyes that scream out! GO OUT! And he gets it through our best friend telepathy.

"Out it is. Now how are we sneaking out of this joint?" Thank God for makeup because I am as good as new and walking out the bathroom door when I realize that both Tanner and Danny are in my direct eye line. Charlie pushes me out of the way before we think either one of them has had a chance to see me and as I'm tumbling over he's saying red alert, red alert and I see Tanner is quickly approaching. Too late, he saw me. I'm up and trying really hard to speed walk, but I'm new to the whole stiletto thing and I'm not as fast as his long legs and comfy shoes. Damn those runners' legs, damn them to H... E.. double hockeystix!

"Elle, is that you? Elle, stop!" He's sort of yelling a bit so I stop before any more attention gets called to us. This is bad. So, so bad.

"Oh hi, funny seeing you here." I'm sweating big, fat, ugly forehead sweats. Be cool. OH MY GOSH, Danny is heading this way and he doesn't see me yet! Mission Control, we need clearance for TAKE OFF!

"Yah, I saw Charlie earlier, he didn't tell me you were here?" He's looking around for my accomplice and so am I and I'm freaking the freak out because it appears he has up and vanished into thin air. He's so dead. You NEVER leave your wingman. This is rule numero uno from the Top Gun Rules for love handbook!

"Well, he had a pair of tickets and we are roommates so it just made sense." Oh my goodness in like a minute this gig is up and blowing sky high. I'm fidgeting like a five year old on the first day of kindergarten and Tanner is eyeing me with super suspicion.

"Oh. So I'm guessing he already told you I'm here with Leslie." He looks worried about my reaction. And until I saw Danny coming this way, he should have been, but now I just don't care. I need to get away. I take a moment to take a mental picture of just how pretty they both are for my future cry fests and then I'm running.

"Yep, Listen I've got to..." Then my luck turns, the fire alarm goes off and I am saved by that rather cliché and annoying bell! A crowd begins surging past and pushes me forward, then my arm is grabbed forcefully from the side and I turn to see Charlie pulling me out the push door entrance at the side of the building. At that exact moment I look up and I'm pretty sure Danny sees me and he looks as stunned as if he's just seen a ghost, but a really fancy smokin' hot ghost that he just so happened to gut.

fifteen

The truth shall set you free…or so I hope…

"I swear Lex, it was her." She was there? God, she looked amazing. "I can't be positive she saw me, so I'm not sure what to do. Lex, she has no idea who our family is, you know this. If she finds out I lied to her all these years I'm screwed." I'm wearing a path in the marble floors back at my parent's place. Can you even do that? Somehow I keep digging myself into a deeper hole. I'm an expert hole digger now. Digging my own grave is getting exhausting.

"Why do you care?" Lex asks flippantly. "We just talked about this like a month ago or something and if I remember right, you were firm in your resolve to stay broken up with her. Are you ready to tell me what's really going on now?" I think I need to tell someone. I'm losing it here and I could use some female help right about now. So I make the decision to go for it. I'm telling!

"First off, I can really get screwed if you ever tell anyone I told you. So do I have your word that your lips are sealed?" This is stupid. My sister is known for her blabber mouth. It's legendary.

"God, you are making this so exciting! Yes, I Swear!! Double swear, pinky swear, okay? GO!" She's almost jumping for joy she's so thrilled by the idea of knowing my big secret.

"Okay. Well, you know how after Ellie J and I got home from school mom and dad were on me all the time about the hotel." I look at her for signs of understanding.

"Yah." She drags out the word looking bored with the direction I'm heading and is now rolling her hand at me to hurry this along and get to the good parts.

"They were more pissed than I realized about my slacking and, well, they made me choose." Now she just looks annoyed and confused.

"Choose what Danny? I seriously don't understand what this has to do with Ellie J." She's waiting for me to drop the rest of the bomb.

"Ellie J or my future with the company. It was the family business or her." There it is and when I say it out loud to my sister I finally realize the depth of my betrayal to Ellie J. I was naïve to think she'd just take me back someday when she heard what happened. What I did was choose money over her, that's just the simple truth of it. I could have made my own life, my own business, and I chose the easy way out and in the process lost the only thing that ever mattered to me and sure, I can see that now, but unfortunately I think it may be too late.

"I.....Oh my God, Danny!" She's yelling at me now. This is not a good sign. "HOW COULD YOU DO THIS TO HER? I can't even look at you right now." Her fists are balled up tight at her sides and she is stiff as a board. Does anyone else know about this?"

"No." My head could not be hung lower. I'm like a dog that's been kicked out of the house for eating my owner's favorite shoes. I guess I won't mention that I signed a formal agreement with mom and dad, especially if she knew I hadn't read the fine print until recently and it's worse than I originally thought.

"Well you have to fix it."

"I know. I just don't know how. That's why I'm telling you now. I need your help. I don't know what to do without her anymore. I really can't take it much longer. I'm seriously turning into a girl. It's disgusting. Seriously, I may start douching."

"You're disgusting…" but I see her wheels turning now, "It all makes sense now. I've been trying to figure out how you've been staving off Carrie's attacks for months. I mean any normal guy would have been all over that, I even appreciate how hot she is. And especially after only being with one girl for six years, it just made no sense, but now…. HA... I knew it…I knew you still loved her!" Biggest understatement of the century.

"Okay, so now you know my big secret. What do I do?" Please let her have suddenly become a genius.

"Honestly? I'm going to have to think this thing through. You've really done it this time. This is going to take some serious thought, and you are going to have to do whatever I tell you to if you want her back as bad as you say you do."

"I do, and fine, I'll do whatever you say. Just help me out here, Lex."

"Stop groveling, it's pathetic. I want Ellie back in our lives as much as you do. We'll figure it out, I promise. FYI, I'm still mad at you though. I'll let you know when I'm over it." She punches me in the arm and leaves the room and I realize I've put all my hopes in the future of my relationship with Ellie J on the most annoying person I know! God help me.

Surprise Tanner!...

"WHAT?!" I shout into the buzzer after the ninth time it's been pushed.

"Hey, it's Tanner, can I come up?" bzzzzzz. Unlock goes the door. Pop goes the Weasel with a capital W!

I hear his smarmy feet bounding up the stairs and am looking forward to letting him have it. I wonder if "liar, liar pants on fire" is too juvenile to lead with. There's a quick double knock on the door and I open it wrapped in a silk zebra robe, shocking Tanner.

"Where's Ellie?" I love shocked boys. So hot!

"Why? You're not happy to see me? Afraid I might scratch your eyes out after what you did to my girl?" Making him nervous is my new thing in life. It's endlessly fun, and easy!

"I want to explain about that, that's the reason I'm here….for the groveling." Good boy. He learns tricks well.

"Well you'll have to do a test run on me because she got called out this morning on a three day, and let me tell you, it was not pretty. Fly girl's hung the hell over!"

Tanner sat on the couch defeated and I had no choice but to listen, he just looked so pathetic. "So on a scale of pissed, ten equaling she's hired a hit man to take me out. How bad is it? Am I in danger?" He's looking around for the gunner he's certain is here. What kind of people does he think we are and why would he come grovel to a girl he thinks would kill him?

"Lucky for you, it's not about you. It was, don't get me wrong. Catching you with Leslie was the reason for our impromptu party crash last night but things changed."

"I don't understand?" You are screwed is what I

should tell him and then wish him a good life while sending him on his way, but I can't. I can tell he seriously likes Elle; she just seriously doesn't like him as much back. He's going to have to climb a Danny size mountain to get to her and I don't have the heart to tell him he might as well try climbing the invisible stairs leading to the moon. He'd have better luck with that.

"Remember the guy I told you about that day I came to pick up the keys?" He nods an affirmative.

"Yah, Mr. No Flowers."

"Well, she's not done working that out." His eyes are squinting and his eyebrows are drawn in wondering and?

"What does that have to do with last night? I saw her and she looked like she wanted to get away from me, what does any of this have to do with some other guy?" Oh Tanner. Poor, poor Tanner.

"She wasn't trying to get away from you. She was trying to get away from him." And there you go…he's got it. His face shows what he's feeling and it's called defeat.

sixteen

Garrett part deux…

Please don't let Garrett be here, please don't let Garrett be here…Please don't…..umphf, "Oh I'm so sorry, I didn't see you, let me…." SERIOUSLY!

"Let you what sweetheart?" YUCKY….YUCKY!

"Oh, hi. Um, I…was going to say let me get that," I say bending to get the bag I knocked out of his dirty, grabby hands. Because as I bend to help him he's firmly planted said hand on my skirt-clad rear end. I need a shower. Instantly he makes me feel dirty and my whole body shivers in disgust. I need a shower –

STAT!

Unfortunately, we're heading in the same direction so he follows me, talking a mile a minute. He wants to know how I've been, where've I been and who with, is flying still scary, blah, blah, blah. I'm sure if I liked him I'd be thrilled that he's so interested, but as it turns out, I can't stand him. And it becomes increasingly clear that we're heading towards the same aircraft as we pass more and more gates. I can only hope with the last two approaching that we'll each head our separate ways, but alas fate has made a mockery of my life yet again.

"Well, how about that. What are the odds that we'd be off together again so soon? It must be my lucky day." He has no idea the irony behind his words considering I'm thinking the exact opposite thing.

"I sure wouldn't have bet on those odds." I say seriously. I've not flown with the same person twice until him. Lucky is not even close to the right sentiment. Flummoxed, definitely flummoxed.

"My night just looked up, that's for sure." Oh my goodness, I'm going to have to use the mugging training on him and flash my maxi pad or poke out his eyeball because no way is he doing any humpy business on me again, no FLIPPING way!

The flight to Portland is smooth, which is odd considering the rain we're flying into, but I'm not arguing here. God is on my side on this one and with the bad karma I've been having lately I'll take a good sign wherever I can get one. Unfortunately this is the end of our day and now we have to move into phase two of the day: Keep Mr. Happy Pants far, far away.

As it turns out this may be harder than it seems, no pun intended. Not only is Garrett confident, bordering on narcissistic but he is also frustratingly aggressive. You here about people who won't take no for an answer and you think, well good for them, they're go getters, get the job done types, we need more people like them in the world and all that nonsense. What you don't see is that sometimes there is a girl behind that aggression who is seriously saying no thank you, with her best manners, and said narcissist won't give up!

The hotel shuttle we're on is crawling to its destination and I seriously could not be in a worse situation. Maverick's plopped down next to me and is currently spewing a sob story about his ex not returning his calls and all I can think is, good for her, be strong sister, solidarity and all that jazz. My stomach is causing a scene of its own with the yowling it's doing so 'Mav' gets me where he can, with a free meal. He knows how poor I am having flown long enough to know what us newbie flight attendants live on.

"Fine, one appetizer, one drink and you should know I'm seeing someone. He's a pro wrestler actually. Met him on a flight, monstrous arms," I say while using my fingers to make a circle the size of a bowling ball. I've moved on to scare tactics and the Neanderthal just smiles while continuing to undress me with his eyes. I'm screwed here and unfortunately this is quite possibly a literal statement.

Thankfully, the bar food was good and the beer exquisite. The combination made Garrett and his boring monologue palatable and I am in a much nicer mood. I say yes and wow, and that's great at all the appropriate times, waiting for a break in conversation to call it a night. I've found out during the evening that tomorrow our flight schedules differ so no more Garrett after tonight. Now instead of worrying about him on the flight I can go back to my fear of flying, which at least I have a plan for when things go wrong. With him I'm winging it and clearly I've proven to be abysmal at flying by the seat of my pants.

The gentlemen that he is NOT, he insists on walking me to my room. The elevator ride is worrying with its creepy classics playing and him inching his way closer and closer to me. First thing tomorrow I'm signing up for one of those mugging classes where you learn to shout NO over and over and next time I'll be prepared for The Mav here. Right as he's about to break my personal space bubble the doors ding and slide open. I'm really starting to love bells and alarms. They are my true friends.

My room is in sight, my key is out and I am about to slide it through the lock and say goodnight when he tries his trusty grab and thrust maneuver. This time I know it's coming and fall to the floor feigning a twisted ankle. Ha! His face is priceless and I'm really howling out like I've broken my poor foot.

"What in the world did you do that for?" Is he serious? The reach and freaking grab!

"What, fall down? I'm sorry I didn't realize I wasn't allowed to fall down. Illegal is it?"

"That's not what happened. You just dropped like a sack of potatoes, I saw you. I was coming in for a kiss and you just dropped out. Who does that?" You have to ask the person who just did it? Really?

"Would you have rather I slapped you?" Hmm? Honesty is refreshing. I'm usually such a weenie, as proven by my fake fallout to get away from a kiss only moments ago. I'm going to have to try this more.

"I would have rather you told me you weren't interested." Oh. He's being really mature here.

"Well, I kinda felt like I was giving you signals that I wasn't interested." Answer that riddle Einstein.

"Like agreeing to go to dinner and drinks with me two times now? Those the red flashing lights of not interested you're speaking of?" His point-making is annoying.

"Okay. Point made. Honestly, I'm not good at this kind of thing. I'm just out of a relationship and have proven to everyone including myself that I am completely undeveloped in the ways of the world. It's really rather humiliating on a daily basis." He's looking at me with something resembling empathy and I realize I've possibly not judged him fairly. Judging someone by a hump fest gone awry probably isn't very reasonable, come to think of it, maybe he is embarrassed about that himself and I'm the jerk....oh man….I did not see that coming!

"So we're good?" He asks sweetly. I can't help but admit he is a cutie and his pleading puppy eyes aren't hurting him either.

"Yah, matter of fact, to make up for my terrible lack of maturity and judgment I'd like to make it up to you. Come in and we can have a grown-up drink like two adults. I have changed and I'm sorry." There. All better. He nods and we enter my room two consenting adults who are currently…friends.

The mini bar does the trick and a couple of drinks later we're laughing about the first time we met when I passed out on the plane and he's having a go at my decision to become a flight attendant in the first place.

I retaliate with, "listen, I realize it was crazy. But, now that you've gotten to know me, surely you see how I would think it was a good idea!" I may have a wee bit of a slur to my speech.

"I get it; you're a girl with a very unique way of seeing things, that's for sure. Mind if I use your restroom? Between the beer at the bar and these, I'm in trouble here." He says pointing at the many empty little bottles. Oops, that's going to cost a fortune. The next two days I'll be eating nothing but pretzels on the plane for all my meals. Rats!

"Sure, go for it." As he enters the bathroom and locks the door behind him, my phone goes off. *Big Me* by the Foo Fighters is playing so I know its Tanner. Great, we haven't talked since the gala and I'm maybe a wee bit slurry with drink and there's a man in my room. The right thing to do is let it go to voicemail, but I'm trying to live more honest from now on. Plus, the part of my brain that makes good decisions is currently drunk, so here goes.

"Hey handsome." Good so far.

"Hey beautiful." Ha, he sounds drunk too. This is ideal!

"Wow, check us out. No weirdness at all, even after I caught you all up in a big fat Leslie lie." That was not supposed to shoot out of my mouth. Drunk brain....ssshhhh!

"Man, I'd hoped you'd forgotten about that?" Dur.

"I'm a girl, we forget nothing." This is so true, except sometimes we forget the nice things boys do when we're mad at them and then we only remember the bad things. Our brains are vicious that way.

"The thing is Elle, I like you. I like you a lot, a lot

and I don't like her that much." All I hear is the 'that much' part and I'm suddenly pissed.

"That MUCH?" I say all snarky.

"I dated her and I did like her, we grew up together for crying out loud, but nowhere close to how I like you. Not even in the same ball park." Not even in the same universe! She's an alien hoe!

"HA. You're just saying all this because I caught you in a lie."

"I never lied. I just never told you about it."

"Same difference." Men.

"You're right." He says quickly without hesitation. What? Say again? I'm too quiet so he repeats this astonishing apology. Call Guinness people, the man apologized and fast!

"I said you're right Elle. It's just that I know about the other guy." Charlie is dead.

"Oh. Well he has nothing to do with you." I'm lost now. All bets are off.

"I know, which is exactly why I haven't asked you about him, but this is getting too real for me and I don't know if I can deal with the unknown competition anymore." Smart boy.

This is getting too honest too fast and I realize I'm not ready to end things with Tanner just as he's trying to back out.

"So, are you saying you don't want to talk anymore?" Then before he can answer the WORST thing happens. The bathroom door swings open to reveal Garrett in nothing but his boxers looking, shall I say, very ready! Boiinggg!!

"OH MY GOD!" I scream. Then I hear Tanners tiny voice coming from my phone hand that's currently shot up to cover my disgusted eyes! "No…No…" I shout as Garrett struts towards me like a damn leopard about to leap on its humping prey! GAH! Before I can think I do the unthinkable, dropping the phone, my training has come immediately to mind and my recently applied maxi is being yanked from its place and thrust in his face!

"What the HELL!" IT WORKS! He's running from me as I chase him around with it. My life has become a made-for-TV movie, and I am now the good girl gone mad. I love it! He did not see this kind of crazy coming from me.

"I'm not coming out until you put that thing

away." He says locked away in the safety of my bathroom. This is too great!

"Only when I see you dressed and the door shut behind your nasty butt will I put this away, capeche?" I say all tough-girl Capone-like. I'm suddenly like an Italian gangster, yay me! He emerges a minute later, dressed and jumpy like attacking him with my pad is a fate worse than being someone's prison wife. Then to scare him worse I grab my phone and thrust it at him, telling him "I've called the police, you better scram." When I shut the door I slide to the floor laughing hysterically at what I've just done. That's when I hear a voice in the background of Tanner's phone and I freeze.

My hands are shaking from adrenaline when I bring the phone slowly up to my ear. "Tanner?" Is all I'm capable of saying.

"Are you okay? What the hell was that?" I can hear him racing around grabbing keys or something in the background? What? He's going to hop in his car and drive here, now, and save me? "Damn it Elle, I was about to hang up and call 911!" I think it's a good sign he's upset. Maybe that means he won't dump me.

"That was this pilot I know and it's not what you think, it's actually a really funny story," he is not going to find any of this funny.

"I can honestly say I don't think I'll find it funny." Mind-reader! "Are you seeing him, too?" Great.

"Gosh, NO! He's like this serial dry-humper! He's gross!" Too much information, I cannot stop the honest part of my brain that is totally taking over.

"Are you telling me he dry humped you?" Blahk! He may be just a bit madder than I thought.

"Listen. This conversation is going nowhere. I have to work early. I accidently got drunk and you are clearly drunk so let's not talk anymore tonight okay. Can we please try again when I get back in like forty eight hours when we're both sober?" Good delivery. No inappropriate hysterical giggling or slurring. I think?

"Fine, I'm at a party anyway." Then I hear him. Danny is there with Tanner and I run to the bathroom and puke with the phone still in my hand for Tanner to hear. The hits just keep on coming.

"Did you just throw up E?" duh?

"Who was that I heard in the background?" I

don't even try to hide my nosiness.

"My friend Tom, Why?" Now he sounds confused, too.

"Just, never mind. I've got to go. Sorry about well, all of this. Bye," and I push end before anything more can go wrong. My life has turned into a circus act where I was once the ring leader and am now the arena's most anticipated clown.

Tanner's Pad...

"You okay man? You look like someone just punched you in the gut?"

"Yah, it's just that I've been seeing this girl. That was her," Tanner says pointing to the phone in his hand wearing a dumbfounded look on his face. "That phone call was a bad move, I should've just let it be and now I've just made it worse. Shit! Everyone knows not to drunk dial, amateur move." He sits against the brick wall of the outdoor patio, his head now dropped between his bent knees in defeat.

"Dude, I'm in it pretty bad myself right now so I got nothing for ya. Sorry man." Tom says while giving me a hard pat on the back. "Maybe we should sit and tell our sob stories like a pair of chicks?" He says laughing and punching my arm. Tom slides down the same brick wall joining me and stares up at the sky waiting for my answer.

"No way man, I need to just forget about this one, she's nothing but trouble."

"Ditto, but mine was perfect and I screwed it up. Trouble or not, some chicks are just worth it."

seventeen

Danny meet my friend Charlie…

"This flight attendant dude won't stop staring at me. It's starting to freak me out, Lex."

"Oh get over yourself, he's probably looking at me," she actually looks up and winks at him, flicking him a wave with her long manicured nails. My sister can be such a moron so I think I'll enlighten her before she embarrasses herself further.

"You realize he's a man and a flight attendant right?" This is the girl I thought could help me with Ellie J. Clearly she's a great detective, very perceptive.

"You are so sexist. That means nothing!" This coming from Ms. Politically correct herself.

"Fine, he loves you, I'm wrong. Besides, that's not what's bothering me about him. I know this guy from somewhere and I can't place him. Where in the world could I know him from? I got nothing and it's driving me nuts."

"You just think you know him. I've never seen him in my life, there's no way you know him." As if I could only know the people she knows, how self-centered can one person be?

"Whatever. It doesn't matter, we need to talk about Ellie J and come up with a plan. That's all that matters for the next three hours while I have your undivided attention and you're tethered down next to me. First class is quiet and we've already eaten so there should be no excuses not to get down to business, I'll even get you a glass of wine."

"They're free idiot." Alex says while thumping her manicured pointer finger against my forehead.

"I know. And what the hell are those claws of yours made of? Frickin' bricks? Damn Lex!" I say while waving over one of the female flight attendants who isn't creeping me out simultaneously rubbing the spot on my forehead that, at present, feels like has a finger nail sized whole in it.

A couple of hours later we're driving back to the Hotel from the airport and I get a text from mom saying she wants to talk, to please come and meet her on the patio when we get in. Alex takes my phone and texts her back for me that we'll be there in twenty. At the same time she's already planning her night while talking a hundred miles an hour next to me. As we're flying down I-95, I'm daydreaming that my mom will tell me that her and my father have changed their minds about Ellie and I. The ultimatum has been thrown out and I'm free to jump on the next flight out to go tell Ellie it was all just one big mistake, and then she forgives me and my problems are solved. Not. Even. Close.

"Hey honey." I see my beautiful mother the moment I step out onto the stone patio and into the humid south Florida wall of air. She's elegant at all hours of the day, always prepared for anything, tonight being no exception. She stands in her pressed white linen slacks and silk white sleeveless top looking like the wind the way her clothes and hair blow so effortlessly in the night breeze. She's a beautiful women and oozes class. She's also extremely smart and not to be taken lightly, she has yet to be outwitted by anyone in our family, my father, the business mogul, included. Lord knows my sister and I have tried enough to pull one over on her and not once has it ever happened, she's got the third-eye mother thing going on that you always hear about, totally freaky.

"Mom," I say kissing her on the smooth, tan, cheek she offers up to me.

"Did Alex go up to get ready for her evening already? That girl never stops to breath does she?" She's smiling thinking about her youngest child with her nonstop social calendar. She looks to be staring off maybe remembering a past life of her own.

"Yah, she was texting and chatting nonstop on the ride home." But, that's not why I'm here so I get right to it and ask. "What's up? You wanted to talk?" I say grabbing a beer from Reggie, my favorite bartender, and he hands me mom's refilled glass of wine. Mom goes back to her spot on the patio while I grab the drinks for us.

Her mood's off tonight, she's not as excited as usual that we're home and she's also not her usual chipper self so now I'm worried. I'm guessing this has to do with what tonight's conversation is about and truthfully she's got me a little concerned. "Everything okay?"

"Well, there are a few things I wanted to talk to you about and it's been a while since we've gotten to talk just the two of us." She's rubbing the condensation on her wine glass in a swirly pattern while looking at it steadily and purposefully not at me. Not a good sign.

"Yah, it's been crazy around here and I know I've been a little distant. I'm guessing maybe that has to do with this?" I'm sure of it looking at her face as I say those words.

"Actually that's mostly what I want to talk about. Your father and I know how hard this whole thing with Ellie's been on you, we see you struggling, but for now it's just going to have to stay that way."

"Then why the talk? I remember what the contract said, two years and then I'm free to see whoever I want and I'll never know why I agreed, but I did and I have to live with that. Damage is done. So what else do you want from me?"

"You don't really mean that, Thomas." HA! The hell I don't.

"Don't call me that! I told you when I signed that

contract that I didn't want to disappoint you guys and I meant it, but I'm not ever going to do things the same way as dad, I'm not him, it doesn't matter that we share a name! I might be his 'junior' or the 'second' but I'll never be HIM! I'm DANNY. Only Danny!" I hate shouting at my mom but I'm seriously approaching my limit.

"Sweetheart, I know that. Your father knows that and truthfully that is why this company needs fresh eyes. A new vision never hurt a company as large as this one. If anything, it's refreshing to everyone, including the customers. That's the reason we're putting you in charge for a while." She says the last part slowly, waiting for my reaction.

"What exactly are you saying? In charge of the hotel?" No biggie.

"No. The company, the entire thing." She waits patiently while I absorb her words.

"Why isn't dad telling me this?" My brow's crinkle in hard when I'm stressed or confused and I tend to rip at my hair. Right now I'm sure I look like Don King in the hair department and I'm going to need Botox after this because I'm completely confused at where she's going with this.

"As you know he's not been feeling well, and the doctor has given him serious orders to take an extended break and it's not a warning. He's very concerned about your father's recent stress test results." This may be the first time I see my mom look genuinely frightened and I know I have to do this. Right now, my family has to come first. Then the worst thing happens. My lovely, put together always calm mom starts to cry and I begin to realize his health problems are more serious than she's letting on.

A needed night out…

Stall's Brew & Co. is packed when I get there. It's a good thing I called and asked Ryan to set a stool to the side for me or I'd be standing the whole night. It never hurts to know the owner. The main part of the pub is dim with low lights hanging above the bar to give the room more of a tavern feel with the brightest lights set in the back room where the pool tables are. Tonight I'm thinking the dim lighting fits my mood perfectly because I feel like the proverbial weight of the world has been set on my shoulders. I'm beginning to realize this is going to be harder than I thought and my plans to get Ellie back may not happen after all.

"You wanna try something different tonight?" Ryan asks as he sees me sulk over and settle in. The ladies are all paying close attention to him and he loves it. Show off.

"Sure, surprise me. Something bold, though. Matter of fact, start me with a shot of whiskey." He lifts his eyebrows and smirks, then pours us each a shot.

"Can't do this alone man. Here's to forgetting our worries," then we tap our glasses once together and once on the bar and down they go.

"Shit that burns." He looks completely fine as I sit there wincing like a girl. I need to man up in just about every area of my life, enough with the boy who can't have his favorite toy routine. I make a pact with myself then and there to pull it together. This pact, this ultimatum, is my own and I've made the decision to take the position that's been handed to me seriously and make the best of it. For a while now I've had some new ideas brewing about the business and now is finally my chance to put those changes in place, make things happen.

"Feeling better already?" Ryan says with a smirk noticing my sudden mood change in the course of a singular shot of some damn good whisky. "I swear man; whiskey is the elixir to life." Yes it is, I think to myself, because my vocal chords are currently unusable to tell him that I agree whole heartedly. Then he's right back to work while I slowly work through my issues about manning up, one of which forces me to truly consider giving up Ellie J for a while, maybe even permanently, unlike what I had planned with my sister only a couple of hours ago. As I'm contemplating, I hear a familiar animated laugh.

I turn around and am struck dumb by the sight of the flight attendant from earlier playing pool with none other than EJ's best friend herself, Becky. Then Ryan's there talking to her and hanging on her every word like he's in love, what the hell's going on? It's like all the different pieces of my life are currently uncoiling and then rewiring at the same time and I'm massively confused by the coincidence of the timing and the people involved.

As I'm walking over, Becky see's me and looks over at her friend with an *oh great* face. I look over at him and he has more the face of someone who wants to find the nearest exit, so I go straight to him. "Hey man, weren't you on my flight from New York earlier?" He looks smug like he's onto me about something and I kind of can't stand him at the moment.

"Yes, yes I was and now here I am. What a small, small world we live in?" He says looking at me like I'm his dinner. Not a chance my friend.

"Danny, Charlie's a friend of mine. Is that a problem?" Clearly Becky hates me and I completely understand and like her more for it. She's one hundred percent loyal to Ellie J and she currently thinks I've dumped her so it makes total sense. I kind of hate me, too. I wish I could confess to her and redeem something about my love for EJ with someone but not gonna happen.

"How do the two of you know each other? And, I have to tell you man, you look familiar and I can't figure out where I recognize you from, it's driving me crazy." He looks high fashion and cool, a perfect fit for Becky.

"I know Beck's here from a mutual friend and you and I met just the other night. I'm flattered you remember my face. I sure remember yours." He says winking at me. What? Where?

"What night was that?" I'm totally lost now, we've actually met? He's smiling at me now. I can see he's finding my discomfort amusing and I'm getting pissed off. Then he plays his cards and shows his hand and…Full House! He wins! JACK POT!

"The Gala in the city. I was talking to a friend of yours, Tanner Stanton, he introduced us." Then I have the light bulb moment and I remember seeing him grab Ellie as the fire alarm went off and click, click, click the pieces tumble together.

"Holy shit."

"Yah, Holy shit" he says while slapping me on the back like we've just become best friends and continues, "you've figured it out have you? So then you know our mutual friend would be your ex, Elle." This could be really good or really bad but one thing's for sure, I think I need this guy on my side. I have a feeling that he may be my ticket back to Ellie. It seems fates stepped in and I'm not going to be moving on without her after all. Maybe I'm the one who hit the Jackpot after all.

eighteen

The kissing's back on...

All I can think about on my way to Tanner's place is how I need to give him a real chance. Sure we've had our issues and the whole Leslie thing's made me a bit (a lot) nuts. But, I've decided to believe that's a good sign because it proves I actually care about him, so I'm going to come clean about Danny and tell Tanner how I feel for real about everything, including him and the crazy zings he gives me. He gives great zing!

It's pouring rain and I'm soaked by the time I run from the bus stop to his doorstep. When I left my place, the strip of sky I saw above the building was beautiful. Unfortunately, I couldn't see the rest of the sky to notice the huge storm that was careening towards me. Hopefully this isn't a bad omen.

When Tanner finally opens the door my heart takes a nose dive. MARY MOTHER! His shirt is off, his jeans are slung low on his hips and the beautiful V that he clearly works hard to maintain is gloriously on display. Dear God I may combust from lust. Is that a thing? My eyes dart quickly up to his face and I see the laugh he's holding in at my expression. Being busted ogling hot boy-toy is uber embarrassing; I have no manners when it comes to his body.

"Well, are you going to stand there while I get soaked or let me in?" I'm shivering with lust. He thinks I'm cold. Afraid not hot stuff, "my chills be multiplyin'". And I may lose control.

"I was waiting for you to finish first," he's laughing at me and steps aside right as I punch him hard in those sick abs I was so busy dying to touch a second ago. They feel as good as they look. "Also, you look pretty good yourself standing there with water pouring over you like that. Very Flashdance of you. Hot." Okay, Paris Hilton.

"Now I'm soaked and I'm on call for work. If they

call I'm screwed. A little sympathy would be nice, you know. Especially from a guy of such high class, you know one who goes to Gala's and all." I get right to the point and he winces.

"We're going to talk about that, but first come with me; we're getting you out of those wet clothes and putting your stuff in the dryer first." He takes my hand and fireworks go off in my lower abdomen, alerting me that I'm in serious trouble if I take my clothes off. We reach his room and he's a perfect gentlemen and I'm not so sure how I feel about that. I was here to tell him I was still in love with someone else and now I'm all hot and bothered. I wish my body would just play along and focus here, but hormones be damned that's not what's happening.

He pulls out a pair of old jeans and a white button up oxford for me to wear while my clothes are drying and I shyly take them from him as he stares at me intently, making the warmth in my abdomen spread to other areas of my body. Screw it, I have to kiss him before I implode. We can talk after I release this building frustration on him.

I shock us both when my cold, wet body slams against his half dressed one and he hisses from the freezing contact, but only for a moment. Then he meets me right where I'm at, kissing me back like our lives depend on it. He pulls my shirt off slowly, as it's stuck to my body and is not coming off without a fight. We both laugh when it gets stuck to my wet head and the wild mane I'm currently sporting that is weighed down with about ten pounds of fresh New York City rain water. "You make everything a challenge for me, you know that right?" he says through a whispered, lust-filled laugh. I can only respond with a rabid head nod, too much to do. Focus man!

I go to kiss him again once my pesky shirt's discarded, but before I do I run my chilly fingers down his abs playing nice and say, "You don't mind, do you?" and goose bumps instantly pop up along the path my hands are taking.

"Dear God, NO. That's what I think I love most about you; I never know what the hell you're going to do next. It makes me nuts but it's working for you," then he throws me onto his big fluffy four poster bed not caring a bit that my wet jeans are soaking everything as we roll all over it.

We are still very PG, just kissing and groping each other frantically when he reaches for the button on my jeans and I am like Heck yeah, it's been so long.

His fingers pop the wet button from the wet seal it's gripped in and as he begins sliding down the zipper my stupid phone starts playing *Learn to Fly* and I let out a loud huff in serious frustration. Duty calls. Worst timing EVER in the history of evers! I grab it from the floor where I dropped it and push it on. I'm in a huff from trying to catch my breath while he continues lightly tickling my stomach with his fingertips, waiting patiently to finish his exploration and I'm about to come unglued. The dispatcher on the other line is suddenly calling out all my check in and flight information. I ask her to wait and sit up, finally realizing I must process this information or risk missing my flight. I hate being responsible. It's so boring. Hate…IT.

"Yep got it, thanks," I say hanging up and scratching away on a discarded receipt I found on his nightstand. "Hope you didn't need this, I'm going to have to take it." I say holding up the wrinkled paper, feeling flustered and splotchy-skinned, in need of finishing the business we've started but clearly unable to. "Do you mind if I wear this home, I kinda gotta haul arse out of here." I say, throwing on the dry clothes he originally set out for me. The jeans are huge but I tuck and roll until I'm securely in.

"Do you ever curse?" he asks smiling, and a

dimple I hadn't notice before pops up.

"Nope. Why? Do you think that makes me immature? Because I can assure you, I'm not," I say grabbing his waist band and pulling him to me for one last hoorah, fully clothed this time.

"No ma'am, not immature. Just another interesting fact about you I'll keep in mind. Does it bother you though when anyone else does?" He says pointing to himself when referring to anyone else and smiling his dazzling smile. I want to stay. Nope, can't. I tell my one-track mind to focus, one step at a time until you're outside and away from the lust-filled haze you're currently embedded in. This too shall pass.

"Oddly enough, other people cursing doesn't bother me. I just can't do it. I've tried and I literally get all tight in the throat, my mouth gets all tickly and I feel like I ate something smelly. So go nuts, no judging here."

He looks at me very seriously then. "We're good, right? I mean I know we didn't technically sort things out but I kinda feel like we sorted things out if you know what I mean?" then he's kissing my neck moving aside my collar and heading down the delicate and sensitive bone it covers. Gah, STOP! I'm dying here.

"Yes, good, we're good," I whisper through short breaths. "I'll call you when I get settled tonight and we can talk more and have a real conversation. But I want us to be good too, okay? I've got to go." He pulls away knowing exactly what he's done to me and grins all victorious while leading me downstairs, still shirtless, and he hails me a cab like the gentlemen he is and hands the guy a twenty. "Tonight" he says tucking me into the yellow cab and once more I'm off to fly the friendly skies. I really hate my job.

"Flight 224 is ready for departure" the pilot's voice fills the cabin over the intercom system as we begin our quick taxi. "We're first in line for takeoff so flight attendants please ready the cabin," he finishes a moment later. I take my flight seat at the rear of the plane and am daydreaming about Tanner when a text dings through, but since the passengers can't open their phones, neither can I. Probably just Tanner again, he's texted me three times since I left his place telling me how much I've made his day and he can't wait to finish what we've started when I get back. Me neither. Honestly I can't wait. I'm desperate.

Rude...

The call light goes off again above seat 43b and I'm about to come unglued. This flight has been the flight from Oz so far and I'm like Dorothy stuck with a bunch of flying monkeys. This guy in particular is testing my already over-exposed nerves. "I nee nother shrink," he slurs.

"I'm sorry sir. I'm going to have to cut you off. Why don't you call it a night and try to sleep? We'll be in Seattle in a couple of hours and it'll be morning. Get some rest. Sleep it off." I say very politely, with just a hint of snarkiness added out of complete frustration.

"Don patron, I mean pardon, paronize me. I not shtoopid," alright, if you say.

"No sir, I'm just trying to help," I'm leaning over the side of his seat now grabbing for the drink he's knocked off the tray, and from there things go completely whack. Before I have a chance to react he's grabbed the hem of my knee length pencil skirt and heaved it up over my thong clad rear. To make matters worse, my elbows are somehow caught up in the upturned skirt and I'm trapped and falling. He's about to grab my girly bits when an older gentlemen who looks about my father's age, aka my hero, stands up and takes over the situation for me. He nicely plops me down on the floor taking me out of the equation and has swiftly tethered both the sicko's hands behind his back.

The other girls are finally clued in to what's happening and getting the safety restraints we have onboard for just these kinds of situations. Never. Never did I think I'd ever see those restraints on a flight and here I am a month in and wham! Restraints! Bells start going off in my head. I take this as a sign that maybe I'm in the wrong business and start having the grand mother of all panic attacks. The pilot, who happens to be a retired Marine (God Bless America), comes out and explains to the gentlemen that the police will be at the gate upon arrival and he'll be the first one off the plane when we land. There justice will be served swift and mercilessly. I feel like I'm being filmed for *Punked* and Ashton Kutcher is going to pop out of the lavatory in a minute with an entire film crew laughing and telling me how great my reaction was and then I'll sign a release to show my butt on TV. There's no place like home, there's no place like home…

By the time we land and the handsy flying-monkey is escorted to his holding cell I'm exhausted. The entire crew is whisked off to the hotel for some much earned rest after one heck of a crazy all-nighter. The crew keeps saying that this story's going to be legendary and I start to feel tears welling up behind my tired eyes as we're driving along the interstate, cars whirring past as the sun is coming up in the distance. I'm getting nailed with questions. Like, exactly how did my arms get stuck in my skirt? That's so funny…..hahahahah goes everyone…..NO it's not! I want to yell but don't. Then, did he actually get his hand in there? I'm mortified knowing that this story will be told in so many ways by the time I hear it again, like that game we all played as kids, I think it's called telephone. Anyway, you start off telling the person to your right one sentence and then take turns whispering it until it comes back around and everyone gets a laugh at the end when after eight people the sentence is completely wrong. Well, my life is telephone and by the time I hear this story again I'll have been shagged by the guy in the aisle until someone noticed and stopped the whole thing. UCK! Flippity UCK!

Never has a hotel room looked more inviting than

this one does. I bee line to the standard hotel bed, lie down and cry a good hard stress-releasing cry. After several minutes of crying off my mascara onto the newly laundered duvet I'm alarmed by a soft knock on the door. NOT AGAIN! Tell me Garrett isn't here and that when I open this door I will not be dry humped. GOD, Say it isn't so. PLEASE! WHERE'S MY WINGMAN?

I swing open the door with my mace in hand ready to spray the ever living daylights out of my current attacker and am stopped mid finger pump by a hand swinging to knock the evil sprayer to the floor. My eyes are all but swollen shut but I'm able to discern the brick wall before me and am so overwhelmed by the familiar face I crumble into his warm chest and start crying all over again. Danny… my Danny.

nineteen

"Lay" over's…

This feels like one of those dreams where you're sure you're still awake but in actuality you've been asleep for like three hours and you've finally gotten to the good part after a bunch of nonsense. This entire day has been the nonsense so we're finally at the good part, only it feels really, truly real. He feels real. I yank his hair and get a loud "What the hell Ellie J?" in response and, surprise! The voice sounds real, too. Then I look up into the eyes of the only boy I've ever loved and he smiles a heartbreakingly small smile that's full of fear and vulnerability. I'm a goner. His eyes are watering along with mine now and before I know what's happening he's kissing me with his warm, encouraging, familiar lips and I fall in love all over again, though I've never stopped loving him to begin with.

He lays me down on the bed without a single spoken word between us, he's only speaking with his eyes now and his body. He strips me down like he's done hundreds of times before and I do the same in return and my world snaps into a beautiful, familiar, focus. He never stops looking in my eyes and though I'm full of questions, I know nothing else matters right now but he and I. There's plenty of time for talking later. After.

This was what I'd call a true *lay* over. We've made love at least three times in as few hours and we're both starving and it's the best kind of starving. As Danny is showering I'm lying in bed with a ridiculous grin on my face, waiting for the room service when suddenly I remember the text I got on takeoff hours and hours ago. It's a miracle I remember my own name after the business that's just gone on in this bed but I'm good like that. My mind is finally firing on all cylinders. Sex with that boy does wonders, honestly. He and his business are like the eighth wonders of the world.

The message icon has a red bubble reading one in

it so I push it open and laugh at the message from my beloved Charlie explaining to me that he's just run into Danny and may have told him where I'd be tonight so, be warned, brother's gonna want an Elle flavored treat. When *my* Danny-flavored treat emerges from the bathroom in all his suntanned glory I'm laughing hysterically and he's smiling his hot guy smile, watching me. Boy have I done a three hundred and sixty degree turn since he first got here.

"What's up?" he says climbing into bed naked next to me and my naked self.

"Look what I just opened," he laughs and rolls onto me tossing my phone to the ground in the process as soon as he's finished reading it.

"That boy saved my life. I've been going nuts Ellie J, and I know we have a lot to work out but if you want to try, just know I'm all in," and then he's kissing my neck, nibbling along my collarbone sending my mind into complete oblivion. I think he just said stuff. Ahhhhhh.....

"Yes, yes me too." is all I can manage when a loud rat-a-tat- tat goes on the door followed by *Room Service.* Danny jumps up, throws on his discarded jeans from off the floor and retrieves our much needed energy in the form of food. Lots and lots of food! He's ordered all our favorites. Cheeseburgers, cooked medium. Steak fries with extra ranch dressing for dipping and two chocolate milkshakes with whipped cream on top. I have died and this has to be heaven. That is, of course, if heaven were to be the land of empty calories and sex I'm currently residing in. But that seems blasphemous, so we'll call it something else. LIKE DISNEYLAND! *Where Dreams Come True.*

I'm terrified to pop the happy bubble I'm in, but I do have some questions that need answering and, as much as I'd like to continue our earlier activities, it's time to put lover boy in the hot seat. I'm wearing one of his favorite feather-soft billabong t-shirts and nothing else underneath, which I happen to know drives him crazy. He's watching me intently, our eyes locked, while I finish sucking up my milkshake. When I'm done getting every last bit of the chocolaty goodness from the bottom I slide over to him and sit on his lap, legs on either side of his hips. He's happy, I can tell. This is a manipulative move because I'm thinking he'll be more honest if all his defenses are down and I need to know the truth if this is really going to happen. And good Lord, do I hope it does. I don't think I can stomach him leaving here without knowing if he's all mine and for good this time.

His hands are starting to roam up my thighs and as much as I don't want their exploration to stop I have to have some self respect now and see if we can fix things properly. "Before you go getting me all worked up....again... I need to know what's going on. I mean, I saw you at a Gala in New York City for heaven's sake, with a hoe! How is that?" I'm giving him my most confused face with just a hint of hurt mixed in.

I can tell he's struggling to think as his eyes are coming in and out of their lusty haze but his hand has stopped its upward trajectory and it's clear he's working out his answer. That doesn't feel like a good sign. "I was there with a friend of the family. It was kind of business related." I can tell he's not lying, but there's definitely more he's not saying. I want the more. "She's just a friend Ellie, I promise." And there it is, the lie. I can see it written all over his face.

"Oh. It's the girl who ruined my boots, though and she's mean and handsy and did I mention hoe-y. I saw her and her hands, it's clear what her intention's are, she wants you. Then there's the night you were with her at the hotel. It sure seems like she's more than a friend, especially if she's traveling with you to such fancy parties. You never did anything like that with me." Now I'm sad and I sound pathetic and whiney, but I also know if I don't get the answers I need this is never going to work.

"There's no good answer here Ellie J. All I can tell you for a fact is she is not, in any way, someone I'm interested in romantically. She and her brother are helping out with the brewery addition. They brew and supply and they happen to be really great at what they do and we always hire the best. That's it, I'll swear to it. Whatever you want, I'll do it." I can see he's telling the truth here. He's not messing with his hair like he does when he's nervous. He's a miserable liar and I love that. I love him.

"The thing is," I say while straddling my naked legs over his beautiful body a little tighter, "I can't take you leaving me again. I know I seemed cool, but I was anything but." Now I'm kissing his neck and breathing in the smell of his showered skin….mmmm.. "I just didn't want to sit and hear you blabber through a bunch of excuses to spare me when you were trying to get rid of me. The minute you said you were breaking up with me I just needed you to go so I could keep my dignity," I whisper still exploring his neck and shoulders with my hungry mouth, giving rise to goose bumps and chills everywhere I'm touching. I love affecting him. LOVE. IT.

"Ellie, I can't think with you touching me like this," he says taking my face in his strong, masculine hands stopping me in my slippery path so I'm able to see the sincerity in his azure eyes when he's talking. "You have no idea how badly I hated doing that to you. Then when you didn't seem to care I thought I was really doing the right thing. Like maybe you wanted a break anyway. I can't ever tell you how sorry I am. I really thought you didn't care. God, I'm an idiot." Then he gives me an evil grin and the mood lightens in a flash as he says, "You want to punish me now?" Neither one of us can take another second of this torture. Our bodies have been apart too long and they are aching to make up for lost time, they seem to have a mind of their own that neither one of us can control.

"I plan on punishing you all night sir, we'll see if you go doing something so foolish again after I'm through with you," and that's it with all the talking. He pulls the only piece of clothing I have on off over my head and we are blissfully back in our comfort zone. Right now all that matters is that he's sorry and I believe him. We have the rest of our lives to work out the kinks and make things right. Tonight we'll just help our bodies get reacquainted.

At midnight I hear my phone ping. Crapola is my first thought followed by Tanner a second later. Oh no, I was supposed to call him when I was settled and we were going to talk. How have I gone and forgotten him? I know how, but still. I'm a terrible person. I can't find the stupid phone anywhere so before it dings again and wakes up Danny I slither like a naked snake out of the bed and crawl on all fours on the floor, listening for the ping again. Then ping. It lights up right next to me on the floor. GAH! I hear Danny roll over and I stay perfectly still until it feels safe again, then I crawl like the nasty creature that I am to the bathroom and shut the door before turning on the light.

I open the text and it's Tanner just as I thought. My hands are shaking and I'm freezing cold sitting on the tile floor bare bottomed so I get up and wrap a towel around myself while thinking how to respond. He says, *hey babe. Just worried about you. Could still be flying I know. Just text when you're safe. X Tanner.* Oh my goodness, I'm a hoe bag. I look at the phone, willing it to type out an appropriate response on my behalf, but nope, nothing appropriate about sleeping with my ex, now non-ex boyfriend when I recently agreed to work on my new relationship with a great new guy.

My fingers punch out quickly, *Hey all's well, couldn't find my phone. Your ping helped. Thanks. Anywho, exhausted. Long day. Talk soon. Xx elle.* Lies, all lies, except I really couldn't find my phone, the ping did help and all is, in fact, well. It's just not well between Tanner and me. But, the thing with Danny is freaking awesome. I'm not a total liar. Hoe bag yes, liar – not all the way. The next moment the door swings open and I'm busted standing there with my phone like a teenager about to sneak out… in only a towel.

"You okay?" he says, looking at me and the phone in my hands, an eyebrow raised with suspicion.

"Yep, I was going to take a shower. Oh and I'm texting Charlie that you found me," I say holding up the phone as proof of my lie.

"It's after midnight. Why don't you shower in the morning and come back to bed with me, you're leaving in the morning and I don't want to share you with the shower right now."

"Well then you come in with me and both my problems are solved. I get clean and you can wash the bits I can't reach. You in?" I say setting down the awful phone as it pings back another message. Danny reaches for it and I panic, but before he can see who the message is from he tosses it in the bedroom and says, "No more distractions, no more Charlie. I'm the only man you'll be talking to tonight. Are we clear?"

"Crystal."

My New Foo's…

In the morning I'm dressed and my girly bits are exhausted as well as my thighs and shoulders and hips. Well, you get the picture, we were on fire. Olympic gold status. I'm staring at Danny while he lounges in his birthday suit on the bed watching me as well. "I've packed and I have to go in a few minutes. I hope I didn't wake you." I say sitting down next to him and kissing him for the millionth time in the last eighteen hours. I need more time!

"No, I woke up a couple of minutes ago and have been watching you pack up. I still can't believe you're doing this by the way," he says gesturing to my luggage and my uniform. "You are the toughest girl I know. I hope you know that? It's one of the thousands of reasons I've missed you so much."

"You really missed me?"

"Everyday Ellie J. Hey that rhymed. Beck's would love that. Speaking of Becky: as I'm sure you're aware, she wants me to die a slow and painful death and I was thinking maybe you could tell her I'm not the total "rat bastard" she thinks I am? She kinda scares the hell out of me every time I see her. I'd swear she's planning my death." And then he's pulling me down onto his very exposed lap for a kiss from the "sexy hostess", his words not mine.

"I'll talk to Becky, don't worry. I know the hit man, I'll call him off."

"I'd really appreciate that, thank you. I have a present for you, by the way. I've just been too preoccupied to give it to you," eyebrow waggle, he's such a boy. "Look in my duffle bag over there. It's in the side pocket." Yay, he knows I love presents. I let out a very childish and ridiculous squeal while running over to the duffel like a lunatic. There's a pretty wrapped package right where he said there'd be so I grab it and run back to sit by him on the bed. I tear through the paper and open the box to find a brand new Foo Fighters shirt and tickets to their sold out show in New York City next month and I almost pass out from the wave of excitement that hits me.

"How'd you get these?" I say holding up the impossible-to-get tickets.

"I know someone. And besides, I'd have done anything to make you this happy again. Does this help me earn back any points or am I still heavy in the negatives?" Duh.

"This gives you tons of points!! You may still be in the negatives but this pulls you close to the zero line for sure! I love you," and as the words shoot out of my mouth I slap my hand over my mouth wishing I could take it back. I should have let him say it first. But he smiles my favorite smile, the one that tells me how he feels and then he speaks it too, "I love you back."

I shove the t-shirt into my carryon bag and kiss him once more for memory's sake and we don't say much more other than we'll see each other soon. As I pull my bag behind me out the door he shouts at me before it closes, "Ellie J," I stop and look back in at the man of my dreams and he finishes, "it's forever this time, you know." I smile big back at him and say my usual, "Duh" back at him and he's laughing when I close the door for good.

twenty

Sorry Tanner, but…

Whoever thinks being a flight attendant is glamorous, HA! Think again. It is a thankless job that deals in grumpy passengers, babies that cry for hours, drunks who molest you and first class passengers who believe a solid butt grab is included in part of their fair. Their money- hungry wives just overlook it. As long as they continue to get to go to Vail for the holidays and keep their nannies, who really cares whose butt's their horny man grabs, right?

I've just entered the smelly lavatory that a woman in first class just exited BARE FOOT! I kid you not!

The fact that this is the only place I have to go for a moment of anonymity should tell you something about flight attending. Sometimes it really stinks.... The bathroom has become my happy place where I can sit and daydream about mine and Danny's future in peace. I'm getting quite used to the smell. It's getting to the point that whenever I smell that blue deodorant disk anywhere, I have triggered thoughts of Danny running through my mind. I know, gross. But also, so handy. Porta-potties aren't so bad to me anymore. Bonus!

This is the last leg on the last day of my three-day trip. I'm desperate to wrap my arms around Charlie's gorgeous boa wrapped neck and thank him properly for sending Danny to me! He's already made plans to come visit us next weekend during my days off and Charlie is on call so it should be fab. First things first, I must deal with Tanner ASAP. Tonight I'm hopeful that Charlie will be able to help me come up with my," it's not you it's me" speech and then a lofty escape plan in which to escape from Tanner and his amazing kisses. When he gets near me I get all hot and bothered and am suddenly incapable of reasoning my way out of a cardboard box. It's embarrassing and immature, but true nonetheless.

Currently I'm eeking towards the hoe-zone and I

need to reverse back into the friend-zone with Tanner. This will be a tricky maneuver but with the proper rehearsal, loads of honesty and the wearing of the most unattractive clothes I own I believe that I'll be able to pull it off. One of the many things I've learned by flying these last couple months is that I can do things that scare me, I just do them better with a plan. So I'll have one heck of a plan ready when I face one of the world's best kissers.

"You're ready Elle. You look dreadful and you know what to say. Go get em', tiger. Or, more appropriately, go get rid of him! Love and luck. Now go!" Charlie is literally pushing me out the door and I feel like I'm skidding across the parquet floor in my rubber rain boots.

"Okay, okay! Stop pushing me. What if he kisses me?" Seriously, I'm in rain boots and my baggy mom-jeans are tucked inside them mushrooming out the top of the colorful rubber. Who am I kidding? I look ridiculous.

"He won't. You're boy proof - and you're stalling," with those final words the door shuts behind me and I'm forced to move forward. I hear the theme to jaws in my head, imagining Tanner's inescapable mouth coming towards my all-too-willing lips and I'm shaking in fear. My biggest worry is that we won't be friends anymore and I really like Tanner. He's been nothing but good to me and is a great, trustworthy friend, which I happen to know are hard to come by. I guess if I want Danny bad enough I'll have to let the chips fall where they may. Dah.. dum ...dah ...dum...dah...dum..dahdumDADADUM.......

The entire walk there I'm being looked at like I'm a crazy person. I want to stop each and every gawker and say, "hey, this isn't how I really dress. Really I'm quite normal outside the overly teased ponytail, man-sized striped Rugby shirt, baggy-jean, rain boot wearing ensemble I've got going on. Then I'd whisper, I'm really on my way to break up with someone," and then they'd be all like "Yes, good move, the ugly clothes move. Good job," followed by any version of fist bumping and high fiving. But alas that's not what's happening; instead people are avoiding me like they may catch my crazy like a flu virus.

Tanner answers after the first round of knocking and is taken aback by my ensemble. "You know it's not raining right, Elle?" he says trying to stifle a laugh with his fist.

"Duh, yes, I know. But if you remember last time, I wasn't prepared so this time I'm being proactive. There's nothing wrong with being ready for the worst," and you're about to get the worst, so get ready. Thank the Shirt gods he's wearing one. This is going to be hard enough without those perfect pecs' staring me down, asking for a squeeze.

We go into the living room and sit down together on the oversized couch next to the ornate stone fireplace. Thankfully it's not cold enough yet for a romantic fire to be blazing. That would make this so much harder. I'm a sucker for a romantic fire. Flames are totally sexy. He pulls me down next to him and looks down at me with a curious expression on his face. He knows something's up.

"What is it Elle? I can tell when you're having a hard time and you are, so spill it." See? He's so nice, and he gets me, he just doesn't complete me. Thanks again for that one, Tom Cruise. Your movie rules can suck it. They've totally messed with my head!

"Okay, here goes. Remember how I said we needed to talk before but then all the kissing happened. Well I really did need to talk to you and your kissing kind of makes me forget that it's really important to talk." I'm babbling and he's smiling. At least I complimented his kissing, that's always nice to hear. "Anyway, I should have talked first because now we have the kissing thing between us and that makes this way harder…"

"I'm going to stop you. Is this about your ex? Because I was hoping to help you get over him. That was part of my plan." Huh?

"How did you know about him? Wait, Charlie told you didn't he? That jerk face! Have you known all along?" Obviously, genius.

"Yeah, but I didn't care. We've all got exes. Look at what I put you through with Leslie. I figured I could work through the ex problem, especially with all the chemistry we have. You're right about the kissing, wow!" He's staring at my mouth, No good, stop. Abort! "I'm sensing there's a problem though so go for it, I can take it." He's trying to make this easy for me and it only makes me feel worse, he's perfect in every way accept one. He's not Danny.

"Well, the ex, Danny, he's kind of not the ex anymore. I know that makes me a total hoe-bag and you'll hate me now but I just want you to know that I really truly don't want to lose you as a friend. It really isn't you because well.. you're hot and tasty, but there's just that he's him and we've been together for so long, I just can't *let it die* without a proper chance."

"That's a Foo Fighters song, isn't it? Let it Die? You have a disease." He's actually smiling.

"I do."

"Friends? I can do that if that's what you want. I won't lie, I still like you like crazy but I'll stop with the 'tasty kissing and stuff' unless for any reason you ask me to and then we can resume. But I don't want to lose you either so I guess I've got no other choice, do I?" Then he sticks out his always warm hand and we shake on our friendship. His hand still gives me the zing though, so I yank it back quick and we both laugh because I know he feels it to.

"Can I ask you one more question?" I shake in the affirmative, "Does this letting me down easy have anything to do with that bizarre outfit you're styling today?"

Laughing at my stupidity I say, "Busted. Charlie told me that if I looked ugly you'd feel relieved to be getting rid of me. I was just trying to be nice." With that he leans forward and does the unthinkable, he kisses me on the cheek and my whole body defies Danny with its reaction to Tanner's lips.

"Sorry, that was just one of the sweetest things anybody's ever done for me, and I was compelled by my good manners to kiss you. But thank you for the effort and just so you know, you'd look good to me no matter what you were wearing or how fluffy you made your ponytail. So please, for the love of all things holy, never do this," pointing from my feet to my hair, "again."

Later that night in Palm Beach…

"Alex, let's go! You look beautiful as always, come on."

"Easy for you to say, you've never had a bad face day in your life. You realize most women loathe you, right Carrie?"

"Let them hate me, it's not like I had anything to do with it. Good genes. Besides, if I'm so beautiful why won't your damn brother give me a shot? God knows I've been throwing myself at him for months now and it's beginning to make me doubt myself." No man has ever turned me down before and Danny is getting on my last nerve, but since my new plan is to kiss up to the sister I've got to be nice. So annoying.

"He's not over an ex yet and he is very much a one woman kind of guy so you'll just have to be patient a while longer, or better yet, give up. I think you might be fighting a losing battle. He and his ex were a perfect match." I want to punch her in her perfect little nose.

"Whatever, I'll figure it out. No nut is too hard to crack, especially when the nut is attached to a penis. Just sayin'. He's just the toughest challenge I've ever had and a little extra work is just sharpening my skills." Alex laughs and I'm sure she thinks I'm just being funny, but I'm not. I'm not stopping until he and I have done 'the deed' and that's that.

"Carrie, you are hysterical! I can't believe we haven't gone out just the two of us before. The men around here better watch out because you and I are going to bring all sorts of trouble tonight."

"Lex, you have no idea."

twenty-one

Angels among us...

One week before Thanksgiving and the city is already decorated for Christmas. It's not as early as my mom's display goes up, but it out-dazzles hers by miles. She's been putting up the same Santa-outfitted flamingos for years, and those crazy little creepers stay up through the Catholic's end of Christmas, which is twelve days longer than anyone else's. We Catholics take our celebrating seriously and I would dare anyone to go up against my holiday-obsessed mom. I always wondered what Jesus would think of those flamingos. They are his creatures, so maybe he'd think they're darling like mom does when she dresses up poor Zha-Zha. I much prefer New York's version of a Christmas display considering I have yet to see one single outfitted flamingo. Keepin' it classy New York, I like it.

To get into the holiday spirit Charlie and I have given ice skating in central park a go, twice. It's a rite of passage if you live in the city, so why not. Well I'll tell you why not. It's stupid. Each time we've tried, both of us have left wet, cut up and bruised. Oh, and also freezing. Why do people say this is fun? All I've learned about myself is that I suck at sliding around on knives. I don't think that's a bad thing. Whoever thought up this brilliant idea to freeze water, strap blades to your feet and slip around on it was an extreme sports person and somehow other people drank their Kool-Aid and decided everyone should do it, even toddlers! So I'd like to suggest the summertime version; we can call it water blading or something equally stupid. What you'd need are water gloves with sharp blades attached to the tips and a pool, easy peasy. Then you see who could do the coolest tricks while balancing on their "bladed" finger-tips underwater, upside-down. Nope, also a bad idea, I say we just get rid of ice skating and nix the water blading idea.

Anyway, the bright side of it being the holidays is that soon Danny will be back for another visit. He's only been up once since we reunited in Seattle last month and I am desperate to have him under, I mean over, I mean with me again. Smiley face. He and Charlie got on like white on rice, or better yet, the vanilla-chocolate swirl yogurt from Costco, SO GOOD! I'm feeling so lucky that we are back together for the holidays and that my life finally feels close to normal again. The one blip on the radar is the job. I mean, I love my lifestyle and I'm having tons of fun meeting so many new people and seeing just how awesome the grand ol' US of A is, but being on the plane really makes my job stink, like a skunk.

My flight attending Yoda, Mary Phelps, sends me notes of encouragement via company mail, and those little nuggets of courage have really helped me to not lose it many a time now. Sometimes she attaches candy to the notes and those are my favorite. Duh. It's kind of like she's my Easter bunny/AA sponsor all wrapped up into one, candy and encouragement and only five steps in her program. So just like they say, I take it one day at a time. Or for me, it's more like one flight at a time. Today I'm off on a trip that should be harmless. It's a two-day turn to Salt Lake City. Shouldn't be too bad because it's only one leg there and one leg back so fingers crossed its uneventful.

I plan on taking the bus to LaGuardia since I've yet

to try this cheaper mode of city transport. Charlie said it's easy, but his life always works out pretty so for him it would be. Seeing that it's the holiday season I really need to save some moolla, so the bus it is. I have my handy route guide in my carry on and as luck would have it, I make my first bus in perfect time. The driver smiles at me in a creeper kind of way as I board, but alas, my flight attending has taught me how to smile through fear. I get off at my transfer where, in about ten minutes, my next bus is due to arrive. So far so good.

As soon as I debark I quickly come to the realization that I'm probably at the wrong stop. Charlie never mentioned this graffiti-styled stop and knowing him and his germ phobia no way would he be caught dead on this dingy corner. I have five minutes until I believe the next bus will be along, so I'll just have to tough it out and wait. In the meantime I'll have to follow my mother's favorite motto and put on my big girl panties and deal with it. Since I'm no longer a weenie I'll brave it out. It's just hard to believe Charlie would send me into such a.....not nice...area. I mean, the only bench that's here to sit on is covered in so much chewing gum it looks like the skittles rainbow landed on it. No way in Hades am I putting my pretty blue skirt down on that thing. I improvise and push the handle down on my roller bag and plop down to wait. Sitting problem solved. Now if only I could get out of here!

I sit and sit and sit some more. My flight is an evening departure so the sky is starting to get dim and as luck would have it the five minutes has come and gone so now I'm running way behind schedule without a single dollar on me for a cab fee or tip. I call scheduling and let them know about my dilemma and they put the standby girl at the airport on ready for my flight in case I don't make it. Their organization and planning skills have no limits. It's impressive! I still live by color coded sticky notes on my wall calendar.

Anywho, it's now dark and my brave face has officially left the so called building/corner in the scary part of town. Then I hear the most lovely voice say, "Sweetie? You out here all by you self?" That's when I turn to see a woman who in no way matches the velvety voice she's been blessed with. She's curvy in the way a three to four hundred pound woman is and wearing spandex in the form of a teal tube dress married with a leopard print faux fur mini jacket. You heard me. I said mini. I know I'm staring but she's smiling at me with her big peachy-glossed mouth and I can't stop. Hello, earth to Ellie?

Manners.

"Hi, um, yes ma'am. I've been waiting for the bus but it's not here yet and I'm really late for work." She's eyeing my outfit and laughing her lumpy buns off.

"Oh girl, you missed that bus an hour ago. No more buses run through here tonight you sweet thing." I know my face shows complete shock and fear. So my new friend stops laughing and is instead smiling with something resembling compassion in her big overshadowed brown eyes. "Don't be scared now, Angel's here and ain't no one stupid enough to mess with me. Come on, we gonna find you a way home."

She takes my hand and leads me into the seediest bar in all of New York City, sets me down in a dark and dingy booth then tells me to sit tight. No problem, I'm not moving an inch. Is she serious, is her name really Angel? Because she doesn't look like any of the angels I learned about in my religious ed classes. But hey, I bet they come in all shapes, sizes and clearly career paths as well. No judgment here. Thank God for Angels!

"Okay, I called a friend. He owes me a favor so

he's gonna pick you up here in fifteen minutes and bring you to the nearest stop that can get you to the airport, no charge. That okay?" One of her breasts is about to escape the torment of its way-too-tight top and I can't help but stare in amazement as it suddenly does an x-rated version of POP goes the weasel! Angel's laughing at my face and says, "I bet you ain't never seen some like these before," as she stuffs the lone escapee back into its holding cell.

"Um, no. I mean sure we all have em' right?" I'm giggling because I cannot think of a single appropriate response to my new friend's wardrobe malfunction.

"Some of us have something a little bit more substantial than others darling. These things," she says lifting them away from her like separate beings, "are my money makers." And she's off laughing again. Oh my goodness gracious, my guardian Angel is a real life hoe-bag, the irony is not even close to being lost on me!

"Lucky for me, my guy is okay with these," I say grabbing my small handful. "But yours really are magnificent." I'm not even lying, I can't take my eyes off them. I know that's gross because I'm totally straight but you have to admire someone when they're so totally over blessed.

"You a funny lil' white girl. I don't ever want to see you round here gain though, you hear me? You lucky ol' Angel here found you and not someone else. This ain't no place for someone rollin' round luggage with panty hose on in a flight suit. Someone's watchin' out for you, that's fo' shor'." A moment later we hear a honk out front and she says, "well, that there's you ride. Com' on now let's get you on outta here."

We step out front to find an old beat up Cadillac and looking inside I see an equally beat up old man, but his smile lets me know I'm safe in his hands. Plus, I can totally poke out his eyeballs if I have to. My training has no limits. Angel grabs me in a big ol' beefy hug and shakes me around, I can't help but smile at her when she lets go. She has a way about her that I just love. Then I find myself kissing her red rouged-cheek, to both of our surprise. "You've been a real nice treat, now get outta here and never come back." Then I'm crawling into the overused backseat along with my luggage. The door slams behind me and we're on our way. I just pretend it's a town car and I'm a fancy lady. The imagination really can be quite a life saver. I turn to see Angel with a new "friend" and am genuinely delighted to be with this old man heading to anywhere else.

Moments later I'm deposited by way of my new friend, Stanley, into a much safer part of town and assured the next bus is the one I want, then he honks and rolls down his window to shout his goodbye, "you bes' listen to Angel an stay out that street from now on, you got'n lucky this time. Bye now." And my chariot whisks itself away into yet another crazy New York night.

Seriously...

When I finally arrive at the airport, the easy flight I had been so happy to get has just departed. I go to the flight attendant lounge thoroughly frustrated and check-in to find I've already been rescheduled onto another trip. This time it's my nightmare scenario. This trip consists of the maximum hours per day we're allowed to fly, for three days, as well as ridiculously short lay over's. Strongly believing that everything happens for a reason- I'm very in to cliché's these days- so I take my getting lost as a sign that for whatever reason this is the trip I am supposed to be on. I board my first flight on time wearing my perfectly practiced smile and decide here and now that optimism will be my middle name from this point forth.

As luck would have it, this trip has been a dream, which is saying a lot coming from someone who hates to fly. Hate is a strong word I know, but if you consider that I'd rather eat fried bugs than do this for a living, then you could see why it's the only appropriate word. The last leg of this long trip is coming to a close as I'm sitting, daydreaming in my jump seat, smelling my new favorite love inducing blue discs from the lavatory through its closed door, anticipating yet another smooth landing thanks to my two new favorite pilots. I'm blissfully sitting in a coma from my love stupor when my cell starts getting messages like mad where it's currently stowed in the coat closet across from me. I can't possibly check them now but something's going on. My phone dings at least twenty times in the final few moments of our descent and I've never been that popular.

As soon as we enter the airport we see camera crews and reporters everywhere. One of them is waiting at our gate expectantly. As we come into view a young women in a tailored, expensive looking dress suit asks which one of us is Elliott Hallowell. In shock that this stranger knows my name I raise my hand like a school child and simultaneously feel the fine hairs on the back of my neck shoot up.

"Hi Ms. Hallowell," she says reaching to shake my trembling hand. "I'm Elizabeth Sturgeon from Evening five news here in New York City and I was hoping to ask you a couple of questions about flight 443, the one you were supposed to have been on. Would you mind? It will only take a couple of minutes." I bob my head to and fro feeling a deep sense of foreboding about what she is here to discuss.

"First off," she says shoving a microphone in my face while mouthing we're rolling, "How do you feel about not making your flight?" What? Why does she care that I didn't make my flight?

"Well, terrible of course. I'm normally very prompt but I got lost getting to the airport and I only missed my flight by a couple of minutes. Matter of fact I saw the plane taxing out as I arrived. This was the first flight I've ever missed in my several months of flying, I feel horrible." She's looking at me like I have a bee on my face and then understanding hits her.

"Ms. Hallowell, are you aware of what happened with flight 443?"

"No, as you can see I've just landed and surely you are aware of flight regulations stipulating no phones or computers on board. I may have been late once, but I do follow all safety rules I can assure you of that." Must plug this so I don't get canned, if management is watching this hopefully they'll overlook my tardiness this once due to my diligence in following their long list of safety standards.

She looks at me with sympathy in her serious media lady eyes and says, still holding the microphone an inch from my mouth, "Well then you are a very lucky girl Ms. Hallowell, because this afternoon flight 443 crashed on takeoff." As soon as the words are finished coming out of her mouth I see the dreaded stars that begin to blink on and off in front of my face and that's the last thing I remember.

twenty-two

Chocolate works when hunks don't…

"Who are you? Put me down. Really I'm fine, just fine," I say, my body in total disagreement with my ridiculous declaration of fineness.

"I'm going to set you down as soon as we get into the lounge ma'am. We wouldn't want you falling down the stairs. Company policy." My rescuer is an airport security guy that I recognize from my regular trips in and out of La Guardia's many terminals. He's built like a linebacker so I'm in no danger of getting dropped, and I suppose a little perspective is in order here considering the news I was given only moments ago. Being cradled in this strong man's arms is strangely comforting.

"Thanks," is all I say to my new found security hero.

The flight attendant lounge is quiet with only a handful of my fellow flight sisters present to witness the embarrassing predicament I am currently in. Unfortunately the few who are here are going to spin this situation into something much more tawdry than it actually is. Apparently Hector, my heroine, is known with the ladies as the airport's equivalent of Garrett the horny humper. I don't mind though, because today my life was spared and I will no longer be infuriated that someone finds me attractive enough to want to dry hump me. It's a compliment. Optimism is a beautiful thing, ladies.

After I've assured everyone I'm not going to drop at any moment, I excuse myself to the ladies room to splash some water on my tingly face and see who was sending me all of those texts. Considering I've had no time in the last three days to contact a single person, I imagine my family and friends are all frantic to hear from me. I'm pretty sure they all think I've died or am severely injured in the plane crash I heard about only moments ago. Thankfully I grabbed my cell from my carryon when we were deplaning because currently I have no clue where my luggage is and I really don't give a flying phooey, either.

My mom's voice shouts through the earpiece after only half of the first ring, "OH MY GOODNESS, JAMES SHE'S ALIVE!" She's hysterical so my father takes the phone from her and gets straight to the point, "We want you to come home, Elliott. This has gone on long enough honey." He's talking in his most soothing voice, mixed with a bit of pleading and it breaks my heart that I've put them through this. The problem is that I'm not ready to throw in the towel yet. Plus I would be ditching Charlie and I just won't do that to my friend, he's been too good to me.

"Daddy, I'm so sorry. I wasn't even on that trip anymore and I'm not ready to quit yet. I've got to prove to myself that I can be independent and strong. Surely you understand. You saw me after the whole Danny thing, Dad. I can't ever be like that again." I'm trying not to cry. Hurting my parents is something I hate doing but I have to be firm here or I'm just going to turn back into the pushover I've always been.

"I know, but understand that your mother and I have spent the morning thinking we've lost our only child so we're both feeling a little desperate to keep you safe right now. Maybe from now on you could text us with flight changes, okay? At least until we calm down."

"Yes, of course. I'm so sorry Dad. Tell mom I love her and for goodness sake give her some chocolate, stat." I can feel him grinning through the phone because we both know my Zumba-obsessed mom has a hidden stash for just such occasions. "On it, already got the bag in hand. You girls and your chocolate. Here honey," he says to my hiccupping mom and I hear the rustling and ripping of plastic as she tears into her favorite, Dove's dark chocolate squares. Mmm, I know what I'm getting on the way home.

"Listen Dad, I hate to go so soon but I have a few calls to make, I know Danny is out of his mind." Seriously, since I've been on the phone with my parents he's texted me at least fifteen times. The interrupting beep is driving me nuts.

"Okay, tell your mom "bye". I'm holding the phone to her ear."

"Love you MOM!" I shout.

"From now on, changes of plans need to be texted. No exceptions or we're driving up there and bringing you home even if you're kicking and screaming. Ca peche?" Dad's so cute when he uses his fake gangster accent. I guess I come by my inner-gangster naturally.

"Yes, Daddy, Ca Peche. I love you too."

"I love you more," he says as usual so I quickly shout back, "No, I love you more," and hang up before he can reply, just like I always have. I'm such a lucky girl to have those two crazy people as parents.

I take the expensive way home, climbing into the back of a yellow cab at the curb throwing caution and money to the wind. After the day I've had, all I want is to be alone and talk to Danny. Like my mom he picks up before the first ring has had time to finish. "Babe, Ellie, OH MY GOD, you're ok?" He sounds out of his mind with worry. I can picture him running his big man-hands through that gorgeous head of hair of his like he does when he's freaking out. I'd be willing to bet its standing up in every direction like he's been shocked all Looney-Toons style.

"Hey baby, I'm so sorry it took so long to get back to you. I only found out what happened after I landed and then mom and dad called, and my supervisor wanted to talk to make sure I was okay.

Anyway, I'm alone, in a cab and I'm so happy to finally hear your voice. I miss you." Now I was crying and rambling on. The gravity of the situation hits me like a kickball to the chest and all I can think is thank God I have more time to live. Then I feel guilt that I made it and someone else maybe didn't because of me. I have to find out what happened and if everyone survived. This realization takes my crying into a howling state and the poor taxi driver looks desperate to get rid of me.

"Ellie J, I am coming this weekend. I don't care what you're doing, cancel it. I have to see you." Note to self, crying hysterically gets me what I want from Danny.

"What about your family? Its Thanksgiving weekend and I thought you said you have guests coming to visit from out of town." He just told me he had family coming a couple of days ago and he couldn't wait to see them.

"I could care less about any of them right now Ellie. I thought after all we've been through that I'd lost you again, for good. God, I don't think I'd have lived through that, Ellie J." I love how much he loves me; I can hear it in his desperation. In a weird way this accident has helped me believe in him again. I secretly felt like maybe he wasn't being honest with me about everything that happened but now how could I not, he really sounds like he'd have given up the ghost if something would've happened to me, so just like that, all my fears vanish.

"I'll be ready and waiting and totally unable to sleep the rest of the week. So two more days until Thanksgiving then it'll be just you and me. Rest up. You're going to need it with the plans I have for you." Lord have mercy. I'm getting myself all hot and bothered. Cold shower, here I come, more like an ice bath.

"You too baby," he sighs all sexy through the tiny electronic thingamajiggy in my hand. "Since we've been on the phone I've already made my flight arrangements and paid so there's no getting out of it now. You and me Friday." Then I hear a knock on his door and his mom's voice all muffly like he's put the phone down in his palm. Next thing I know his voice is back on the line and he says oddly serious, "Okay, great plan. Talk soon," and click, he's gone. Bewildered, I still hold the phone to my ear waiting for him to come back on the line but when I see my screensaver pic of the two of us pop up, I know he's really gone. Weird and definitely NOT COOL!

Walking through the heavy apartment door I'm met with the most delicious smell, brownies! MY FAVORITE THING IN THE WORLD! They fix everything and Charlie knows they're my go-to treat of choice, even more than Dove chocolate! So of course I'm surprised when it's Tanner in our small, friendly kitchen with Charlie M.I.A. "Hey," he says walking over and folding me up into the world's best and most needed hug ever. I do what I do best lately and cry in his arms releasing all the coulda-shoulda-woulda's that keep playing through my frazzled mind.

When I'm all done, Mary Kay be damned, Tanner leads me to the bathroom and wipes the black streaks from my splotchy cheeks. Then he kisses me, only once and very chastely, before leading me back to the kitchen where there is an enormous pan of warm brownies....with icing, my very extra favorite, to greet me. "Charlie called me after you texted him and told me this was an emergency and, I quote, "of the brownie kind", and I was to bring a pan of these here immediately," he scoops a piece out with a spatula and puts it up to my mouth, offering me a chewy, warm bite.

"What would I do without the two of you?" I say while hopping up onto the tile countertop.

"You'd be just fine. You're Miss Independent now. A totally different girl than the scaredy cat I first met all those months back. The real question is what would I do without you?" He's looking very serious as he comes to stand in front of me wearing an expression that scares me, because I know what he's trying to show me through his eyes and it's coming through crystal clear. He loves me.

"Tanner," oh God, why do I have to like him so much? "Don't. Don't look at me like that, I can't." Then he does that annoying thing where he kisses the socks, or in this case stockings, right off me. Lordy, he is truly excellent with his mouth! He stops abruptly and tilts his forehead against mine.

"Listen, Elle, I know we said we could just be friends and I meant it when I said I could. The problem is that its way more than that for me and you know it." Bingo, he's right. I'm being incredibly selfish and can no longer have my proverbial cake, or brownies, and eat it too whilst also having Danny cake a la mode on the side.

I look sheepishly into his lovely eyes, catching my

raggedy just kissed to death breath and I know what I have to do. "I'm sorry Tanner but I don't think we can be friends anymore. This isn't fair to you or Danny. I can't love you both and I've already chosen him." This is so sad.

"The thing is, I know you love me too, Elle, I can feel it when I'm kissing you."

"I do love you, okay. But that doesn't change that I love Danny more. He's my lobster, Tanner. Like from that episode of Friends when Phoebe says lobsters have soul mates and they stay together forever and they'd never survive apart. That's me and Danny. We tried being apart and it almost killed us both."

"Then how do you explain what happens to you when I kiss you?" Heck if I know? I don't respond because I have no explanation and he doesn't deserve a made up one so I just look at him. "You feel it too I can tell by the way you kiss me back."

"I do feel it, I've just told you I love you too, it's just not enough. Besides you really are an exceptional kisser." Then a tear slips down my cheek along with a half smile.

"Right. Well then I guess this is it. I'm sorry for

how this turned out. I'm sorry I'm incapable of just being your friend Elle, I tried. I promise." Then he kisses my cheek and walks down the hallway, out the door and is gone. Just like that, Poof! I pick up the pan of brownies and head for my room heartbroken by the loss of one very kissable and lovable Tanner.

When Charlie gets in that night he finds me passed out in his bed all cuddled into his massive pile of velvet and silk pillows with a half empty pan of brownies on his nightstand. In the hand curled under my chin is a picture of Tanner, Charlie and I from the week we moved into the apartment. That's all Charlie needs to see to figure out what's happened. He is a relationship genius, after all. Charlie quietly changes into his silky pj's and curls up behind me. Then he does my favorite thing and wraps me up in his secure, loving embrace. As soon as I feel him, I'm awake and the waterworks start again. Doing what he's best at, he comforts me and right now that's all he can do because the guilt I feel for first surviving and then breaking Tanner's heart is breaking me.

twenty-three

New friends and surprising secrets…

Two days later I'm in Indianapolis on a dreary Thanksgiving morning, feeling hollow. The Macy's Day Parade is on and I'm watching it from my hotel room, feeling incredibly sorry for myself. I realized in my cry fest the other night that I've never told Danny about Tanner, convincing myself that it was not important and that we were just friends, HA! Then I feel guilty for leading Tanner on the way I know that I did. I'm not stupid. I saw the way he looked at me and I chose to ignore it because I didn't want to lose him and now look at me. And of course there's the whole crash thing that really freaked me out. Thankfully there were only a few major injuries but no deaths and that's the positive nugget I'm holding on to right now. The girl who took my place has two broken legs and will be well taken care of by Blue Skies for the foreseeable future while she heals. Thank God she's alive or the guilt would have been unbearable and I just can't take anything more right now.

When I see Danny this weekend, I'm going to tell him all about Tanner and let the chips fall where they may. My mom always says if you have guilt do something about it, use the feeling to propel you into action. It's only fair that I come out to him as a Tanner-kissing hoe-bag. It's starting to weigh on me that I've been such a hypocrite. I guess my inner hoe is about to be revealed. I swear he feels my turmoil because in the middle of these thoughts my phone rings Danny's Foo Fighters anthem and on the display it says Mr. Hotpants himself wants to facetime, yippee. I love his face, have I mentioned he's H.O.T....HOT! Two seconds later there he is staring at me and all the yucky feelings I'm currently drowning in magically sail away, he's my very own pain elixir at a dose of 220 lbs.

"Hey Ellie J. Happy turkey day baby." He's still in his boxer briefs and nothing else, straight from the shower. He purposefully puts the phone back where

I can see ALL of him -he does not play fair- but….I'm not complaining.

"Put some clothes on, would ya? Or this is going to get x-rated very quickly." He laughs and pulls a shirt over his head giving me a lovely view of his well maintained bod. Clearly he's too busy for what my look is saying I'd like to do, otherwise, he would've stayed undressed and made a girl very happy. Wink, wink. I've seriously become a perve. Thank you Charlie!

We chat about how I'm feeling being all alone for the first time on such a big holiday. He knows how my mom is about celebrations and traditions and Thanksgiving does not take a back seat. It's fantastic at our house. I don't even care that football is on all day because we play board games, sip on wine, and like the rest of the world eat until we're sick. He's about to ask me what my plans are for food today when his mom comes in the room. Right before the line goes dead and the screen goes to black I get a good look at the expression on his face and I'm surprised because he looks busted. For what, I have no clue. I mean why couldn't I say 'Happy Thanksgiving' to his mom? He knows I'm all alone here and that I'm missing family big time, yet he looked afraid for her to see me. My gut is telling me

I'm missing something, but what it is I have absolutely no freaking clue.

After calling my parents and hearing them cry about how much they miss me, the frustration I'd been feeling about Danny is momentarily replaced with guilt for ruining their lovely holiday with my absence. The hits just keep on coming. I am the equivalent to a human emotional wrecking ball in all the lives of the people I love most. I should wear a sign that says beware, insert skull-face picture, come too close to this person and bad juju may get tossed at you with the ability to destroy your day/life. What I need to change my mood is some good food and a long walk. I do just that by getting all bundled up for the cool weather in my warm new camel colored Uggs, black skinny jeans, a warm Florida State sweatshirt and a knit beanie my mom made for me. I hurry out of my depressing room in search of both a clear mind and a full tummy.

It becomes apparent after several blocks of walking that the city is shut down. There is not a single open sign or unlocked door in all of downtown Indianapolis, which translates to yet another snafu in my already unconventional and frustrating day. Since I was just a filler on my morning flight, I am the only person from my crew that laid over in

Indianapolis, thus leaving me to fend for myself. Normally I would have someone with me to save the day but I'm realizing this is an opportunity to prove that I can take care of myself and make my own fun, save my own day!

Danny has yet to return his call and I'm pretty stinkin' mad. The old me would've sat around and wallowed in it but this new girl I'm becoming takes this opportunity to prove to herself that she won't let him bring her down. My new motto is WWCD: what would Charlie do? So instead of heading back upstairs to my empty room where there is no room service, I walk…far. Then I see a bus and I'm tickled pink or whatever color makes you happier. The driver looks less than thrilled to be working but in spite of this still greats me warmly. We're both making the best of our stinky holiday situations.

"Hi there," I say getting a nice smile in return. "I'm alone and looking for something nice to do today, any ideas for me?" Locals always know what's going on.

"No family?" I reply "no" with a simple head shake so he continues. "I hate to be the bearer of bad news, but the city closes down on Thanksgiving and Christmas, so if you don't have anywhere to be there's not too much to do but ride on this here bus with me where at least you'll be warm, or you can walk around the city here and freeze to death."

"Well, that's the nicest offer I've had all day, and the only one." I wink at him and he blushes under his full brown cheeks.

"Alright then. Well, I guess I should ask if you've ever been here before?"

"Nope, first time."

"Then while I'm doing my route I'll be your personal tour guide. Sound good?" I can tell he's proud of his city by the way he's puffed his chest up and grabbed the big round wheel, ready for our city bus adventure. This day is going to be fun. I can feel it in my numb, tingly toes.

My chauffer for the day's name is Fred and he is my new and only best friend here in Indy. We spend the afternoon driving his route while talking about our families. Turns out Fred is a war veteran, a father of six grown children and a grandfather of fifteen. What an interesting life this man has lived and if I hadn't stepped onto his bus today I would've missed meeting this amazing person. He and his wife run an organization for underprivileged youth out of their small home and this bus route is what mostly funds it.

Honestly what have I been doing with my life? The perspective I'm gaining talking to him is priceless. I look out the window biting my lip, deep in thought when a huge sculpture of the word LOVE comes into view. Obviously I missed what Fred was saying about it because I point and ask, "What's that?" right in the middle of his explanation he laughs and says, "that's what I was just talking about," and we both laugh at my flightiness.

"My bad. Can we stop? Just for a second. I just want to take a quick picture." I give him my pouty pretty please eyes that work so well on every man I know and he says yes. I kinda knew he would, pouty eyes are rarely turned down.

"Go on out. I'll take your picture." He says exasperated with me and my silly demand.

"Great idea, yes please." I race over to it and lean over and kiss it and I hear him laughing at me from the bus doors. I'm hoping he's snapping pictures like I'd be. I want to send one of these bad boys to Danny tonight and tell him I forgive him and his bad manners.

"Be careful not to put your tongue on there, it'll stick." He's teasing me but in all seriousness I'm glad he said that. I've been known to use my tongue stupidly, but that's another story.

"Duh, Mr. Fred. I'm not a complete ninny." I actually am. He snaps a couple pictures and we're on our way circling back around to the hotel. On the way my stomach is trying to hold a conversation with anyone who will pay attention and it's pretty embarrassing. Noticing the one way conversation of the growling kind Mr. Fred says, "Where you planning on getting this dinner you're growling for when I drop you off?"

"Oh, don't worry about me; I've got several bags of peanuts and pretzels…oh and a coke. Besides I've had such an unexpected and fabulous day I'll be asleep in no time. Really I can't thank you enough. You've really turned my day around Mr. Fred." There he goes blushing again. What a great man, and so cute. Lucky Mrs. Fred.

"Tell you what. I'm off in twenty minutes and my wife and kids are waiting for me to eat. When dinner's done, her and I are gonna drop off a big ol' plate of homemade goodies for you. Just don't tell me you're a picky eater. Mrs. Fred will have none of that and believe me: you don't want to make her mad." I can tell he's serious and has maybe been on the wrong end of her mad before.

"No sir, but you really don't have to do that. I'll be fine, I happen to be extremely independent." That feels so good to say out loud.

"I know. You've mentioned that a few times" he says winking at me, "but if I know all you're eatin' the rest of the day is pretzels and peanuts I'll be up all night praying for forgiveness. Now go call your parents and let em' know you're alright. Be back in a bit with your dinner." With those parting words he slides open the heavy glass door and I'm back where I started. Feeling like a totally new me. Sometimes perspective really is the rock star of a crazy day!

"Charlie, I'm home!" It feels like forever since I've seen him last even though it's only been a couple days.

"There's my girl. How was your Thanksgiving? Did you get my text? I got yours." I notice right away what a good mood Charlie's in. He's rambling and he doesn't do rambling. Something's up.

"Yes I got your text and my Thanksgiving was fantastic. Started off a bit rocky but it turned around thanks to the kindness of my new bff, Mr. Fred. What about you? You're not telling me something, it's written all over your pretty face. Does this have anything to do with love?" I've not seen him out with a single person since we've lived together so I know he's ready.

"Let's just say going home was good. I saw an old friend and, well, things are new again if you know what I mean," he's singing his words, he's got it bad, "I don't want to jinx it but I think he's moving here soon for work. So keep your fingers and toes crossed, okay?"

"Whatever you want, I'll do it. Toes crossed. And I'll have you know that hurts but since I owe you my sanity if toes crossing is what you desire, toe crossing you shall get. Seriously though, I hope you know how grateful I am for you. You being happy makes me happy, plus you have great taste so I'm super stoked to meet him. I bet he's a stud. Now, watch out, world's biggest hug coming your way," I say diving at my bestest friend in all of New York and most of the world.

"You, my friend, are a dork. Hey, isn't Danny

coming tonight? You better go get pretty."

"Yes, and he'll take what he gets and be happy about it." Wow, snarky. I guess maybe I am still a little miffed at Danny.

"Trouble in paradise?" What gave it away?

"He hung up on me yesterday in the middle of our conversation, knowing I was all alone in a strange city. It was so weird, it was like he didn't want his mom to see he was talking to me. Matter of fact, I know that's what he was doing. It was written all over his *caught* face. The problem is that I just don't know why. And when he tried to call me back *hours* later I decided I didn't want to hear some lame excuse, so here we are."

"When will that boy stop being such an arseface. Well, I'll make sure to be out late tonight. I don't want to accidently get sucked into his tornado of suck," he says, heading to the bathroom. "I've got big plans so just fix it before I come in, pretty please. I don't want to walk in on you and Mr. Make-up-Sex! Even though I'm sure you're both great at it. And Lord knows I'd like to see Danny…" and with that I slam the door shut on the conversation.

Oddly, I have yet to hear from Danny today. I

thought he'd at least text me to ask if I still wanted him to come but nothing all day and he's due in soon. I decide to take a bubble bath as soon as Charlie finishes in our deluxe spa- NOT- and then I'll primp the next couple of hours away because I want to look my very best for the grovel fest that's going to go down this evening. Ellen is on in fifteen minutes so I'll watch her in hopes of seeing some of her thumbsy funsy texts segment. Auto correct can seriously shift a mood in the right direction. My favorite spot in the corner of the sofa is calling to me as I grab the remote and flick on the flat screen, waiting patiently for my turn in the bathroom.

The moment the sound comes on I freeze. What I'm hearing the newsman on the screen say makes no sense. Especially when you apply the words he's saying with the picture of Danny in an extremely expensive tailored suit walking into the Trump Plaza. Along the bottom of the screen the words *New acting CEO Thomas D. Lovelle the third has just landed in New York and is headed to an emergency meeting following his father's heart attack late last night. At 23 he has quite a big job on his hands; many people's livelihoods depend on his ability to run a fortune five hundred company at such a young age. Tonight we'll have more on this breaking story and a statement from the new CEO himself.*

WHAT???

twenty-four

Pain and suffering can both suck it…

Heartbreak does different things to different people. Something I've learned about myself the past several months is that, for me, the response changes each time. I'm the human equivalent to a chameleon when it comes to pain. I try to hide from it by changing my colorful response's but nothing works. I show up despite those subtle changes and the people who know me best can see my hurt. Charlie's had no luck convincing me to talk to Danny all weekend. My 'acting fine' color scheme is not a reaction he's seen me use before. My classic move has been to lay about crying in my underwear so this is a transformation that scares him. He's now in unknown Elliemy territory and it's got him rattled. I don't know 'rattled' Charlie, he's a stranger as well.

Apparently Danny's a very popular man, over the course of the weekend he's seen all over the city and touted as the new "it" guy by all the major networks. In two short days he's given the status of bachelor numero uno in all the tabloids and silly me thought he was mine. HA! He's given me the consideration of two phone calls, each one coming in after midnight. The messages he left were sorry enough, he did sound exhausted and maybe even a little remorseful but I've heard it all before and I'm exhausted from all the lies he's been spinning.

One of the networks reported that his father was no longer in any immediate danger but has been given strict instructions by his cardiologist to take it easy for a good long while. Looks like Danny may be taking on the CEO position for the indefinite future and the media loves it…loves him! His laid back surfer boy looks all wrapped up in a tailored suit along with the ability to charm the pants off any available sucker doesn't hurt his current cause. Accept of course if that victim is me, because I've officially taken myself off his list of prey. I'll be checked off and left behind soon enough, receiving my rejection notice in the mail, probably sent by some sleazy secretary with big boobs and a slutty uniform.

Charlie has called in the troops and before I leave on the trip I've just been called out to he informs me that next week Becky is coming in for some Elle recovery program he's cleverly titled, 'Tanner, part deux'. I've told him repeatedly that it is not my intention to bring Tanner into this mess yet again, so call the plan something else, like 'Ellie turns lezbo because men are pigs and their pork does not taste like bacon', or whatever.

"BYE CHARLIE," I shout as I run to the door already fifteen minutes behind schedule. I'll never be late again.

"What do I say again if Danny calls?" He wants me to talk to Danny and at least let him explain himself, but Charlie doesn't understand how weak I am when it comes to my mysterious ex. I need a nice clean break. I'll give in, and I'm done being that girl. She was a PANSY!

"Charlie," I stop, almost catching my roller bag on my hose and say for the last time, "NO! I've puzzled it out for myself, I don't think I need to hear his excuses. And, if you answer it he will try and swindle you so DO NOT TALK TO HIM!" My aggressive tone shuts him right up. He looks stunned and maybe even a wee bit impressed by this new super B in front of him so he smiles and says, "Well then, excuse me for livin'. I didn't know you had that in you love, but Daddy likey!"

"You are such a weirdo. But, that's why I like you. I look so normal next to you, it's a beautiful thing. Love you, ciao!" And I'm off to fly the friendly skies hopefully leaving Danny, also apparently known as Thomas, far behind in my wake or, more precisely, my jet stream.

As luck would have it when I arrive at the Flight attendant lounge to check in, my flights been cancelled. But no worries, scheduling has already reassigned me to a different trip. As I'm printing out my new trip info an old friend from flight school comes in and we get to chatting about how our lives have been. So in my distraction, I don't see my trip, just my gate number. She's in a hurry as well so we run together through the terminal while sharing our funny flying stories. It's comforting to know I'm not the only one who's had some crazy flights. She's been barfed on twice and almost had to deliver a baby, GAH! At the time I thought that training would be useless, but guess not!

I see my gate and we part with a big hug, a see you later and a promise to get together soon. What happens next changes my mood quicker than a snake bite. I look down at my schedule and sure enough my first flight is at gate 25. Its destination, Palm Beach International Airport. Click, click goes my brain as it places together the pieces of the rest of my day. My snake stands and starts towards me, so I do what any girl in my situation would do. I run away.

"ELLIE J," he's shouting as I zip around the row of chairs that take me the long way to the ramp. He can see that I'm on his flight though and gives up, aware that in the not-too-distant future, he'll have me cornered on this death trap in the sky.

"Are you kidding me?" I say out loud in my most flabbergasted voice when I get onboard and see that a familiar face is co-piloting. "You again? Are you following me?" What are the odds today?

"No, are you following me?" HA! YOU WISH!

"You're kidding, right? You are a PIG," I whisper harshly through my front teeth as Garrett stands and takes my arm, leading me to the back of the plane where we can talk in private.

"Okay, listen. I promise I had no idea you were on this flight. Let's just make the best of a weird situation and act like adults here."

"Oh, so now we're going to be grownups." I hiss back.

"I don't have time for this Elliott. I'll stay away from you, especially if you're on your cycle. So gross, by the way. And you stay away from me." He can NOT be serious! He thinks he's the one who was wronged in this misguided relationship!

"Something's very wrong with you if you ever thought for a second that I'd go anywhere near you. So fine, plan accepted. Excuse me, perve." And with that he rolls his eyes and saunters off like the stud he thinks he is.

The crew meets before boarding and we are assigned our positions for this leg of our journey and as luck would have it, I'm placed in the rear with a newbie. Knowing now that Danny is some super-rich socialite, I'm sure he's bought a seat in first class so I should be safe during boarding and take off. After that I may need to hide. The flight attendant I'm working with this leg is rather….sexual, I think is the best word. She's kind of driving me nuts the way she's going on about this guy and that one as they board and I'm fairly certain that by the end of this trip she may be getting humped by Garrett, maybe even without clothes on. EW! She's beautiful but not too bright and extremely endowed in the 'girls' department. The shirt and vest she's wearing look about two sizes too small and I fear for the eyes of anyone she happens to lean across. They're in real danger of being poked out.

We've finished boarding and all the girls are running around talking about the "hottie" in 2B. While strapping in next to new Emily, my super-sexy flight sister says, "Have you seen him? You know Mr. 2B? He's so dreamy. He's the guy who, you know, is all over the news. Super young, rich and HOT! I'd do anything for a taste of that!" I want to tell her no, you don't but I'd be lying.

"Since you're so eager to get a better look how about when we do service you work front to back and I'll do back to front?" She gets eager puppy eyes at my suggestion and her tongue darts out to lick her lips.

"Yes! God you're awesome, I was gonna try and trick you into letting me have that spot but you're so thoughtful. Doesn't he do it for you?" If you only knew how often he'd done it for me and to me.

"Nope, he's all yours." Put your heart away though. He'll smash it.

An hour into the flight and still no sign of Danny here in the back with us commoners. Emily and I have done our drink service and are about to deliver a light snack when the curtain separating the haves from the have not's is parted. There's Danny all wrinkled and glorious, scanning the plane looking for me. I drop to my knees in the back galley and hide. Emily hurries over to see if I'm okay so I tell her I think I'm going to be sick and I crawl across the germy rubber floor to the nearest bathroom that says OPEN in green across the slide bar screwed into the flimsy door. I hate how everything feels so flimsy on this machine that propels us all through the air.

"Ellie J, I know you're in there. I saw the door open and shut without a body in sight. You're hiding from me. Gigs up, come out." He even sounds rich now, it's so unfair.

"You're not the boss of me. Go away, rich boy." It's quiet. No response. Then, "Ellie J, I love you. Please talk to me."

"Alright, I'll talk," I answer through the closed door, "You know what I realized the other day when I saw you on the news. That I didn't even know your name was Thomas. It's over Thomas, Danny, whoever the junior you are. Please, just go away. You've embarrassed me enough."

"That's it? After all these years, all I get is a go away through a bathroom door?"

"That about sums it up. Our relationships officially in the toilet."

"I'm sorry." And through the flimsy door I hear him put his head down against the thin metal separating us and pause. Then after a couple of minutes of silence he gives up and walks away. I sit down with a thud on the counter top and then there's frantic knocking on the hollow door.

"Elliott, it's me Emily, Psst," make her go away. Anyone, please. Are you there Heartbreak gods? It's me…Elliott. "I'm dying out here, what was that all about? Have you had sex with that man?" This girl is sharp as a tack.

"Emily, if it's all right, I'd really like to stay in here for awhile. Can you handle the rest of the snacks or do you need me?" I say, completely ignoring all her other felacious questions.

"Yah, okay. Sure." She sounds so disappointed but right now I only care about myself.

I wait on the plane until the very last passenger has gone and the creepy perma-smile I wear at deplaning is cleared of my face before I think about stepping off the safety of the plane. Just as I expected Emily is departing the aircraft with Garrett's sleazy arm draped over her overexcited shoulder. Maybe they'll be the perfect couple, he needs a puppy like her to have as his weird love slave and she needs….sex. I hope it works for them. Truly, nothing warms my heart like two sleazy people giving love a chance. BWAHAHAHAHA! In the moment I realize that I may actually be losing my mind and I race to find my mother at curbside pickup.

Thank God she's on time. She's all dressed up in one of her wild gym outfits like she's going to some kind of Zumba night club. This is what makes my mother so unique and this is also why I love her so much, she's herself and it's refreshing. "Hi honey," she says pushing open the door from the inside. "I'd get out but the security officer over there is giving me the stink eye because I've been here exactly one minute longer than allowed. So hurry that little hiney of yours up and get in the car already."

"Gracious, give a girl a second to stow her bag. Good to see you too, by the way." And then I lean over the center console and receive the most lovely motherly hug, full of her vanilla smells and sticky hairspray. *You can just wait security man, a girl needs a hug* I think to myself as his rubber baton goes rat-a-tat-tat on the windshield. My mother smiles and blows the old man a kiss as we leave like nothing ever happened and he's not a complete 'A'. She's where I learned to fight my battles with kindness. One of her many mottos is the ol', *"you always catch more flies with honey than vinegar"* and I'm thinking, who are all these people who want to catch flies? That's way weird!

By the time we get home she's all up to snuff on the Danny fiasco and I'm wiped out. I look over at my beautiful Jeep and say out loud to my metal baby, "I love you Daisy, mommy will get up early to drive you in the morning," then I hear my crazy dog Zha-Zha going mad through the front windows and I run to go see her. She meets me with a zillion little doggy kisses, nearly licking my face clean for the night and I feel so unconditionally loved. I miss this…all of it.

Dad comes in from the family room with his arms open as mom hurries off to the restroom and I launch myself at him, almost toppling us both over. "Hey baby girl, I've missed you."

"Me too, Dad." Then he holds me out at an arm's length and gives me a once over, "You look good, kid. I was worried you'd come home a different girl, but other than that fancy outfit of yours you look like the same old Ellie."

"I am the same old me, except I'd like to think I'm a bit smarter now."

"Oh really, and how is that, my young *Padawan* learner?"

"It's a long story. You'll just have to take my word on it for now. I'm exhausted." The bags under my eyes are screaming sleep STAT' in the dark, ringy sort of way that eye bags sometimes do.

"Right, well mom said you don't leave until noon tomorrow so off you go. We'll go get some breakfast at John G's in the morning." After he drops my bag by the bedroom door he leaves tapping the white molding one time and looking over his shoulder saying, "Glad you're home sweetie, even if it is for only one night. Sleep good, and I do."

Daisy…help…

Driving Daisy with her doors off and the top down is hands down my most favorite way to spend a sunny south Florida morning. With my Foo Fighters drowning out the howling wind that's currently blowing my hair into a tizzy around me and the volume maxed out, Dave Grohl does his musical best to calm my frayed & slightly tattered nerves. The song *Pretender* comes on and there's nobody around to hide my pain from anymore. The tears begin to fall before I arrive at my usual thinking spot so I do the safe thing and pull-over across from Juno Beach into a new shopping plaza parking lot.

I sit for a while thinking about the last month of my life. I've still got so many unanswered questions. At the top of the list is the reason Danny hung up on me Thanksgiving morning. I'd like to know if he did it because his mom came into the room and he didn't want her to know he was slumming with me again. She was always a glamorous woman and now I understand why. They are worth millions, maybe even billions, and that requires a certain amount of posh that I will never have. For goodness sakes, flip flops and cowboy boots are my favorite shoes and I seriously doubt the Trumpster and his hotel cronies will find this very sophisticated. The bottom line is Danny is just way out of my social league and now that I know his big secret, he's no longer someone I can picture in my future.

"Hey, Ellie James. Is that you? Dude, check it. Ellie J!" I know that voice and the motorcycle that pulls up beside me.

"Hey Kyle," I say stepping through the doorless frame with a swipe to my eyes and a big embarrassed smile. I haven't seen my old high school buddy in years, and never would've expected to run into him now.

"I knew it was you, saw Daisy here." He says slapping her hood as a sign of adoration. "Why you crying? Who is it? I'll killem'." He says, looking around for the culprit knowing full well there's no one around.

"I'm okay, really. Just been a long couple months but enough about my drama. I have no desire to bore you with all of that. What about you? It's been a long time. Tell me what's up with you?" I'm so happy to see a friendly, familiar face.

"No shit, man. Ouch….. sorry, forgot about the no cussing thing, my bad," he says as I teasingly slap his lean arm and we both laugh. "It's all good here. Matter of fact it's cool I ran into you, serendipitous to be exact. I know you kill it on the guitar and me and the guys own a music shop downtown now. We're looking for a few new teachers and it'd be rad to have a lady with mad skills like yourself at the store."

"Wow, I'm flattered. Really, I am, especially coming from you, oh Guru of all things rock-n-roll, but I can't. I'm living in New York right now. Flying the friendly skies and such, though your gig sounds way more my speed. I hate my job."

"Life's too short to do something you hate, man. Why don't you just let it sit awhile and see what happens?"

"Thanks Kyle. You've given me something to hope for," then he hugs me and fist bumps me, adding our old school snap at the end.

"Love ya, little lady. Next time you're around come check us out, maybe then you won't turn me down. Lates," and with one last contented smile shot my way Kyle, straddles his hog and is off to live the dream. What I wouldn't give to feel that kind of peace in my life again. One thing's for sure: I'm not going back to the city without my guitar. Music has always been my happy place and if Taylor Swift gets relief from writing songs about her ex's, then I might as well give it a try. I'm not trying to reinvent the wheel here, just need some simple heartbreak 101 therapy. And then it hits me. The Foo Fighters show is in a week and Danny has the tickets. Well, Fiddler on a hot tin roof!

twenty-five

The Dob's saves the day…

Bzzzzzz….Bzzzzz.. "Charlie can you get the door? I'm in the shower." I shout from the steamy bathroom. Really, he can be so lazy. I can hear the darn thing buzzing all the way in here for goodness sake! Several seconds pass before I finally hear his feet begin to strut down the hall. The front door is opened and I can make out a mumbled exchange between two deep voices. A moment later the door shuts and Charlie comes into the bathroom poppin a squat on the spongy zebra printed toilet seat cover.

"Delivery for you darling, and that delivery boy was H…O….T….HOT! Sad for you, I flirted with him and he was definitely straight. Should've jumped out all wet, he would've fallen out at the sight of your hot little bod."

"Sometimes you sound like such a guy, it's disgusting. Now, if you don't mind, I'm conditioning. Set it on the counter and go away."

"Moody much? Lord, Becky can't get here soon enough," I hear him mumble as he walks out leaving the door wide open just to peev me off. Men. They're all the same, even the gay ones.

I towel dry and lotion up from head to toe - my mom says it's the number one way to fight wrinkly skin. Considering I grew up on the beach, this is one step in my beauty regimen that I take very seriously. Besides, I have yet to find a man, straight or otherwise, who doesn't love the smell of a woman slathered in cherry-vanilla. It's for sure an aphrodisiac, unlike the package Charlie deposited on the counter that has Danny's company logo stamped along the side of the envelope.

Deciding I'm not strong enough to open it I march into the cozy little family room and toss the package at Charlie as if it contains some kind of explosive. Of course this only makes him more curious. He saw the name on it and is well aware of who it's from. "Would you like me to do the honors?" He says, already slipping his index finger under the space in the corner and sliding it along to release the sticky seal.

"Help yourself… Well?" I say, impatiently waiting while he reads the note tucked inside.

"Here, read this first." Charlie hands me the note and all it says is

I'm sorry. I hope you'll still come.

All my Love,

Danny

aka The most sorry boyfriend in the history of the world

'Ex-boyfriend' is my first thought, followed immediately by *'you can say that again'.*

Then Charlie hands me a single Foo Fighters ticket. WAIT, WHAT? WHERE IS THE OTHER ONE?

"That, that……MAN! How dare he hijack my other ticket? Those were meant to be a present, which means they're both MINE! Well this is just not going to happen. I'll show him. I was so looking forward to this show and he knows it, he thinks I'm so desperate to go that I'd sit by him. HA! I couldn't get my proper Foo Fighters high sitting there next to *him*!" My cheeks have turned red and splotchy and alas I've hit the angry stage of grief. This is the real deal and I am over that S.O.B. and his sneaky tricks. I draw the line at using my favorite band against me, that's totally, like….. immoral!

"Do you have a plan for that ticket, or should I figure it out for you?" Charlie says reaching for it a little too quickly.

"Not on your life. I know exactly who that ticket is going to and it's not you. I just wish I could be there to see Danny's face when his date arrives."

"You are finally starting to get scary and it suits you. I like it. A lot."

The New York club scene is legendary and Becky is desperate for a good time. She said she'd tried to hook up with Ryan from the pub back home but it turns out he's kind of a bore. He's way too "into his job" and "not much fun" so she had to give him a pass, regardless of his "yummy bits" her words, not mine. Tonight she is on the prowl and Charlie and I are enjoying watching her stalk her prey. So many years I've watched her in action and never really grasped the extent of her skill. She is brilliant at this whole boy vs. girl thing, one after another she drops em' like rotten socks and they never see it coming. She does a maneuver she calls 'the wink and the wave'. It's exactly what it sounds like, nothing tricky, but it gets her free drinks all night.

As I'm witnessing yet another wink and wave attack I look across the bar trying to spot the poor guy who's about to be trapped in Beck's flirting vortex. The look on my face alerts Charlie to where the next victim is and we both are overcome with a fit of drunken giggles at the utter impossibility of it all. Of all the bars in this city or in this quadrant or even on this particular block, what are the odds that we'd be staring across at Tanner 'The good-frickin'-kisser-but-still-not-Danny Stanton?

"Look at him, he's so yummy. I still can't believe you could have had that man and it didn't happen. Crying shame, that's what that is." I find this whole situation hysterical while in my drunken stupor.

"I had Danny and you saw him. Don't feel sorry for me, I'll die a happy lady. Woops, scuse me," and now I've got the hiccups. Charlie and I watch as the master pulls Tanner in and I'm surprised to find that

I'm not jealous in the least by their very obvious flirting. It's clear he's into her by the focused look in his eyes. Every time she talks he leans into her, his ear just a breath from her pouty overdone mouth while she possessively rubs her hands up and down over his chest. Dear God, Becky you just met the guy and I'm heating up just watching the two of them, no wonder boys love her so much.

"Here I was thinking you and Tanner would have another go at it but guess not. How bout we go over and mix this up a little. Wanna have some fun?" Charlie's all about the mischief.

"Do first class passengers go barefoot to the john? Heck ya!" If you remember, they totally do sometimes, it's gross!

Charlie tells me to follow him and since I'm too tipsy to be making any solid choices I do whatever he tells me to do. We get over to the two lovebirds in time to hear Tanner say, "You wanna get outta here?" Wow! Moving quick, Tanner. Geesh, he's not as broken up over me as I thought, but who cares, I love both these people and I say, if they get on, then go get it on.

At his question, Tanner follows Becky's gaze over

his shoulder and sees both Charlie and I standing pressed against his back listening to their sexy conversation. BUSTED! Charlie's laughing his face off like we just pulled off some great sneak attack….dork. That's as good a plan as he could come up with after all the darn margarita's we've tipped back tonight. Oh well, it's good enough because Tanner looks like he's been attacked by rattle snakes, and his expression is priceless. Baffled, Tanner says, "What the hell, Elle. What do you think you're doing?"

"Don't be mad. It was Charlie's idea," I say pointing and falling over. Now it's Becky's turn to look confused.

"Ellie J, what's going on? Why are you two laughing like a couple of hyenas? Seriously, you're snorting. It's embarrassing, stop." She heard about Tanner but how could I expect her to put it together with all the Tanner's that must live in New York City, that this is 'The Tanner'?

"I'm sorry, but this is Tanner, you know. The one I've told you about." I say pointing and talking over Tanner like he's not even there. Then I see the switch go click in her mind and she's right there with Charlie and I giggling away.

"Okay, I'm lost here. How do you all know each other? Help a guy out here?" He looks confused but is smiling at the drunken lot of ditz's currently falling apart in front of him.

Taking pity on him I explain, "This is my best friend from home, Becky. She's here visiting and tonight we were out on the prowl and, well, you've been prowled." The three of us snicker like this is the funniest thing one of us has ever said, but Tanner is not laughing anymore.

"Oh, so I guess that's a no then." He says to Becky and then continues, "Well I wish I could say it was good to see you Elle, but considering," he gestured at the three of us laughing, "that I am now a joke of some sort, I'll be going."

As he turns to leave Becky's whole face sobers up and I know what I have to do, "Wait, Tanner. Don't go or do go, but with us. Come on," I say grabbing his arm and flinging him at Becky. "We were headed to get food someplace, come with." I say without asking, only telling.

"Or," said Becky in her pathetic pleading voice, "Tanner and I can head home and you and Charlie can go get food." Her eyes say a whole lot more to me. They say, and I quote, 'you never slept with him, and I'm about to die if I don't have my way with him and if you loved me you'd let me have this one last thing. Please oh pretty, pretty please. I want this toy.' It was the most pathetic best friend mind chat that we've ever had but like I always do with her, I give in. She's always been there for me and I've done nothing but hurt Tanner, this gift I am going to give him should bring us back to even. Becky is legendary as far as the male population is concerned. If I'm right I'll end up with a thank you note from Tanner within the next twenty four hours.

"Why don't the two of you just go back to Tanner's place, I happen to know he's not an ax murderer so you'd be safe."

"Oh, why didn't I think of that? You wanna?" Tanner says, full of renewed hope.

Without so much as a second look back at either Charlie or I, Becky answers for them both. "Hell ya I wanna. See ya BiAtch'esss," and they're off looking for a cab. Tanner is going to have the best night of his life, all thanks to me. As far as I'm concerned I can now put a check mark next to his name on my to-fix guilt list. Better yet, that deserves a shiny gold star.

We don't hear from Becky for almost twenty four hours, unless you count the time I call her phone only to have it answered and set aside so I'm able to hear her and Tanner in the throes of some serious passion. Of course I tossed the phone at Charlie, who listened and said all sorts of nasty things while narrating for me. They are all so gross! We finally receive a proper phone call at two the next morning if the middle of the night counts as proper. I need to set some proper boundaries in place with my friends.

"Well, you're alive." I answer after the first ring.

"I don't know if I'd say that. I think I've killed my vagina. Or Tanner has." Gahk!

"Too much information, even from you. Will we see you today, or are you shooting for the gold in the Vaginal Olympics?" She's laughing her head off and repeating everything I say to Tanner so he replies loud enough for me to hear, 'she already won that. Think of something bigger.'

"That's what she said." More laughing.....this could go on all night. They are in a sex-filled haze of euphoria and cannot be communicated with.

"How about you just call me tomorrow. Charlie's on call but I'm good through Tuesday and it's only

Saturday, so you have fun and call soon. Do you need me to bring you any of your stuff. Or some food and water? I sure hope you two are hydrating." I say, giggling and thinking of Mary Phelps rules.

"Nope, I'm fine. Tanner has the best shampoo and conditioner. Smells like man. I love it. Anyway, thanks for being cool. You know I love you best."

"I do. Talk soon, bye you slut." I hang up before she retaliates. I look over at a still very wide awake Charlie. "What do we do now?"

"I can't sleep now thanks to Becky and all her sex talk. I'm all worked up and no offense to you, but you're not my type."

"Ditto," I say bopping him over his gorgeous head with one of our many velour couch pillows. "Movie? I've got chocolate and a new bottle of that yummy Cupcake wine you like."

"Yes and yes." He answers quickly

"Good. You're in charge of the entertainment. I'll get the snacks." As I head over to the small fridge in the corner of the kitchen I hear my favorite movie come on over the surround sound and scream to Charlie, "that one, stop. I want to watch that." I'm back a minute later with two very full glasses of pinot noir and a bag of the Dove dark chocolates I've been dying to dig into.

"What is this? It looks old?" He cannot be serious.

"You've never seen *Say Anything*? What planet have you been living on for the last twenty odd years? We're fixing this right now. Sit, eat, drink and prepare to have your heart stolen and your mind blown by Lloyd Dobler, the ultimate smartgirl heart-throb." He laughs at me, but in a moment he'll see just what I mean. 'The Dob's do-me eyes are legendary.

When the movie ends Charlie and I are both caught up in some kind of *Say Anything* love coma, silently staring at the blank screen, gripped by the awesomeness that is John Cusack. He looks down at my face nestled in his lap and says sweetly, "You know you're going to be alright, don't you?" The concern in his voice and the tale of desperate love that I just watched are too much. Together they undo me. Tonight is the night my heart comes to terms with the fact that it must at last release Danny. This is the moment our love story ends. I want Lloyd Dobler to come and rescue me. Really, any other heartthrob would do. I am desperate to believe in love again.

twenty-six

Change of plans…

The next morning finds my heart sober and my mind made up. I take the bus across town, focused and alert with the sole mission of dropping off my birthday ticket and thanking my new friend for all she's done for me. She opened my eyes to a lot of things and a ticket to the almighty Foo Fighters is the best I can do as a thank you. I hope she will enjoy it as much as I would have. I find her where I last saw her and hand over my most precious possession. I explain why there's only one and she does what any friend would do and tells me not to worry about a thing, everything's gonna be alright. After parting with a big hug and nothing else to do for the rest of the day I decide to walk home with the words of Bob Marley playing on repeat through the iPod of my mind. I rewind and repeat *'don't worry bout a thing. Every little things gonna be alright.* Choosing to focus on my future, I know exactly what I'm going to do. I'm going to learn to walk again, this time without the pretender. I scan the playlist in my mind until I find Bob Marley's everything's gonna be alright. Repeat…repeat…repeat.

No problem…

"Charlie, are you home?" I shout as I unlock the third and final lock to our apartment and push open the heavy door.

"In here." I find him zipping up his bags on his bedroom floor in a hurry.

"This will only take a sec. I've decided something kind of big." He looks up from the floor and stops what he's doing when he hears how resolute and serious my voice is.

"Well, don't leave me in suspense here." I'm afraid. But fear hasn't stopped me in a while.

"I'm quitting, Charlie." Silence.

"I guess I should've seen that coming. What are you going to do?" He says without a hint of anger in his voice, even though I know he can't afford this place without me.

"You don't hate me? I mean, what will you do?" I say pointing around our little home.

"I'll figure it out. I always do. Don't worry about that. Tell me what the hell is going on." His love is the real deal.

"You know I love you, don't you? I mean I wouldn't have been able to get through any of this without you. I'm not breaking up with you, you know. You'll have to come see me all the time."

"Does that mean you're going back to Palm Beach?" He half smiles with his I already know but still need to ask look.

"It does." When I say it out loud I realize how much I've missed home and am buzzing to get there now that I've made up my mind.

"Well then, I'm gone until Wednesday so message me as soon as you know what you're doing. Living with you and all your crazy has made my life so interesting, it's not going to be easy to replace you, but I will." He ducks. Smart man.

"Hey," I say, slapping his arm and then kiss him big and wet on the cheek, which I know he hates. "You better not forget about me." I say while squeezing him tight to me. If I could pack him and take him with me I would.

"Stop pouting. Your breath smells. Brush your teeth." I can tell he's trying not to cry and his being mean trick isn't working, because his lips starting to tremble as he realizes this may be the last time I'm here with him in our happy little home.

"I'll brush right now," I say. Then I give him one last kiss and scurry off to the bathroom to save us both from what's sure to otherwise be a devastating goodbye.

Who knew it would be so easy to quit my job. I call the supervisor on duty, whom I've never met before, and ask her what the protocol is to quit my job. She asks me when my last day will be and I decide then and there that today is the day, I'm done. The only flight I want to be on is the one that takes me home for good. While I'm on the phone receiving my instructions and how to schedule my final flight back

Becky and Tanner come giggling through the front door. "Okay, thanks for all your help." I say, finishing quickly with the helpful supervisor while hanging up simultaneously.

"Ellie J, we're home," Becky sings pulling Tanner along behind her down the hall and into my room to chat. "What are you doing?" she says shocked when she sees me emptying my once over-stuffed closet into my few barely-used bags.

"Hey," I almost shout at her, caught up in the excitement that I'm leaving. "I've quit my job. I'm going home. Isn't that amazing? No more scary job, no more Danny. I'm a free woman, I'm starting over. Yay ME!!" Tanner looks at me like I've spontaneously grown another head and chimes in.

"Why have you finished with this Danny guy… again?" he asks confused. The last time we really talked I'd dumped him for my perfect relationship with Danny.

"It's a long story. Let's just say he's a big fat liar and I hope he chokes on all the crapola that comes spewing from his big fat handsome face hole."

"She's normally not so vial. You know you just said crap, out loud, which is technically a bad word.

Adding the 'ola' at the end does not make it sound less like a bad word."

"Don't look so smug. I know what I said and be glad it wasn't something worse because right now I feel so free, who knows what I'm capable of. I could have used the S.H. word without a single mouth tingle." I'm so proud of me. I'm growing up more and more every minute.

"What about Charlie? Who's going to take your room? You can't just go leaving him with your half of all the bills." Becky sounds indignant on his behalf. This is what makes her such a great friend, she's always looking out.

"Why don't you take it?" says the sex king himself.

"What?" We both say in unison, turning to look at a very serious Tanner.

"Well, I've spent several days with Becky and in the course of that time I've heard on more than one occasion how much she hates her job and that she's ready for a change. So why not do that here? I mean, there are tons of salons, surely there's at least one that's hiring." Neither of us is saying a word as he's talking. We're both coming to understand that he's being genuine.

"You'd be okay with me moving here? I mean, that wouldn't be too soon for you?" Beck says, shocked by a guy who isn't playing games for once. He's like some allusive wild animal that's going extinct and Becky's simultaneously intrigued and horrified.

"Hell no. You've been the best thing that's happened to me for a long time. No hard feelings, Elle," he says, smiling down at me. Then he focuses again on Becky. "I like you, a lot. More than that even, but I'm sensing some real fear here so I'm going to leave it at that, for now, and say no, you moving here is in no way too soon for me." He makes his point by grabbing Beck by the waist and kissing the daylights out of her already chapped mouth.

She looks at me for some kind of assistance so I do what I know she won't do for herself and make the aggressive and obvious decision, "I say yes. Becky, Say Yes to my Mess. This here lovely room can be yours as of today because I'm leaving in an hour." She laughs at my pop culture reference and gives us a resounding and satisfying, "YES! YES! YES!," while jumping into Tanner's arms, who happens to be the first boy to win over her fragile guarded heart, I think, ever.

We set up plans for me to go to Becks place and put what little she's accumulated over the past few years into a storage facility. I'm going to send her what she needs ASAP and *WHALLA,* the move is complete. Talk about the glass slipper fitting the princess, this could not have gone down any smoother. My room fits her perfectly.

"Hey, where'd you get this?" Tanner says, holding up the receipt I used to write my flight info on a couple of months ago.

"From your place. Remember that day I got called out. I snagged that from your nightstand," I say looking guiltily over at Becky. What I just said sounds so bad. I told her we never did *it* but this lets her know that we came close enough and I was in his bed. "I didn't think you'd care, it just looked like some old receipt." I say feeling guilty that maybe he needed it.

"I don't care. It's my friend Thomas's. He was looking for it and called me to see if I'd found it lying around. He thought he'd need it to return his tux."

The night at the Gala comes back to me and I flash to the memory of the two of them talking. I assumed they were just gala acquaintances but holy cow, maybe it's more than that if his receipt was on Tanner's night stand.

"Wait a minute. Are you talking about Thomas Lovelle? This is his receipt?" I say, causing Becky to do a double take between me and Tanner.

"How do you know Danny, I mean Thomas?" Becky says to Tanner. This is all so confusing.

Tanner see's my face has gone ashen and is hurriedly trying to compile the information he's been given into some kind of relationship algorithm. Then his face goes blank, "Tell me he's not *your* Danny? The one you dumped me for? Holy Shit this is too much. Is there something I can drink here?" He says, leaving the room and heading directly to the mini bar in the kitchen.

"Ew gross, I almost slept with my forever boyfriend's best friend." I say through shivers that rush from my head to my toes.

"Let's stay focused on the positive's here. 1) We now know how the boys know each other and 2) Tanner is my new boyfriend." Becky finishes at the moment Tanner comes back through the doors carrying a bottle and three shot glasses.

"Good, you've saved me the embarrassment of having to ask such a juvenile question. You're my girlfriend. Excellent." Becky moans mortified that he walked in catching her sounding so immature. All I can do is laugh at how ridiculous this is all becoming. Forget the six degrees of Kevin Bacon. It's more like the three degrees of Ellie James.

"All right, so now that we've all exposed our deep dark secrets let's do a couple shots of whatever this is to wipe out the last couple moments and get me out of here. Then the two of you can get to whatever filthy things I know she has in mind," I say waving my hand over the lingerie Becky is pulling out of her overnight bag happily waving it at Tanner. Really who did she think she'd be seeing when she was packing to come visit me? She gives wishful thinking a whole new meaning.

"To Ellie J and her fantastic choice of friends," Tanner says as we clink our glasses together before swallowing down the lethal liquid filling the bottom third of each. I want to spew out whatever it is but Tanner said that there are actual gold bits swirling about in the thick syrupy liquid so I choke it down vowing to never try it again.

Everything's gonna be alright…

Leaving Tanner and Becky was not as hard as I'd thought it would be. Their happiness brings me so much joy. I've never seen Becky serious about a guy so Tanner better watch out. If he hurts my girl he'll rue the day he met me. The thing is, I know he'll be good to her so leaving her behind isn't as painful for me as I imagined it would be. She's in good hands, literally because as I leave I turn to see his hands have a death grip on each of her cheeks and not the facial ones. The two of them will be just fine. Perves.

Tanner sends his company car to get me, which saves my life in numerous ways. Becky and I know we'll be in contact daily so it'll be just like when I was here and she was home. Besides Christmas is in a couple of weeks and she's always spent it with me so we both assume we'll see each other then. Before I leave I put out a message via company email that I'll be selling my uniforms to the first quality bidder and within thirty minutes I have a taker. If ever I knew this was the right move it is now. Everything I need to do to make this transition smooth is happening without almost any effort on my part. Within a twenty-four hour period I've quit my job, found a replacement roommate, gotten rid of my concert ticket and sold all my uniforms. The ease at which this is all happening only fuels my belief that I'm making the right decision at the exact right time.

The only thing I regret is not being able to see the look on Danny's face tomorrow when my replacement Elle shows up. Talk about ruing the day. Oh well, I see my plane taxing to the window and there's no looking back. This time when I leave him I know it's for good.

twenty-seven

Foo the what the…

Waiting for Ellie J to show up is excruciating for a number of reasons. First I've got the worst seats in the world, depending on your perspective. Ellie would say they are the best because front row center gives her the best view of Taylor Hawkins and his "rad drumming skills," but I've somehow managed to seat us amongst what appears to be some kind of raging fraternity social. At a damn concert! Right before my eyes, I witness the group coupling off left and right. It's like some kind of speed dating social except they aren't talking. The technique is simple. The male picks his target, stares her down, she walks over slow motion style, and they make out. Done, couple paired. This goes on until I'd swear there is a perfect number of matched couples. I keep thinking how much fun this would've been to watch with Ellie J. She does this thing where she narrates what she thinks people are saying or thinking and this would've been a gold mine of funny with her.

I can't think about that right now though, because she should be here any minute. Normally she shows up at least an hour before a Foo Fighters show just in case they come out to set up or something. It's never happened, but she's a big dreamer. Now it's five minutes until the opening act and still no sign of her. This is not a promising start to my night. She'll probably wait until the last minute so she won't have to talk to me and this scares me the most because I HAVE to talk to her. I've been incredibly patient waiting until today.

The last couple of days have been miserable. When I walked away from her on the plane it was not that I was giving up on us, because that's the last thing I'd ever do. I wanted her to see that I would respect her space, her need to think things through. Without a doubt I have a serious hole to dig my sorry ass out of, but I'll dig for her. I will dig as long as she needs me too and this is what I plan to tell her. Currently I reside at evacuation-station, party-o-one.

Then the next step in my plan is to be completely honest. I want to tell her everything. Why I didn't tell her who my family was all those years ago, about my parents and the ultimatum that changed both of our lives, and most importantly that I've never and will never love anyone the way I love her.

It becomes clear she's not coming when the lights go down and the opening act comes on stage. I grab the gift I'd brought for her off the seat and turn to leave. That's when I see a woman who in no way fits in with this crowd coming towards me and my empty seat. Stunned is not the word that describes the look on my face when she stops at Ellie's seat and looks at her ticket and smiles as she says, "You Danny?"

"Ah, yah," unable to think of any other words I continue to stare at this sizable woman in front of me. All I want to know is how did she get Ellie's ticket.

"You okay? You look like you never seen a black woman before. Tell me you ain't no racist, that little girl seem too smart to date a racist." Okay so she does know Ellie, she didn't sell the ticket on line to this person. "You got any manners, boy? Or you normally just stare at people like this?" She asks, circling her hand in front of my eyes trying to get my attention.

"You know Ellie J? Where is she?" What is this woman wearing? It looks like she's tried to squeeze her bodacious body into one of Ellie's size four dresses and nothing is staying where it should be, if you know what I'm saying.

"I don't know where she is, sweetie. I do know you in trouble though. She told me to make sure I gave you this," she screams at me over the music and hands me a note with my name scribbled across the front in Ellie's quirky handwriting. My heart beat is keeping pace with the wailing drum beats and I'm starting to sweat as I tear open the envelope. One sheet of folded paper falls out and on the front she's written *this made me think of you, thought you'd like to learn it.* Suddenly this note feels ominous. Immediately I see that it's a piece of sheet music. Actually this is one of Ellie's most favorite songs. The image I have of her banging away in the air is running through my mind as a sad defeated smile comes to my face. In true Ellie style she's calling me out using her favorite Foo Fighter song, *The Pretender.*

I want to ask this woman how she knows Ellie but the note in my hand keeps me silent. My replacement Ellie is staring at me waiting for me to say something, but in this loud room I can't concentrate anymore. She interrupts my thoughts after a second, "I know one thing. You good lookin, and if a girl threw you out, you musta done somethin real bad. I'd never throw you out baby," she says, reaching for my pants. What the hell?

"Whoa. I gotta get out of here," I grab my jacket and start to push past my attacker when she grabs my arm and breathes some advice in my ear with her big sticky lips. "You wanna fix this thing with Elle you betta be true. No girl like a liar and what Elle told me, you a liar. Good luck baby, you gonna need it." She says, sucking my earlobe into her big, wet mouth to finish off the task of freaking me the freak out.

Once I get free from the replacement Elle from Hell, I try and run only to be slowed down every few steps by overexcited jostling Foo Fighters fans. I hear her laughing at my retreat and she says loud enough for me to hear over the banging in my head and on the stage, "You don't worry about Angel, baby. I always find me some new friends." Sure enough when I turn around she's got her hands all over one of the frat boys that clearly found her and her voluptuous bod more entertaining than the teeny little sorority girl left pouting by his side. I did not see that coming. Knowing Ellie J the way I do, their unusual friendship makes perfect sense to me. This lady, as odd and inappropriate as she just was, has the same unique sense of spirit my Ellie does. She's all about adventure and being yourself.

I turn and yell back at her when it hits me, "HEY, I'M GONNA FIX IT! I'M GONNA GET HER BACK!" With her dress rolling up and down at either end she gives me a rousing thumbs up before she grabs frat boy and shoves his face into the crevice of her breasts, causing an uproar of cheers from his surrounding brothers. All I can think is*, I think I've just had my ear sucked on by a hoe.*

As soon as I get outside, I see I have three missed texts. I can only hope that at least one of them is from Ellie explaining to me that there was a mugging and her ticket was stolen. Unfortunately that's not the way my luck has been going as of late. Instead all three are from my sister, each one with more capital letters than the last telling me to CALL HER ASAP! Hailing a cab I get in, give the driver directions and hit return call. On the first ring she picks up, "What the HELL! How hard is it to answer a text or call me!" she shouts through her digital megaphone.

"If you knew what I've just been through you wouldn't be asking me that. All I have to say is my ear was in a prostitute's mouth only a minute ago. So as you can imagine it *was* rather hard," she's silent for a beat while she processes what I've just said.

"Okay, clearly there's a story here but first I have news. Oddly enough this news may disturb you more than what you've just gone through. Are you sitting down?"

"I'm in a cab, whatever it is just rip the Band-Aid off," Lord help me.

"Carrie found the copy of the ultimatum I had. Danny, she took a picture of it and I think she may have sent it to Ellie J."

All I hear is a buzzing sound coming from the phone after that. She's clearly going on with the story but after that last sentence the how's and why's don't matter. I didn't think things could get any worse for me than they already are but if there's one thing I've learned over the past couple of months it's that things can always get worse. And they just did, by miles.

The universe is right…

The flight to Palm Beach International leaves right on time, which also happens to be the same time my Foo Fighters are set to start playing. They'll be playing through my ear buds for the next several hours so I'll survive. This would've been the first time I had front row center, though, and that pill is a little bitter to swallow. I have no doubt that Angel will make up for my absence. Matter of fact I bet she's a big hit with the crowd around her, how could she not be with what little she's sure to be wearing.

As I sit daydreaming about all the possibilities of Danny's night I'm tapped on the shoulder and look up at a face I was sure I'd never see again. "Well, look who's here. I was just thinking about you and lucky me you're here. I was just in the flight lounge trying to leave you this," she says, handing me a pack of Dove Dark Chocolates and a note, "and guess what? Your box number was reassigned," she says eyeing me with suspicion.

"I was going to write you a note on the flight and have one of the girls send it company mail to you, I swear. Pinky swear," I say holding up my little finger. She takes it in hers and we shake.

"I'm in coach tonight so we'll talk when things settle down." With that she gives me a motherly pat on the shoulder and is off to do her preflight checks that I'll never have to do again. God is GOOD!

We're an hour out, snack service in coach is concluded, and Mary finally has a minute to chat. She sits down and holds her hand out for a piece of chocolate, so I one up her and fill her hand up. "So talk," she says, ripping into her first one and putting the piece on her tongue, ready to listen.

I fill her in on all the gory details of my life as of late and she just quietly takes it all in, never interrupting and letting me get through the story in record time. After I explain to her that I believe all my crazy flights and the ease of my transition are all signs that I'm not supposed to be doing this she laughs. I did not expect that from her of all people, my guru. I thought I'd finish the tale and she'd be like, yes my dear you are right. The universe is telling you this is not the life meant for you, and so on, but her laughing at me I didn't expect. Shocked is the only word to describe how I feel. Or maybe hurt.

"I know you think I'm laughing at you but I'm not. I'm laughing at *the universe is telling you something* bit." That I can handle. I give her my best please precede face and she obliges, "These things that are happening are just life, sweetheart, and the ease in your transition is simply results made from the good decisions you are making. You, my friend need to give credit where credit is due. What I just heard was a story of a girl who's been through quite a lot over the last year but despite all of it she didn't quit. Then when she'd had enough she made the adult decision that was right for her and no one else. Then, after making a bunch of good decisions everything worked and she made a move, a great move. That isn't the universe working, that's you making good adult choices that ended up yielding good results."

I sit silently, eating my chocolate and drinking the glass of wine she so graciously brought for me. "I guess I should take the compliment and tell you that you have had a big hand in changing my life Ms. Mary. You always knew when to listen and when to intercede and I can't thank you enough for all your help."

"How about as a thank you, you go home and kick butt. That's the best result of our relationship, don't you agree?"

"I agree." Then I lean my head over on her motherly shoulder and sigh. This will probably be the last I see of Mary and the thought leaves me feeling blue. She senses my mood and leaves me with one last pearl while standing to head back to her duties. "You better never give up on love, little girl. Your heart is pure gold and one day when it's all healed up and beating strong again you are going to find *the* guy and trust yourself again."

Sitting and thinking about what she just said leaves me feeling confused. Surely she meant that one day I'd trust a man again, not myself. We'll chalk that up to a Mary oops. She's entitled to one after all the good advice I've received from her.

The captain announces we're about twenty minutes out and that there are reports of some severe turbulence in the area so for the rest of the flight he'd like our seatbelts to remain fastened. Considering this is my final flight I refuse to let fear win. Then it happens. The plane falls. This sounds dramatic…BECAUSE it is! What's currently happening is not turbulence: I know what that feels like, and this is falling from the damned sky! That's exactly what it is, the sky is damned. There's no other explanation.

I look and see Mary's small frame smack into the ceiling while trying to get to her jump seat. Thank God she doesn't appear to be injured because as soon as she's back on the floor she crawls over and is helped into her seat by her fellow flight attendant. The look on her face is one that I'd never expect from her. It's……FEAR! Unbelievable. After all of this, I am going to actually die from flying. Months and months of getting over my fear, only to end the whole darn experience in death. Clearly Mary's forgotten all her steps because she looks to be in the throes of a massive panic attack, gasping for air. I know one when I see it.

This goes on for several minutes and then wham, just like that we're landing, the tires are screeching down the runway and there is the loudest silence you've ever heard on the aircraft. Sometimes silence is the loudest noise, and this is the perfect example. If you listen hard enough you can make out the sound of the person's heart beating next to you, pounding as hard and as loud as your own.

The captain's voice breaks through the terror induced trance that we are all in and he apologizes profusely for what we've just been through. He explains this was not ordinary turbulence but something much more harsh known as wind shear. Our flight was the first to come in during this particular storm and there had been no indication of shear on the radar. He asks us to please accept his apology on behalf of the airline and with a click of a button he's gone.

The plane comes to a halt and empties in record

time. As I pass Mary at the door she takes hold of my upper arms, looks me in the eyes and says very seriously, "In all my years flying, I have never experienced anything remotely like that before. I take back what I said before. The universe doesn't want you flying. Now go." She pats my bum and scoots me off her airplane before my bad juju sets in on the aircraft. When I'm halfway down the ramp I turn around and wave. In return she puts her delicate fingers to her mouth and blows me one last kiss goodbye. I reach up to grab her thrown kiss and my secret guru, Mary Phelps, is gone from my life; forever.

twenty-eight

Home is where the lovin' is…

The cab ride to my house in Palm Beach is nothing like the cab rides I've grown used to in the city. The driver is quiet, respectful of all the standard safety laws and, bonus, he lets me pick the radio station. To say I'm relieved to be home is the understatement of all understatements. The salty smell of the air alone is enough to bring me to my knees in gratitude, but then you add in the warm temperature, the open views of the sky and the fact that tomorrow I will be safely on the ground driving around in Daisy, well, enough said.

As I exit the cab I notice there are no lights on in

the house so I grab one bag at a time from the curb and bring them to the porch. I fumble around in my purse until I locate my key chain from inside my giant purse while standing in the dark on the front porch. My mom hates leaving the light on because she says it draws in too many bugs, but it's seriously frustrating when you have to dig around in the dark. After several minutes I find the chain in question and quickly unlock and push open the door, happy, finally to get away from the mammoth mosquitoes that have been torpedoing my exposed skin for the last five minutes.

The minute the door is fully opened I rush in, pulling my roller bag and am stopped dead in my tracks by the sight of my mom's naked butt in the air. Only a second passes, but it feels like hours as my mom slow motion rolls off my very exposed and naked father and covers them each up with one of my favorite throw pillows. OLD FAVORITE! My hands fly to my face but it's too late. I will never be able to unsee this, NEVER. Why do images have to burn in our minds? WHY? Now that she's covered her lady parts, my mother seems completely unfazed with the position I've caught them in. "Well, surprise!" I'm pretty sure that's my line but she wins. "Why didn't you call honey? Daddy or I would have come and picked you up from the airport." She's looking past me trying to see how I got home.

"Oh. I took a cab. I was hoping to surprise you," note to self; never do that again.

"Looks like you're the one who got the surprise," she says, unable to help the laugh that escapes behind her words.

"You know what? I'm gonna go for a walk. Get some fresh air, clear my mind. I'll be back in a couple minutes. Tootles." I say, backing slowly out the door. Right before I've got the door all the way closed my mother yells back at me, "You know what honey? Better make it a little longer than a couple minutes," followed by giggling.

It's official. No way am I moving back into my childhood home with them. It's become a sex chalet and they've clearly grown accustomed to a lifestyle that I was blissfully unaware of until this evening. I hate to be the one to take away their fun. Besides, I can no longer sit on my favorite sofa so what's the point? Since I'm in my casual travel clothes and I have my purse on me I decide to head around the corner to the pub we went to before I left for New York. Thank goodness it's in walking distance because I have no plans on heading home for a while. When I do I can only hope and pray my parents will be asleep because I don't think I can face them again tonight. It's going to take quite a few drinks in order to dull the image that's currently trying to upload in my mind. Seeing parental sex is life altering and in NO way, good for me!

As I push open the pub door, all my senses are instantly engaged. The jukebox in the back is playing *Melissa* by the Allman brothers. Several people are playing pool and by the looks of it, someone just had a great first shot landing several solids to start the game. The kitchen door bursts open sending the delicious smell of frying onions and good sirloin pulsating throughout the room. By the amount of cash pouring over the top of the tip well sitting at the bar, I'd say the bartender is having a stellar night, as well. It's perfect and I'm home.

As I approach the bar I recognize the guy serving the drinks immediately. He lifts his head and smiles with ease at the girl in front of him, at home behind the bar. Becky had a date or two with him, so hopefully he won't hold her wild behavior against me. All I know about their short-lived romance was what she told me and that was only that he was boring and too into his job, whatever that means.

Thank God I know for a fact that Tanner is not boring and that he won't put up with any of her BS. Otherwise, I'd never have left her in his care.

"Hey," I yell over the crowd around me when Ryan makes eye contact with me. I can tell he's trying to place me so I help him out. "I'm Becky's friend, Ellie, but we only met briefly a while ago so don't worry, you haven't forgotten who I am."

"Thank you for that," he says leaning over the bar so we can hear each other better. "If I remember right she said you moved to New York? You back for a couple days?"

"Actually I'm back for good. Turns out I'm a really bad flight attendant."

He laughs at my response, "I highly doubt that. A pretty girl like you must have been adored by the passengers. I know if I saw your face at boarding I'd feel lucky." I think Ryan is flirting with me. If I wasn't so over boys I'd give it right back to him but he has no clue how over his kind I am. I'm a day away from lezzing out, for real.

"That's sweet, but if your flight attendant is having panic attacks in the bathroom and using up all the airsick bags to hyperventilate into, you wouldn't feel any sense of peace, I can promise you that." He laughs and I can see he thinks I'm kidding, but I'm not. "Anyway, I missed the beach. I'm not really a big city girl after all. A visit now and again would be all right but permanent residence is not my thing. What about you?" I ask, making friendly conversation, no flirting in my tone whatsoever.

"I'm with you. I can't imagine being anywhere else but here. Plus, I love my bar, so it's an easy decision." He sees me eyeing the guy's appetizer next to me and offers me a menu. Of course I take it. After a three-hour flight and nothing but pretzels I'm starving.

"Thanks, but I don't need a menu. Can you order me up a cheeseburger and fries? Medium, please."

"Of course," he says while simultaneously punching it onto a computer screen. "Drink?"

"I'll have one of your house brews. Surprise me, I love beer. I'm not into IPA's so much so anything but that." He gives me a wink and leaves to fill a mug with something at the other end of the bar. He returns after a sec with a frosted sixteen ounce mug filled to perfection, the top inch of the mug a solid wall of beige foam followed by a rich dark brown that sinks to the bottom of the deep glass. It looks like heaven in a cup. I take a sip and my eyeballs roll into the back of my head. "I love this," I whisper after my first sip, and I notice his satisfied smile as he walks away to take an order at the other end of the bar.

As I sit and wait for my burger I reflect over how quickly things have changed in my life. I went from being with the love of my life, our future wide open to suddenly being at home and alone all in the span of a couple of unpredictable weeks. During the long flight home I had a lot of time to plan out what I was going to do next. Hopefully Kyle hasn't filled the position he was telling me about, because that's step one for tomorrow followed quickly by step two, find apartment.

I'm drinking my beer, engulfed in my own thoughts when Ryan places a big warm plate of yummy in front of me. "Need anything else?" he says, handing me a roll of silverware.

"Ranch dressing if you've got some handy. Otherwise I'm set. Thanks." I've already got my napkin in my lap and a fry in my mouth before he can turn away. "Oh, and when you see this empty, I'd like one more. Amazing," I say, tapping my frosty mug of goodness.

"I'll keep an eye out then, wouldn't want you going without," he says jokingly before handing over a brand new bottle of ranch from the kitchen.

"You have no idea how glad I am you all opened so close to my parent's house. Honestly, you saved my life tonight. At the very least, my mental health."

"I'm sure there's a great story that goes along with the sentiment, but I've got to get back to the ass at the other end of the bar who won't give me a rest. I'll watch out for your beer, enjoy your burger," and with that he leaves me to eat in peace.

After cleaning my plate and finishing my second beer, Ryan brings me the check. He hasn't charged me for either of my beers and when I try to protest he tells me not to argue, they're on the house as a welcome home. I pay for my food and stand to leave when the door swings open and along with the scent of the fresh night air comes the hoe-bag herself. The sight of her alone causes my blood pressure to shoot through the roof and the hair on my arms to stand up tall. I have to get out of here before I say or do something I regret, so as she makes her way to the pool tables I sneak out. I don't know if she'd even recognize me from the stalking incident at the hotel but I'm not willing to take the chance. I've humiliated myself in front of her enough as it is.

The walk home is quiet unless you count the chirping of the crickets and the chorus of the frogs. Walking around the city at night I only heard bar chatter, sirens and taxi cabs being hailed. The novelty wore off much quicker than I thought it would. In my imagination I was going to live a long fancy life in the city just like you see girls doing in the movies or on TV, but it turns out that's not the kind of adventure I'm looking for. The next adventure in my life will be one of self fulfillment and not one of self destruction.

I won't call it all a wash though, because without that time I would've never found out Danny was such a liar, Becky wouldn't be living her fantasies out in the city with a guy who is absolutely perfect for her and I would never have met Charlie. Not to mention the fact that I now feel secure in the fact that this is where I know I want to live out my days, doing the thing I love most in life, music. Until this all happened I was living a life that Danny had planned for us and I was desperate to do what worked for him. Now I plan on living the life that I plan and I'm desperate to do what will work for me.

I'm almost home when my phone beeps in my

hand alerting me to a new text. Before I have a chance to see who it's from I'm distracted by my mother's loud voice shouting my name from the front porch a few doors down. It's late now and I'm shushing her as I jog towards her so she'll see me and be quiet. She stops mid holler the minute she sees me jogging toward her with my hands up in the air giving her the *'are you serious'* gesture.

As I approach I see she's wrapped in her favorite terry robe and lord willing something is underneath it but I can assure you I don't plan on finding out either way. I stuff my phone in my pocket forgetting that I have a new message and give her the huge hug I had planned on initially. She hugs me back just as hard and when my Dad comes into view I lean back and say with a huge grin on my face, "This time, I'm home for good," and as I look around I realize my dad's already brought everything up to my room and he's got the sweetest, most sincere, single tear dripping from the corner of his eye. Man it's good to be back. I missed these people.

twenty-nine

Starting fresh…

The next day I wake up with the bright sun I've missed for months streaming through my open curtains and onto my now pale skin. I plan on remedying this within the next forty-eight hours but first I need to go and see Kyle. My only plan for the day is to get that job he'd offered me before I left, so I dress in my best Foo Fighters tee and tightest skinny jeans to go secure my place as guitar teacher extraordinaire.

When I push the door open to the shop I'm immediately overcome by how cool the place is. The first thing I notice is the amount of square footage.

From outside you can't tell that there are two stories and it looks like the second floor loft area is where the classes take place. There are all sorts of instruments littering the loft with chairs and music stands strategically placed in a semi circle towards the rear of the space. It's magical. The downstairs is where the music and instruments are sold. The walls are painted raven black and covered with graffiti style musical pictures as well as famous lyrics penned from the best of the best. The stairs have been spray-painted the same bright teal that is present in so much of the surrounding graffiti, tying the color scheme together and really popping off the bright white tiled floors.

Impressed is not the word I would use to describe how I'm feeling. Amazed, shocked, dumbfounded are just a few that come to mind, considering the last time I'd lived at home Kyle was a drop out stoner who could jam on his guitar and that's about it. Who knew in just a few years he'd get it together enough to create this. I'm contemplating what to look at first when I hear his familiar voice coming from up above. "Dude, you came. Sweet."

He comes down the steps as I come up and we meet in the middle with a good ol' fashioned bear hug. "I thought you said you were leavin'? Wuz up?"

"I did leave; I've just decided to come back is all. Still need a teacher?" I say holding on to him, pulling back to look into his baby blue eyes.

"Hells ya I do. This is crazy man. When you wanna start?" He says full on in his own personal chill style of joy.

"Monday would be cool. I've got to tan up," I say gesturing to the pale skin covering all my exposed parts.

"Monday it is, then. Let me give you a tour while you're here then we'll get paperwork done and you on the schedule, cool?"

"Yah, cool."

After about an hour at the shop I'm headed to Becky's place to grab the stuff she needs sent to her and to check out what I have in store in the way of packing the place up. It doesn't take me long to realize I could live here. It's only about fifteen minutes away from work, a skip to the ocean and if Becky could afford it off the money she made at the salon then surely I can. I hadn't planned on the generous amount Kyle offered to start me on but he said the business does well so I didn't argue with him, clearly he knows what he's doing.

I call her as soon as I've got the plan worked out in my head and she answers laughing. I hear Tanner in the background tickling her; seriously I'm so glad I broke up with him. All that darn tickling is nerve racking, you never know when he's going to attack. "You at my place already?" she asks gasping for air.

"Could you tell him to stop with all the sexy stuff for like five seconds so I can talk to you?" I know I sound annoyed but I do kind of miss being manhandled and it's only been a couple weeks since I last saw Danny. This alone thing is going to take some getting used to.

"What's up, grumpy bear?"

"Nothing. Actually, a lot." I fill her in on the job and then the apartment idea and she loves it. This saves her having to find someone else to take over her lease and I know that she's really thinking if her and Tanner don't work out she's got her place to fall back on so it's a no brainer.

"I'll have your stuff sent Monday morning. You're good until then?"

"I haven't had on clothes since you left girly, so I think I'll be fine," then I hear her growl at Tanner.

"Okay, well, you're gross. On that note talk soon and peace out."

"Hey, Wait! Why do you have your mom's phone?" she asks right before I'm about to hang up.

"Last night I must have dropped mine when I was out or maybe when I got home, who knows. All I know for sure is I've looked everywhere this morning and mine still hasn't turned up. I'll have my mom's until I find mine. I guess I should say thanks for answering if you thought it was my mom calling to harass you."

"I knew it was you, you're always loosing that stupid phone. You'd lose your own head if it wasn't attached!" I hear sexy time music turn up in the background then Beck's hand must cover the phone because all I hear now is muffled voices.

"Tanner says I have to go now. Thank you for him, by the way. Peace." And just like that I'm alone with my thoughts… again… and all I can think is how over the last couple months my life has been like a circus side show. For the first time in a really long time I'm starting to feel in control of my life again.

It's amazing. No boys, no distractions, just me, my new pad and maybe my mom will let me bring Zha-Zha here to live with me. I feel an overwhelming sense of peace come over me and I know that what Angel said is right. "Everything is gonna be alright."

Moving on…

The weekend goes fast with all the things I have on my growing to-do list, first being to move out of my parent's house…again. When I told them my plan to live at Becky's it was obvious they were sad. But, my parents excel at being supportive so they do what they always have done and they help me. My dad carries down all the bags he brought up just the night before and loads up my precious Daisy for me. Mom helps me empty all my other stuff into plastic bins and even agrees to let me bring Zha-Zha so I won't be alone. She's super yappy so she'll be a great alert dog. Besides, I'd just look like I was always talking to myself and I feel much less weird if I'm talking to her.

My mom follows me to Becky's and we have all my stuff emptied and unpacked into her place in under an hour. The two of us work like Ben and

Jerry's together, chill. After we're done mom says she'll be back shortly and mysteriously leaves, only to return with her arms loaded down with bags full of my favorite groceries. After a giant stinky thank you hug she shoos me off to go take the shower I've been dying for.

When I come out she's sitting on the back patio with a glass of wine poured for each of us and I'm overcome with appreciation for my life. "Hey mom, thanks for today," I say sitting down in the oversized papasan chair sitting across from the mismatched lounger she's curled up on. We both take a big ol' chug from our glasses of pinot grigio out of a couple of those funny redneck wine glasses Becky paid too much for at some silly boutique.

"You know daddy and I will always help you, sweetheart. You're always going to be our little girl. But, I'd like to know what brought you home so hastily. The last time we talked you were doing better with work and I thought you were trying to make a go again with Danny, but since you've been home today I've noticed his name hasn't come up once. What's up?" She asks, giving me her best spill it eyes. They work like a charm, as always.

"It's a long story. You heard about Danny right?

You'd have to, considering he's been all over the news," she shakes her pretty brown hair in the affirmative. "I just can't do it anymore, mom. I feel like every time I give him a chance or think that I'm safe again he's going to lie to me. You know, I am a forgiving person but I just don't think I can live with feeling like I was never good enough for him. All these years he's been someone I felt equal to in every way but now. Now, I just feel like he was using me to….."

"To what honey? How was he using you? The way I always saw the two of you it was the opposite of that. That boy loved you and I would imagine there's a reason he never told you about his family and all that comes along with them. You haven't even given him a chance to explain, have you?" She asks, trying to make me see reason.

"Mom, trust me, the two of us have put each other through too much the last year and at this point I think enough is enough. One of us has to end this stupid unhealthy cycle we've created. I love him and I'm pretty sure I always will, but I can't take the pain anymore. In all our years together we never once broke up. Shoot, we barely ever had a fight outside of who loved who more. But somehow over the past couple of months all we've been able to do is hurt one another. Now we're stuck with all these questions about who's done what to whom and it feels like we've just become two different people than the ones who always were good to each other. It feels like it was all a lie, we were a lie and I don't know how we can ever fix that."

My mom knows me well enough to know that when I've made up my mind I can be pretty stubborn so she doesn't push the issue any more tonight, though I can tell by the twitch in her eye she's dying to put in more of her two cents. She doesn't, though, and I appreciate it because I just need to rest and let this all go. I went right from being in school with Danny, then home to my parents, before I fell right into Charlie's arms and then finally Tanner's. This is the first time I've just been by myself, EVER, and I need this. I need to depend on myself because I've learned that I can. After the last few months one thing that's happened that I'll never regret is that I have become independent. I know I can take care of myself, and now it's time I start proving that to everyone else, too. Eventually this hole in my heart will have to heal. After all, isn't that where the phrase time heals comes in. I'm counting on that one to be true. It has to be.

Music moves me…

The next couple of weeks can only be described in the dorkiest of ways. They've been a complete dream come true. I know, dorky right? Only it's a dream I had no idea I ever wanted. I'm teaching guitar to several students and I love them each for different reasons. Some remind me of me when I was starting out, they pick it up quickly but want to skip all the necessary steps at learning different skills and just want to jump in to the rough stuff with all their enthusiasm to play music. I keep thinking of how patient Danny used to be with me and I'm filled with gratitude. It's nice to be able to bring back good memories of him and not simultaneously feel like dying. It feels…healthy.

The very first student I meet is the one who brings me the most joy, her name is Jenny. She reminds me of my friend Fred's granddaughter up in Indianapolis. Teaching her has taught me some amazing lessons about life. The first being that music, if you let it, can help you manage the pain in your life. She's on scholarship thanks to a wonderful program Kyle started here to give underprivileged kids a chance to learn about and play music. A year ago her father was lost in a terrible car accident and she and her mother are trying to make it but it's been a real struggle for them both emotionally and financially. The two of us have been writing simple songs for her to practice that incorporate all her new skills, along with the words that she needs to express herself in a safe and healing way.

By teaching Jenny, I've been healing myself, as well. Sometimes after work I go home and for hours I just sit and write music. I've been listening to my Foo Fighters all these years and now I'm inspired to make my own music. I love them for the healing they've given me but now I need to heal myself, and man if music isn't the way I'm doing it. Jenny and I play our newest creations for each other at each lesson and sometimes we laugh at our crazy lyrics and sometimes we cry but whatever the feeling is, at least we're feeling it and not running from it.

I've been in touch with Fred since working with Jenny and told him I'd like to start fundraising for his and his wife's afterschool program to add music time to their schedule. To say he's overjoyed is the understatement of the century. He calls me, sometimes daily, with new ideas and ways they've found to make money for the instruments they need. They've had bake sales and car washes and they've earned a little but nowhere near enough. When Fred started learning about instruments he was shocked to hear how much the good ones cost. All of us here at the music shop have agreed to make instructional DVD's for the instrument we teach best. Kyle is sending one for beginning base, I'm sending one for acoustic guitar, Sam is our resident slayer so he has the drums covered and by the time we're done we're hoping to have one for each instrument we sell.

Things are moving along well in the fundraising department. I've had T-shirts made up to sell in the shop with the majority of the profit going towards Fred's program and the rest coming back to the scholarship program we have here. The guy who designed them is the graffiti artist who did the work in the store and the shirts came out amazing. They're black like the walls in our store and he used the same fluorescent color scheme to pop them off the black like he did here. On the front is an artistic expression of a child done in a bright teal holding a shaky purple music note in the air above his head and the phrase "Music saves, music heals, music inspires" is scribbled beneath his urban-styled body. When you flip the shirt over the lyrics from one of Jenny's most recent songs is covering the back of the shirt in a bright pink for all the world to see.

The shirts are by far our best moneymaker for the program but it's not nearly enough for what Fred needs. I was under the impression that he and his wife had a manageable number of children in the afternoons but apparently that number has increased since adding the music lessons. He says he's having a hard time with the number of children applying to the program and for the first time he has to turn kids away. The intention of the program was to help. The stress and heartbreak I hear in Fred's voice from having to turn kids away is all I need to get myself motivated to amp things up.

After a long conversation with Fred I realize he needs a bigger space to work in as well as more instruments and it's time we added some real instructors as well for some much needed one on one instruction. This means more money - a lot more money - and I'm the one who started this, so I need to make this happen. Out of the two of us Becky is the party planner so when I decide to have a fundraising concert/party, she's the one I call.

"First of all, you are my hero Ellie J. When I grow up I wanna be just like you," my best friend in the world says through the phone. "Second, you suck at throwing parties. What are you thinking?" She so knows me.

"That's why I'm calling you, smarty pants. I know my limits. Can you help me or what?"

"I can, I just need to know the date because we're going to the Hamptons the first week of July with Tanner's family for some big gathering "the fancy people" have every year, so as long as it's not that week, I'm in."

"Fine, perfect. I want to do it soon though before school starts up in the fall, so is the week after that okay for you or is that too crazy?"

"Done. No prob. Is there a theme?"

"I hadn't thought of that. Any ideas pop into that pretty little head of yours?"

"Duh, of course. How about……..Music is the Art of the Heart or something like that?" She says flippantly, like that isn't freaking brilliant.

"YES! YES! YES! I LOVE THAT!" I shout through the airwaves to her genius mind. "That's exactly what music is, Becky. It's your heart. Thank you, I love it…..really. I really, truly…love it."

"Okay already, got it. You love it. So I'm the boss, right? You have to do whatever I say?" She knows I will.

"Yes Becky, you are the boss. Whatever you say goes. Where do we start?" The excited energy is pulsing through me as I wait for her instructions.

"Get a pen, I've got a couple minutes right now and then I'm off to be fabulous somewhere," I know whatever she says I'll do because if Becky knows how to do anything, its party.

thirty

Things always get worse before they get better…

Lately it seems like everywhere I turn I see Danny and I'm feeling P.O'ed all over again. He's either on the TV doing some stupid interview or looking incredibly sexy representing his hotel chain in a series of new commercials they're running where he is their new spokesmen. His advertisers got smart using his pretty face to sell their hotels. He's literally a money maker. Here I am, rubbing pennies together and loving my life and he's rubbing millions together and probably loving his. As happy as I am for him because I genuinely am, I'm also human and maybe a tad bit jealous. Okay… I'm a lot bit jealous.

The other night I was watching some silly E! Special featuring Hollywood's Hunky top 20 bachelors and he was on the list. First of all, he's not from Hollywood. Second, he doesn't make movies. Apparently he received his SAG card for making commercials and so now he's considered Hollywood. Kyle is constantly teasing me about it. "Looks like you lost out on the new Bachelor," or something equally annoying like, "Looks like you're not going to get anymore of his Hollywood. Get it? HollyWOOD?" drp....dee...drp....drp. dumbarse.

It's not easy seeing and hearing about all the beautiful women he gets to hang out with, but I made my bed and I'm very literally laying in it. I've got the flu. Not the twenty-four hour barfing one but the real ten-day fever, chills, coughing want-to-die one. This is the first time I've been sick like this and all alone. Of course my parents live nearby and bring me your typical sick person supplies, but there's no cuddling at night to help my chills or kisses to check for fever on my forehead and for the first time in a long time, I realize I miss Danny. These stupid ads of his aren't helping one little bit.

In my fever-induced hallucinations he keeps showing up and is lying next to me in the fancy suit that he wears in the commercials and he's rubbing my arm the way I like saying, *"you can come stay at my hotel for only a hundred and fifty dollars a night. And that includes breakfast."* He says it in his sweetest voice, like he's doing me some big favor. Next thing I know he evaporates into thin air and I'm left with the sound of his voice and his face on the tv screen in front of me and I feel so alone all over again. It sucks to love someone who you can no longer have. I'm writing a song about that when this fever breaks, if I can remember.

Becky calls to check up on me in my time of need and to give me a few updates. She starts with the party and lets me know that everything is set up for the second week of July and the vendors and venue have all been arranged. Then her voice shifts into serious mode and she gets to the good stuff.

"I hear Danny's been asking around about you."

"So." I answer, trying to sound completely unaffected by this revelation even though I'm over the moon happy to hear maybe he misses me too, or maybe he just wants to make sure I'm okay because he's being nice? I wish I knew. I don't feel like I know him anymore and it hurts.

"He wants to know where you are. Dumbass

hasn't figured out you're home yet. How can he be so rich and successful and yet so stupid? Doesn't he realize he can hire someone to find you? Really!" I miss her so much. "Anyway, that's just what I heard from people I talk to at home. He still has no clue about you having dated Tanner either, by the way. Or for that matter, that I'm dating his BFF."

"Good, let's keep it that way. I still can't believe I haven't run into him or Lex. I guess I'm not supposed to, huh?"

"Listen, I'm going to be serious for like the first time ever here. You have believed all along that these things are happening how they're supposed to and I've been on the same page with you, really seriously I have. That's the only thing that explains my having met Tanner, who happens to be my perfect match, by the way, and again thank you," she says this EVERY time we talk. "The thing is, I still really believe that you and Danny should be together. It feels wrong to me that you're not. And I know you don't want to hear that and all but, well, I just had to say it once so I can let it go. Love me still?" She can't know that I'm crying because she'll feel bad so I answer her quickly with, "Love you still." We hang up after she tells me she loves me one more time and I cry for the first time in a good long while. I literally feel every kind of pain right now and all I can do is hope that it will pass soon along with this god awful flu.

After the flu incident I'm having a hard time getting my groove back. Things are going great at the store. Business is booming, teaching is going great, the concert is coming up and the planning's pretty much done. The Danny-sized hole in my heart just refuses to go away. Even driving around in Daisy isn't helping, writing music isn't helping, and the beach, my go-to for bad days, isn't helping. It's that bad.

Everyone at the shop has been noticing my funk. So one morning Kyle asks if he can talk to me in private. We go to his office and sit facing each other on the overstuffed, purple velour couch that he got on eBay. It's his prized possession. "Okay. Here's the thing. The party's in a couple of days and I was thinking, we both need a date." And? Is my first thought. Then realization hits me, oh crud, and it's too late. I can't stop him. "Wanna go?" he says with so much hope in his eyes, I want to crawl under this disgusting couch and die a slow death. Why KYLE?

"Kyle, I....I'm not dating right now."

"Duh, why'd you think I asked you? I know that.

Anyway, I like you, like you and I think it's time you go out. With me."

"Don't you think that would screw up things here at work Kyle? I love my job. I don't want to risk it." There. I said it.

"We'll always be friends, no matter what Ellie." Apparently he doesn't understand what I'm saying. More direct it is then.

"Listen, I know we'll always be friends, but I just don't feel like more than that.......at all." Understanding shows in his eyes and I feel like such a tool. After all he's done for me I can't muster the strength to go on a single date with him. Danny has ruined all men for me. I should just stop now, cut my losses and join the nunnery like my dad had always hoped I would.

"Can I do something to try to change your mind first?" He's got a mischievous look in his eye which makes me wonder about the "something" he has in mind.

"Depends."

"Close your eyes."

"Only because you're my friend." I close my eyes

hesitantly. Then without any warning his lips are on mine and it feels……lovely. It's been so long since I've been kissed that even though I have no lustful feelings for the guy kissing me I am still enjoying it. His hands that were once only music makers in my mind start roaming over the exposed skin on my arms and up to the back of my neck in order to cradle my head and help deepen this intimate kiss between friends and coworkers. Shite! COWORKERS!

"Stop….Whoa, I can't. I'm so sorry. I love my job and I can't do both. Please." And with my final request he stops. He looks so sad for being such a cool rocker and it makes me feel like such a tease. "If I led you on in any way I want to apologize. Swear to all things wonderful that it has nothing to do with that kiss because that was….let's just say, you can kiss." With that he leans over and gives me one last kiss before standing up.

"Hey, you can't blame a guy for trying. It would have been rad if you were into it, but I get it. You still love Danny, we're all good. No worries. Feel free to take a minute. I've gotta go check on something," and he smiles at me when he turns to go and closes the door behind him, leaving me alone to go over that kiss one more time and wonder if maybe there's more to Kyle than I thought.

I sit in the office for what feels like hours, daydreaming about kissing and how each kiss in my life has meant something so different. The problem is that I don't trust myself to make decisions in this arena anymore. This is the one part of my life that I always let the experts handle, ie. Charlie and Becky, and seeing how the two of them aren't here to analyze said kiss between me and my bad-boy boss, I'm at a loss.

So I take out my phone and dial Becky's number and for the first time in a long while she doesn't answer.

The Hamptons in July…

"Tanner, are you sure I'm going to fit in? I mean look at these ladies. For God's sake they're in twill in the freakin' summer! SUMMER!" I say while wearing a very cool, very urban mini skirt, tank top, linen blazer combo.

"Beck, listen to me," he says turning my cheek to him while looking into my totally geeked out eyes. "You are the most beautiful, most unique and, without a doubt, the sexiest woman I have ever seen.

Please do not for one moment think these society snobs are better than you. Besides, your confidence is one of the things I'm most attracted to. Please don't lose it now," he says kissing me beneath my earlobe in the place that he knows drives me insane.

"Well played my friend, well played," I answer with a soft moan as he continues kissing down my neck until I'm brought back from my necking high by a very familiar voice. A voice I have not heard in many, many months.

"Becky? Becky is that you?" He says approaching me from behind, without a doubt recognizing my unique hair color and the long legs that are always getting me into so much trouble. I turn from Tanners sexy nibbles in time to see one very confused and stunned Danny/Thomas Lovelle walking straight for me.

"Hey Danny. How's it goin'?" I play cool like Ellie would want me to.

"Fine, I guess," he answers, slowly looking from Tanner to me. "How do you know Tanner? And why are you here?"

"I'm here as Tanner's date dumbass. What? I'm not good enough for your snotty society friends, either? You sure have some nerve, Danny. If you'll excuse us, come on Tanner, I'm not interested in talking to douche bags." I turn and start to stomp off, leaving Danny standing there in complete and utter shock.

"Wait." Tanner grabs my arm and turns me to face him, and Danny is still standing there stuck to the floor like he's incapable of speaking. "What did you just call him?" Even though he already knows what's up, he plays along.

"Danny. Why? That *is* his name." I say rolling my eyes heavily at poor, sweet Tanner.

"As in Elle's ex. Like the Danny she broke up with me for." And he's back. That gets Danny's attention because he looks like a dingo just ate his baby or his girlfriend.

"Did you just say Ellie J was your girlfriend? What the HELL, TANNER?" He's shouting. Good God.

"Okay, we need to get a few things straight," I say stepping between the two boys because Tanner has no idea that the look in Danny's eyes is one of death. "Danny. You broke up with Ellie J and when you did that she then became available to the rest of the free world, idiot. Second, she broke it off with Tanner here when you tricked her into taking your sorry ass back because for some reason she always believes you and she loves you. I mean, loved you," Shit. "And third, Tanner and I have been together for like a while now and we live together, so chill. He's no longer your problem."

"This is crazy, Becky. I just can't believe this is Elle's Danny. I'm sorry man. I swear I wouldn't have gone after her if I knew you were the ex, but dude, wow. You broke up with her? What's the matter with you?" Tanner is begging to have his ass kicked. I've seen Danny do it for way less.

"The only reason I broke up with her was… never mind, it doesn't even matter anymore. Besides, I don't even know where she is. I thought she was still in the city but no one will tell me. I've been asking everyone."

"Why?" I will help him if he answers this question correctly. Otherwise, he's screwed.

"Why? Because I freakin' love that girl. Since she's been gone I feel like…. I feel like when it's raining and it won't stop, I feel like when you have a fever and your body hurts, I feel like when you sit on the bottom of the pool and you can't breathe anymore. I feel like my life will never…ever…be alright again unless I get her back." Wow, he's good.

"Whoa dude, you have it bad. That's great, isn't it babe?" Tanner asks, breaking the silence that followed Danny's heartfelt confession.

"Well you haven't been looking very hard, Danny, because she's been home since before Christmas. Matter of fact, she moved home the night she was supposed to go to the Foo Fighters show with you." I wish she could see his face right now.

"She's been home this entire time? Where? I've driven by her house like a million times trying to get the nerve to talk to her parents but I can only imagine how they feel about me and I've never seen her car there. NOT once."

"She's living at my place, working at Kyle's teaching guitar, and I've never seen her happier." A little dig is in order here.

"Oh." He hangs his head and pulls his hands through his hair. "So I guess she wouldn't want to see me then?" he says still looking down.

"I didn't say that. I said she was happy, not that she couldn't be happier." Now I've got him. His head shoots up and his eyes are wide open, pupils dilated and all.

"Don't mess with me, Becky. Are you saying you'll help me out? Because if you are, you are officially my second favorite person of all time."

"I'm saying I want my best friend to have what she deserves and if you were serious about what you said, about how you feel about her, then yeah, I'll help a brother out." Then he lifts me up higher than my 5'9" frame has been lifted in quite some time and twirls me like a tiny ballerina. Tanner is laughing and yanking me out of Danny's arms all possessive like.

"Get your hands off my girl, Tommy. I can't have you taking another one from me." Before he sets me down I pull back and put my hands on either side of his handsome face, making sure he can see my eyes and the seriousness in them. Then I say without blinking once, "If you hurt her again, Danny Lovelle, I will hunt you down, rip your nards off and shove them down your throat. Are we clear?" He nods in understanding and I see his Adam's apple gulp as he sets me back down on my feet. He knows this is not an empty threat, I'm for real.

"You, Becky…are scary."

"Thanks. Now let's go plan a reunion."

thirty-one

Humpty Dumpty…

After Kyle's surprise kiss I sit – no, hide - in the office, seriously contemplating walking out of there and agreeing to that date with him. But that's not exactly how things go down. Instead I walk out to find the TV tuned in to the evening news, alerting us to an approaching hurricane that is due to make landfall within the next seventy-two hours, right here in Palm Beach. Yep, right in the middle of my fundraiser. Then, to make matters worse, Danny's commercial is the next thing to pop up on the screen. Really Universe? Back the H.E. double hockey sticks up!

Its official, I'm going to have to cancel the party. When I saw the forecast a week ago I wasn't worried. Everyone knows the path of these storms changes frequently during the first few rounds of projections. A true Floridian doesn't start planning for IT until its a couple days out and a sure thing. Unfortunately, this stubborn storm, known oddly enough as Becky, also a sure thing, has decided to stay right on target. This reminds me. I need to talk to the human Becky ASAP about our party disaster.

I text her again and still I get nothing back. If it wasn't for her rabid sex life with Tanner and her frequently forgetting to return my calls lately, I'd be scared that something happened to her. But it's a pretty safe bet to say that she's currently tied up with Tanner somewhere….literally. I decide to go ahead and let the vendors know that it looks like we'll have to postpone until a later date and I make the call to Fred I was dreading having to make.

He answers the phone after only two rings and I can tell he already knows what this is about, "Hey little girl, bummer about the storm huh?" I can cry hearing his voice. Even now he's not defeated. This man is my hero.

"Bummed does not even begin to describe how I

feel right now. Fred, I am so sorry. Don't worry; as soon as this thing passes we'll get on setting up another date. We have everything we need lined up, so it should be a piece of cake and..." he stops me mid sentence.

"You don't need to worry about it anymore." He says laughing. HUH?

"Wait.....what?" I answer shocked by his happy mood.

"Elliott, I don't know who you've told about us but today we got a call that's a real game changer. I mean...life changing, for all of us. Most importantly the kids."

"Well don't keep me hangin'! What's up?" He goes on to say that earlier in the day, just about the time the news was predicting a direct hit to Palm Beach of all places, he received a phone call from some fella who tells him he'd like to remain anonymous. "The nice man goes on to say he'd heard about what we were doing here in Indianapolis, was a music lover himself and was hoping he could help us out. He agreed to help with whatever expenses we needed in order to get the program running full speed ahead. "The only thing he asked is that he be able to make the donation in your name, Elliott. Can you believe it?" We talk a while longer and we hang up with plans to talk about what is needed to get things moving after the storm has passed.

I hang up the phone and sink down onto the floor feeling an overwhelming mixture of relief and joy. Relief that this storm isn't going to ruin things for the kids after all and joy that, for whatever reason, some stranger loves music enough to share it so generously with children that he has never and probably will never even meet. I seem to be back in the universe's favor and I won't take it for granted. Operation Changed Woman is back on. Funk officially over.

Kyle sees my smile when I get off the phone and tells me that since we've got nothing planned for the rest of the day I can take off. I gladly take the bone he hands me and kiss his cheek as I leave in thanks. I'm sure our kiss earlier has left him feeling as awkward as it has me, and a day apart will probably help smooth things over for us both and hopefully my well-played kiss on the cheek will let him know we're all good. As I'm walking to the car my cell beeps, alerting me to an incoming text from Becky. *HEY, was so busy all morning. Sorry didn't get back to ya sooner. We'll figure everything out, no worries. Kisses.* Yah, I bet you were "so busy all morning." I wish I was that kind of busy. Sigh. It's all good, I'm fulfilled and happy. Fulfilled and happy….

When I'm walking up to the apartment, I see Zha-Zha jumping like a lunatic in the window and I smile big at her sweet little face. I'm so thankful my parents let me bring her with me so I'd have company in the evenings. She's my current best friend. Matter of fact, tonight I have big plans for us. On the way home I stopped and got us each a treat. I got her the vanilla peanut butter puppy ice cream that she loves and me, Ben & Jerry's. We're going to watch Lloyd Dobler profess his undying love to Diane Court, boom box style and then daydream while eating our ice cream about the day our very own Lloyd will come boomboxing into our lives.

Unfortunately things take a nasty turn when I open the door. Zha-Zha comes slipping and sliding around the corner into the entry way and I'm shocked to see her soaking wet. As soon as I turn the corner into the living room it becomes clear why my sweet little girl is drenched, because my floors are! I call the landlord's emergency maintenance number and tell him about the flood currently happening in my apartment. As soon as he tells me he's on his way I decide to leave.

I quick pack an overnight bag, put Zha-Zha in her carrier with a warm, dry blanket from my bed and head to my parents'. I call my mom to warn them I'm on my way so that if there's any hanky panky going on they have ample opportunity to move it into the bedroom or some other place out of my field of vision. I will never make the mistake of showing up at their place unannounced again; message received loud and clear on that one. More like message seared into my memory. Eckk.....Mom's at the door to great me as soon as I walk in holding out the cell phone I'd lost the first night I moved back months ago.

"Are you serious? I was so afraid I'd lost all the numbers from my contact list forever. Mom you are a life saver. Thank you, thank you, thank you," I say while dotting her bronzed cheek with kisses. Zha-Zha is frantic to get out of the carrier, she sees her second mommy and is whining like a mad woman. She shocks us both when I put her down because instead of attacking my mom she runs for the back door to resume her squirrel hunting. She's unpredictable like the rest of us Hallowell ladies.

"So what are we watching?" Mom asks, even though she probably has already guessed it's my go-to favorite. I've never hid the fact that I adore a good love story with a happy ending. It's not that I don't see the value in realistic endings, because I do. I'm living one. But, when I want to believe there's hope or feel that love still exists, I'm not into realism. I'm into fiction. Fiction is where I dream lately, but if that's what it takes to keep me from going back to the dark place I was in last year then that's where I need to be. Fiction is my therapy and Lloyd is my hope.

"You know what we're watching. Will you put the ice cream in the freezer for me? I'm going to go change out of these wet pants and put my bags up. Be down in five."

Twenty minutes later I hear my mother's heavy footsteps as she comes up the wooden stairs. "Honey, are you coming?" She asks, pushing my door open. "Ellie, honey? What's the matter? Why are you crying?" She comes to the side of the bed and pulls me into a loving motherly embrace and I pass her the phone she gave back to me just a few minutes ago.

She opens the text sent from an anonymous "C" person and then the attachment that came with it and starts reading. The entire time I cry into her shoulder and she just keeps reading and rubbing my back with her free hand letting me have my moment of release. When she's done she sets the phone on the bed beside her and sits contemplating what to say next. We're both silent for several minutes, taking in the message that was clearly sent to hurt my feelings, maybe even break my heart. Too late for that though, it's been broken since the first night Danny broke up with me and has yet to be put back together. I'm kind of like that humpty dumpty guy, no one can put humpty back together again. What a sad story for children to learn. Realistic, but sad.

My mom's the first to speak, "You know what this says to me? It says to me that the only way his parents could get him to give you up is to take everything from him, even his dreams. This is how much he loves you Ellie," she says holding up the phone to me with that ugly love-stealing attachment staring back at me. Then she continues, "This does NOT say he gave up on you, don't you see that honey?"

"I wish I did mom, but I don't. The only thing I see in those words, followed by his signature, is that he loved me that amount of dollars. His love wasn't infinite like I thought. When push came to shove, he didn't push back for me - for us - he caved. I keep thinking if maybe I'd do the same thing if the shoe was on the other foot, and I just don't think so, mom. I would have chosen to live in a box in the woods with that man for the rest of my life and his signature on that piece of paper shows me that he wouldn't. No, that he didn't choose the same ."

"That signature is from a young man who was backed into a corner, honey. When we're young and we have dreams as big as Danny's have always been and they're threatened, well sometimes, we make the wrong choice in your push comes to shove scenario. Without a doubt he made the wrong choice, Ellie. Believe me I want to ring his neck. But....he's not perfect and neither are you, honey. Just think about that before you go hating him more. Okay?"

I give her a small smile and stand up. "Come on," I say, grabbing her hand and lifting her off my childhood bed. "I need me some Mr. Dobler. Let's go watch someone get their happy ending." She laughs at my ability to lighten the mood so quickly and swats my butt as she walks out of my room. "Mom, I hate it when you do that."

"I made that butt, so shut it," she says back, laughing while skipping down the stairs. She knows that I'll take to heart everything she just said and work this out. I'm just going to need a little bit of time.

When I fall asleep later that night I'm staring up at

the glow-in-the-dark stars that my big, hunky boyfriend helped me put up so many years ago. I remember that day so well. He told me that every night when I went to sleep to think of him when I looked up at these stars. That night when I did, I noticed that my clever boyfriend had spelled the words I LOVE YOU in my stars. You can't fake that. I know he loved me. As I fall asleep I wish upon those very same stars that he'd just have loved me enough. I wish I was enough.

Right isn't awkward…

The next day starts crazy at the shop. We're hearing the storm is getting stronger and that it's time to start boarding up the windows. Kyle leaves to go load up on wood and I'm running the shop. I get a phone call from Jenny and she asks if she can come in for a short lesson in a few hours, she's got some new music she wants me to hear. I tell her of course because I need the distraction from the now continuous running stream of mental Danny images flowing through my over romanticized brain. We're in the calm before the storm and it's a beautiful day, but no one's shopping for music; only plywood.

I'm on the phone with one of the vendors when the door chimes alerting me to a customer. Danny's sister Lex, who I haven't seen in forever, is standing there giving me a great big smile and I realize then, just how much I've missed her. I'm finishing with the vendor and hanging up while simultaneously walking over to my long lost ex-sister-in-law to be.

"Hey Ellie J."

"Lex, oh my goodness it's so great to see you," I say with tears in my eyes. Just seeing her is making me weepy.

"E, I've missed you so much. I just heard from someone you worked here and I came right over. I can't believe you've been back and you haven't come to see me," I can tell I've hurt her feelings when I release her from the tight hold I have on her and look into the very same eyes as Danny's.

"Honestly Lex, I know this is so uncool and now that I see you I know I was wrong but I thought it would be too hard to see you. Plus, I kinda haven't told your brother I'm here so, there's that."

"You're totally right, uncool. Luckily for you I'm a forgiving bitch." There's the girl I know and love. "Let's go out soon, kay? You can fill me in on your new love life then." She says this like it's no big deal but I can hear the question she's really asking. She wants to know if I'm over Danny and just isn't saying it. I know how her devious little mind works. She's good. But, two can play that game.

"Love to. I have tons to tell you." No, I don't. We talk about all the mundane things going on in our lives and make a dinner date for next week after hurricane Becky's moved on. She kisses me on both cheeks like the fancy, super rich girl that she apparently is and leaves. I was sure that the first time I saw anyone from his family it would feel awkward, but after seeing Lex I realize when you love people it's never weird. That's what love does, it takes away the weird.

Jenny's coming soon so I get working on her next lesson. She has picked up the guitar quicker than anyone I've ever taught. She's even starting to learn some of the easier Foo Fighters songs and she's doing it on her free time, just for me. We jam out together at the end of our lessons and I'm always spellbound by her voice. It does something amazingly beautiful to Dave Grohls lyrics.

The morning flies by and before I know it it's the afternoon and Jenny's bouncing through the doors, her Converse squeaking along the smooth tile floors. She asks if we can sit downstairs today since the store's empty and heads to the nearest set of lounge chairs before I've even agreed. I'm still at the counter finishing up some lyrics I've been working on when she starts to play. My heart stops when I hear the melody she's playing and then her smooth angelic voice begins to sing out some of my favorite words Dave Grohl has ever written;

If ever you think you're not the one, I'll remind you.

If ever you think you're about to run, I will find you.

Come on to me, just let it go.

If ever you think you're not the one. I'll remind you.

Come on my love

Come on my love

I'm approaching her slowly from the counter watching her through tears I didn't even feel myself making when a small piece of paper floats down in front of me. I reach out and grab it before it hits the ground and stifle a sob when I read the words. In Danny's chicken scratch it says the very same words he wrote to me so many years ago; *your legs did look "rad" in these. I couldn't imagine them on anyone else.*

Call me 555-4477. This time he added just one more sentence, *look on the stairs.*

With the music still being played and my crying reaching an ugly level I warily approach the stairs and sitting there on the third step is a box that I've seen before. I lift the lid and am met with the most beautiful sight. New boots. They are even more beautiful than my last pair and hold no bad memories. The design is subtly different but both the heal and the color are the same. I can tell just by looking at them they are going to come to the perfect spot on my calf and I immediately kick off my Teva's and stick my feet into the softest leather I've ever felt. Home is what these shoes feel like. As I bend to pick up the box a deep voice is added to the melody making for a beautiful duet. I close my eyes to try and pull the sound of his voice deep into my soul, making sure I never forget this moment.

I turn when he starts the next stanza alone and stare into eyes as deep and rich as the ocean, he stares back as he sings. Jenny has disappeared and it's only the two of us.

If ever you think I'm not the one, I'll remind you.

With everything under the sun, stars above you.

Come on to me, just let it go.

If ever you think I'm not the one, I'll remind you.

Come on my love

Come on my love

Come on my love

Come on my love

If ever you think you're not the one, I'll remind you.

If ever you think you're not the one.

By the time he finishes, we're only a foot apart. He lays the guitar down reverently next to him and we are stuck in a staring contest. My hand reaches out first and I place it over his heart, I can feel it beating as fast as my own and I know he's feeling the fear I'm feeling.

"I like your shirt."

"Yah, some girl I know inspired me to buy it, actually. I heard the money's going to a really great cause."

"It was you, wasn't it? You're the one who gave Mr. Fred the money?" Of course he did, he's still the boy I love except now he wears suits more than jeans, but not today. Today he's in my favorite loose fitting pair of Levi's. They hang just right off his hips exposing the muscular V shape that leads to the Promised Land. The t-shirt is a bit tight but I'm not complaining, I've missed that body. He's watching me watch him and one side of his mouth turns up into one of the most perfect grins I've ever seen.

"You did a good thing helping them, Ellie J. I wanted to be a part of it somehow even if you wouldn't see me."

I look up into the eyes of the only man I've ever loved and I see the same thing staring back at me; forgiveness. There are so many definitions of this word when you look it up, yet the idea is so simple. It's when your heart can at last just let go of the pain that you've chosen to focus on. We've both said, and done, so many hurtful things to one another, that we can't take back over the last year and a half. But, with this one look it's undone, it's forgiven. The debts of our injuries are pardoned. Then, he does something I've dreamt about since the moment I first laid eyes on him, when I was only a girl who loved a boy.

He drops down onto his right knee in front of me and takes my shaking left hand into both of his solid, strong, determined ones and while gazing up into my eyes says, "Do you remember what I wrote in the stars for you so long ago Ellie J?" I shake my head yes slightly in response. "It never changed. I might have, but not my feelings. Never my feelings." He puts an emphasis on the NEVER so I will understand that he's never given up on us. I realize I need to stop him because he doesn't know that I know about the ultimatum and I want all of our secrets out in the open before this happens.

Before he can continue I press the three middle fingers of my right hand to his beautiful, soft lips to shush him. "I need you to know that I know all about the ultimatum." He blinks his eyes in confusion. "Someone with the initial C anonymously sent it to me. I think this person was trying to upset me, but unfortunately for them it backfired. All this time I thought you just didn't love me enough, that maybe you wanted more. Then when I found out who your family was and what that meant about you, I assumed you were ashamed of me. Like maybe I wasn't good enough for you." He just shakes his head back and forth, showing me his feelings. "When I saw you at that party in New York in that tuxedo, I was so confused, especially when I saw the woman you were with. She was nothing like me, in any way, so it was easy for me to think that that's why you left me. I thought all along you wanted more……until I read that ultimatum. A very wise person told me that if I read it closely I'd see that the only way you wouldn't be with me was by force… not choice. At first I thought you were weak for making that choice, but then I started going over the last year and a half of my life and I realized that maybe if I had been you I would have done the same thing. Maybe before all of this, I would have been weak."

A lone tear rolls down from the corner of his eye with my admission and I reach over to wipe it away and go on. "Before *we* were broken, I was on autopilot for you. My focus wasn't clear and my path wasn't my own. I was essentially being guided by everyone but me, and that was something I had to grow up to learn. I realize after reading that ultimatum that you were in the same place and you did the same thing. The difference is that you wanted the cards you were dealt and I didn't. I didn't want to just work at the hotel and follow you around my whole life. I just didn't know it, and now I do. As much as I love you, my dreams are not the same as yours but it doesn't mean we can't share them."

"What you don't understand, is that I never cared what you did. I'd support you no matter what that means. You can do anything you want, as long as you're by my side. Well, within reason. I don't want you on a pole for the entire world to see that cute little ass of yours but," I slap him before he can go any further, but he knows I love his silly sense of humor and that he's just trying to lighten the mood. So, I play along like I always have. Some things were never meant to change.

"Too bad, I was hoping to do just that. That was my dream." Cue sad face and big doe eyes. "Hmm? Maybe you aren't the supportive man I thought you were after all," I say pretending to retreat because no way, in you know what, am I leaving him now, not even for pretend.

Before I can go on, with my fake diatribe, he stands and pulls me against him with a passion we have never exchanged before until this moment. I thought I knew all his kisses, but I didn't. This is a soul shattering, mind changing, life altering kiss and we both need it. This one kiss is the reset button on our story. It changes everything about whom and what we were and is now the perfect seal, on the covenant of what we will become.

He reverently slides down my body, back to his knee, leaving me winded and gasping for air. He retakes my strong, yet delicate hand in his and slides on the most exquisite and unique ring I've ever seen. The setting is perfect for my slim fingers and, though he could afford to go over the top, he knows my style is minimalist. It's a solid platinum band with nothing on it but a lone square cut diamond - I'd guess a little over two carats - but those two carats are perfect in quality and color, causing a remarkable glitter to shine around the room….. almost like little stars reminding me of his love.

"Ellie James Hallowell," Pause….stare… "I've loved you from the moment I set eyes on those rad legs," I can't help but laugh, "And more than anything in the world I want to take care of those legs, these hands," he says kissing them each once, "that beautiful face, for the rest of my days. Marry me. Say yes." Then he flips his hand over, and on the ring finger of his left hand he's gotten a tattoo and all it says is *I'm Yours.*

Epilogue

Lloyd who?

I'm in room 3555 reapplying my Mary Kay I love Black mascara, on this, the happiest day of my life. Danny's mom and my mom are the last to leave the room, giving me a couple minutes of much needed alone time to gather myself. Today has been a dream, but unfortunately, I cannot get my crying under control. In less than half an hour I will be marching down "THE" aisle of love - cheesy, but true - to marry the stud to shame all other studs and I will be doing so with cheeks caked over with my favorite mascara. There is no mascara strong enough for these heavy weight tears I've got going on. My "mom's" assure me that Danny will find my messy face adorable but I assure you that I will not find the pictures "adorable".

This morning I was fine. No, I was deliriously fine. Cue birds chirping and the sun shining through my window, all whilst I lazily stretched on my bed dreaming of the wedding night to come. Bliss. Then I hear him, my soon to be husband. I CAN'T believe I said the "H" word……ahhhhhh. Anyway, I follow the lovely tenor of his deep voice over to the heavy, hotel room door. As I begin to turn the knob he stops me by saying, "No, just listen."

He's giving me my Lloyd Dobler moment but it's much better, because the music isn't from a heavy contraption held up in the rain but from him and his hunky heart in the echoey hallway of our soon to be love-nest. He's singing me the song he used to propose to me with, *If Ever.* He's reminding me that I'll never have to worry about his love. That no matter the problem he will always be there to come home to. He's reminding me that he IS my home and that I am his. But, he's doing it in the most romantic way I've ever heard.

Well, needless to say, from then on I was kind of a wreck. A happy wreck, yes. A pretty, put together one, no. As soon as he was done belting out his love for me I heard all sorts of whistling and hollering and

I knew that he had just sung to me in front of my entire wedding party. His love for me knows no boundaries. After he hushed the girls, and Charlie, I heard his head touch the door. I could imagine him there in his favorite billabong tee and worn Levi's lookin' like heaven in pants. I put my head on the door as well so we would only be separated by one small piece of lumber.

"Ellie J?" Sigh.

"Yes?"

"I love you more than the stars." Swoon. Literally, I swooned. Fell right to the floor.

"ELLIE? Oh my GOD! ARE YOU OKAY?" I do not fall quietly or gracefully. Ouch! He can kiss it and make it better later. Lord, now I'm sweating.

"I won't be if you don't stop being so romantic. Your romance may literally kill me. Hey I need to write that down. What a great song title." I can hear him laughing at me. He loves me.

"Alright. Well since your harem has arrived, I will leave you ladies to do your…..lady stuff." As he gets further down the hall and my door is shut he shouts loudly, one last time, just to make me smile, "More than the stars Ellie J." How could I stop the tears after that? I mean, he's been telling me since we were kids he loves me like the stars and today I finally get to marry my stargazer. My supernova.

THE END

ABOUT THE AUTHOR

Jamie Nicole is well on her way to a degree in what appears to be a lot of things according to her college transcripts. Unable to pick a major in college, she essentially studied the entire course catalog, which included everything from Jazz dance, Scuba (no joke, this was a college class) and aerobic sciences. While she's accumulated all of the required general education credits one needs to graduate, her real major is real life, for which she should probably be a doctoral candidate.

What was obvious from her choice of classes was one thing…she was curious. This curiosity served her well in becoming both a mother and a wife, which has proven to be way tougher than either the scuba diving or the Jazz dancing. She considers herself an honorary nurse after raising 3 kids, as well as an unofficial part time psychologist, (again – 3 kids!). Her steadfast curiosity, along with living a life full of surprises and her love of reading are all what led to the creation of Flighty.

Her mind is now chalk full of characters she's excited to explore and dying to introduce you to. Her next novel, *You've got Game,* is full of more quirky characters who struggle through some of life's greatest challenges, all the while hoping desperately to find some peace and with a little luck that elusive beast: LOVE.

www.ingramcontent.com/pod-product-compliance
Lightning Source LLC
Chambersburg PA
CBHW030619250626
47154CB00006B/1849

* 9 7 8 0 6 1 5 9 3 1 8 8 3 *